Viking Kingdom

Book 4 in the
Dragon Heart Series
By
Griff Hosker

Published by Sword Books Ltd 2014
Copyright © Griff Hosker First Edition

*A CIP catalogue record for this title is available from the British
Library.*
Cover by Design for Writers

Prologue

Those who devoured the dead and the dying were gathering; carrion beasts were coming to my home. The human creatures which feast on the dying and the weak were closing in on us. Since the death of Prince Butar others, such as the ones the Saxons called the Vikings, had been sniffing around our island of Man to see if we were weak enough to devour. They could not believe that someone who had been a slave and born a Saxon could rule somewhere like our island haven of Man.

The only things which kept the sea wolves from the door were my sword, Ragnar's Spirit, and my resolute warriors. All the warriors who heard of the mystical blade both coveted and feared touched by the gods. No-one wished to fight an enchanted blade. It had never been beaten in battle. I hoped that the illusion would last. Since Prince Butar had been killed I knew that there were many who thought that they could rule Man

As I sat, on Snaefell's peak I pondered such matters. I no longer gazed to the west and the island of the Irish. We had struck fear into their hearts. Other sea wolves like us might take over that troubled land but the Hibernians themselves would not risk war with me. They had been hurt too many times and their women and children sold as slaves. I gazed to the east and the land of the Angles and the Saxons. I looked to the land where I had been born. It was a land full of riches. It was the land of my mother and her ancestors.

Since my mother's death I had learned much about her and her people. She had not been a Saxon. She had been descended from the last Warlord of Rheged. That had been the last vestige of the Roman Empire and the old land of the Britons. Rheged was now merely a name, a legend almost, but I had found the tomb of the warlord and his wizard, Myrddyn. I knew that it was real. Perhaps I should say I was led to the tomb for I know that the spirits from beyond our world wished me to find them. And then I was buried and found the ancient sword of the warlord. When I emerged from my earthly tomb I knew that I had been reborn. I had been dead and now I was alive.

All of that had been some time ago but I had had time to reflect and to think. Once a month I would ascend, alone, to the soft top of Snaefell and I would think. My warriors and my family knew what I did and respected my vigil. I was as high as I could be on the island and I believed that those who had died before, Ragnar, my mother and Prince Butar, could speak with me. Their words filled my head. I was close to the Gods and I could see all of the lands which surrounded us.

We had been visited by many Jarls over the last year: Ragnar Hairy-Breeches, Magnus Bare Legs and Olvir the Child Sparer. They had all come, apparently to offer us friendship and support but we had seen them assessing our defences and seeking weaknesses. We were not fooled. And then there were those that we knew were enemies: Harald One-Eye Butar's cousin had driven us from our Norse home many years ago. He had hated him as he hated me. There were others too: Thorfinn the Skull Splitter and Sihtric Silkbeard who made no pretence of friendship but coveted what we ruled.

They had all settled either in the land of the Angles or on the islands to the north. We, on the island of Man, were too strong for them. My warriors controlled the nearby island which had been the ancient home of the druids, Anglesey. My warriors there were protected by the holy mountain and it prevented others from using that rich island as a base from which to raid us. But I knew we could not just sit and wait for them to come. If we did that we would lose. The voice in my head, which had been Ragnar's, told me so. The voice had changed of late. I still saw Ragnar but it was not his voice. No matter whose voice it was, the words in my head had never let me down and I would heed them. I descended the mountain happier than I had been for some time. I knew what I had to do.

Chapter 1

By the time I had reached my home at Hrams-a I was decided. I had the plan in my head. Of course, as with all things, I would speak with my wife, Erika. It was not to seek her approval; I did not need that. Rather it was to have her apply her mind to what I had decided. Oft times her sage advice had made the plan work better. I believed she might be a volva but she denied any such powers. The Otherworld worked in mysterious ways.

My daughter Kara was now toddling and was proving a handful for Seara who watched over her. As I approached the hall I heard her squeals as she fled from her nurse and I heard Seara's voice as she tried to control my child. Arturus my son had grown rapidly over the last year. He spent every waking minute practising to be a warrior. If Aiden was available then he sparred with him and if not he used his bow and the targets. At other times he would happily wield an axe to strengthen his muscles. He wanted to be an Ulfheonar and he knew that required a high standard of skill.

Aiden was the Irish boy I had adopted. Although he used sword and shield he was no warrior. He was a fine worker of metals and had made the wolf charms for my oathsworn. He had become something of a healer for my warriors and could stitch the deep cuts they sometimes suffered. He could also read and had shown himself adept at conjuring cunning plans. I knew that when Erika had refined my thoughts Aiden would add his own opinion and ideas. I would welcome them. He was as loyal a man as any of my warriors and I was not arrogant enough to believe that I knew it all.

Arturus ran to me when he saw me. I noticed that he was now as tall as my shoulder and was filling out. Another summer or two and he could begin raiding with me as a warrior rather than an apprentice. "You are back father. Did you dream the dream?"

I smiled, "Not this time my son, but the sky and the mountain cleared my head and allowed the spirits to talk with me.

I cannot always dream but I can speak with those who have gone before."

"Will I be able to do that when I grow older?"

I had no doubt that he would for his mother was fey too but it did not do to put such ideas in a boy's mind in case it turned out not to be the way he would walk. "It may be. When I was your age the gift had not come. You will need to grow and see what the Allfather has planned for you."

His face showed disappointment tinged with resolve. He would still believe that he could be exactly the same as me. "I will continue to work then father."

"Good. The gods help those that help themselves."

Erika was a good organiser and she had finished the chores which needed completion. She was a master at ensuring that others worked hard. She was sitting by the fire weaving a new kyrtle for Arturus. He was growing rapidly and would need one when winter returned. She looked as I entered and laid down the spindle whorl and went to the barrel to get me a horn of beer. She did not need to say a word. She knew that I would speak when I was ready. I had chosen a good wife or perhaps she had chosen me; I was never sure.

The ale was freshly made and refreshed me. It must have been made with the waters from the Garlic River; that always had a distinctive taste which I liked.

"I have decided that I will not wait for our enemies to determine that we are weak and take this land from us. I will strike first."

I drank some more of the ale and waited for her comments.

"Would you leave us undefended?"

"No, for I have done that twice and both times lost someone dear to me. The last time Harald One Eye nearly had you. No, I intend to leave Dargh with a healthy number of men. There are many who have fought with Prince Butar and are no longer fit to go A-Viking. I will gather them and they will guard Duboglassio and here. I will also ask your brother to use his drekar to watch for enemies here."

She looked up sharply. "Perhaps he will want to raid too."

I smiled, "I think his wife wishes him at home a little more. She is not you, my love."

She laughed, "And is that a criticism?"

"No, I would take you over ten such wives."

"And where will you go first?"

I thought back to the last raid which had come from Harald One-Eye. I had almost caught him but he had fled with many of his men. More left their bones bleaching the hillsides of Man but he would be rebuilding.

"One-Eye is the closest and the one who needs the lesson first. It will serve as a warning to others that Dragon Heart and his Ulfheonar do not forgive treachery."

"And then?"

"I would take my men south. Now that Eardwulf is no longer king, Eanred, his successor, will take time to gain control of his lands. It seems a perfect time to clear the land and join up with Jarl Thorkell. With that part of Northumbria under our control I could venture north."

She laughed, "I can read you as Aiden reads those Latin books. All this talk of preventing our enemies from attacking us is not the real reason you wish to go across the waters."

I looked to the ground. She was a volva.

"You wish to visit and conquer Rheged. The sword you found in the water has haunted you since you brought it back."

I nodded. "It draws my mind to it. The sword belonged to a warlord who fought the Saxons. I was meant to find it and if I was meant to find it then, perhaps, I am meant to use it to drive the Saxons away from the land of my ancestors."

She nodded firmly and took my empty horn to refill it. "Good. You are being honest with yourself now as well as me." She handed me the refilled horn. "There is nothing wrong with that. Who are the warriors you will take?"

Apart from the Ulfheonar, Jarl Rolf and his men I do not know. I will just take *'Wolf'* and *'Bear'*. When those are filled with volunteers then I will leave the rest to guard here."

"That is not many warriors. Will you have enough?"

"It should be enough. I can always send back for more men."

"Then you will be away some time?"

"I expect to be away for the whole of the summer." I shrugged, "If I can get back by winter then so much the better."

"So you will use Alf and '**Serpent**' to keep me informed of how you fare?"

This was not a question it was an order. Our captured Hibernian ship was used to trade with other peoples. She could also be useful for ferrying messages and new warriors too. I laughed and kissed her on the cheek, "Of course, my love."

"Good, then I am settled and I look forward to all the treasure that you will send back to me."

We had much to do in a short space of time. I sought out my Ulfheonar. We were growing smaller in number as it was hard to replace such warriors. There were just eight of them left with me. Not all were dead. Some had opted to stay in Gwynedd but I only had eight of my elite warriors. I joined them in their hall. It was more spacious now. After explaining my plan I waited for their comments.

Cnut nodded as did Haaken; they had been with me since we had lived beyond the seas in the land of ice and snow. "It will be good to pay back Harald One-Eye."

"Remember Haaken, he has no honour, as he showed when he fled our shores to leave his oathsworn to die for him. It will take more than just courage to defeat him."

"And in you we have that something extra. You have a mind as well as the sword touched by the gods."

Cnut asked, "What of the others? Will they oppose us?"

"Ragnar Hairy-Breeches is as slippery as an eel. When he smiles then you watch your back for the dagger. He has based himself around Caerlleon. We will be heading in that direction to reach Thorkell. I will approach him as though he is on our side but I will expect him to betray us."

"That is a dangerous game to play, Dragon Heart."

"I know, Beorn, but when he does betray us and attempt some underhand trick it may work against him. He has good warriors with him. He has warriors who have honour. They may join us. I am only taking two drekar."

There was a gasp from one or two of the younger Ulfheonar. "A small number then."

"Yes Ragnar Siggison but I will not leave our people undefended. We all know what happened the last time we did that."

Many of them had recently married and they nodded as the import of my words sank in.

"You will take Rolf and his warriors then?"

"Yes Haaken. They are now well trained and a doughty band. We know that we can rely on them. Many now have a mail byrnie. We will be as well armed as an army five times our size."

"And when do we leave?"

I smiled. "When I return with Rolf and his warriors then we will sail east. Say your goodbyes soon for I already have." I took Arturus and Aiden with me when I rode to speak with Jarl Eric. He had to be willing to watch over my family or we would not be able to leave. He had changed over the years I had known him. There was a time when he wanted to sail with me and raid as much as any warrior. He had even wintered in Gwynedd and raided the Saxons and the Welsh. His wife, however, had fallen pregnant. He was besotted with his child and when she was with child again he lost the urge to raid. I hoped to use that to protect my family and his sister.

I smiled when I saw his new defences. This was a warrior watching over his home. When I told him of my plans I saw the look of fear flit across his face. He wondered if I would ask him to come with me. He had sworn an oath to me but I would never take a man, even oathsworn, if his heart was not in it.

"I do not need you to come with me, brother. I need you and your ship to protect my island and, most importantly, my family."

The relief on his face almost made me smile. "Of course. I swear that I will give my life to protect Erika and your children."

"I hope it will not come to that but you should know that I take Rolf and any of the younger warriors from Duboglassio who wish to join me. Remember Sihtric Silkbeard is now carving out a kingdom in Hibernia. He may decide to expand east."

He smiled back at me, "Brother I have learned much from you. Look at my walls. I promise that I know how to defend."

As I left with my son and Aiden I felt happier knowing that my family had a guardian. Of course bad things could still happen and he might fail but I knew that he would try with every fibre of his being.

Arturus said, as we rode through the pass to the east, "You promised that I could come with you on your next raid."

I closed my eyes and cursed my own promise. He was right and I would have to keep my word. "And I will keep my word but you will not be fighting. You will be on '*Wolf*' and you will be working as Aiden worked and Snorri too. The fact that you are a Jarl's son will not give you an easy berth."

He seemed relieved, "I know and I will not let you down."

When we reached Duboglassio I felt the same sadness I always did when I visited the scene of Prince Butar's death. Many of my people said that I should live there for it had a better location and more lived there. I preferred Hrams-a and I left Duboglassio to the warriors who had followed Butar. They had all sworn allegiance to me and I knew that they were reliable warriors.

Ulf the Squint-Eyed now administered my justice. He was older than I was and was one of the warriors who had sailed around the island of Britannia when we had first settled here. He had, like me, survived. There were not many who remembered that voyage in the '*Ran*'.

He greeted me as an old friend. We had once shared a bench and rowed together when I was a mere youth. "Good to see you Jarl. You do not visit nearly enough."

"I know but I keep seeing the ghost of the prince and it brings back sad memories."

He looked at me askance. "Why? He had a sword in his hand and he is in Valhalla. He is talking with Old Ragnar and your mother even as we speak."

"You make it sound like a good thing."

"It is. We all must die and it is the manner of our death which is important. Prince Butar had a good death. Just think of him as though he is still alive but somewhere else."

"I tried that but when I return here I see the empty throne…"

"Everyone would like it if you became prince and occupied the throne."

I shook my head. I have no wish to be prince. When the jarls have enough of taking my advice I will retire to my hall."

"They will never tire of your advice Dragon Heart. So, tell me what brings you here."

I explained my dilemma. He understood it immediately. "There are many young warriors who would dearly love the chance to raid with you for you are lucky and that is as important as a good sword. And I will find warriors to help guard your stead. All love the Lady Erika and will defend her with their lives." His voice became hard. "Were I not beyond my warrior days I would come with you and slay this treacherous One-Eye myself."

Although he wished us to stay I knew I had to speak with Rolf. I could not refuse to stay with Rolf. He would know it would be a long journey home. It would have been too much for both Aiden and Arturus. "Besides," Rolf said, "we can sail back in *'Bear'* and save time."

He, of course, was quite happy to be raiding again. The quiet life of a land bound jarl was not for him. He had many men who he could choose from and all were sound and hearty warriors. When we left, the next day, we would be taking the very best warriors from the southern part of the island.

At the feast I restrained myself. I did not want a thick head. It was because I was so sober that I learned what a fine poet and singer Aiden was. Haaken had been the one to write all the sagas and stories about me but Aiden had created a few himself and he entertained the warriors well with his words. Perhaps because he could read he used different words to those used by Haaken and the stories seemed more musical somehow. Aiden was a youth with much depth. I was so grateful for the day he had chosen to follow me and leave his family.

The voyage home helped me to gauge the mettle of these warriors and I was pleased. They rowed well together and they sang as they rowed. I knew that meant they would fight well together. I would keep this as one crew and mix the other volunteers with my Ulfheonar. We would be taking just sixty warriors. It did not dishearten me for I knew we left more behind to defend what was ours. The men would fight all the better knowing that their hearths were safe.

When we landed I sent Arturus back to his mother with Aiden. He would need to prepare. Before he took him I charged Aiden with another task. He almost ran with my son to complete his two tasks. Rolf took our men to the warrior hall and I headed for Bjorn Bagsecgson. He was my blacksmith and I had a task for him. I was returning to Rheged and I hoped that it would soon become our home again. I could not return empty handed.

He saw me coming and left his smithy to greet me. "I hear you are going to pay back that snake One-Eye."

"I am."

"I wish I could come with you. My father hated that man. I was just a child when we left our home but I had never heard my father speak of anyone in that way before. I knew then that he was evil."

"We will, the Allfather willing, punish him." He put his hands on his hips as he waited for me to continue. He knew my moods and my ways as well as any man. He knew that I measure my words much as a housewife would weigh out her flour in her hands.

"The sword I brought from the land of the Welsh. You remember it?"

"Aye Jarl. The sword you pulled from the pool in the stone cave. It had been a fine weapon but it had seen better days."

"It was not killed. My ancestor who threw it down the hole did it to save it. He did it so that it would come to me." He nodded his understanding. "It came to me but I know that he would not want it left in the state it was. Can you do anything with it?"

"That is a tall order but I would need to see it again. I had the briefest of viewings when you first returned with it."

Just then Aiden raced up with a sheepskin. He bowed and laid it on the floor before us. "Then look now Bjorn Bagsecgson and tell me if it can be saved."

He took the sword out and held it reverently. It was still a fine weapon but the jewels which had adorned it and the gilding were gone. The wrappings around the hilt were no more and it was pitted with rust. He examined it closed and, after, an age he laid it down.

"This weapon can never fight again. It would be like sending out Old Ragnar to face a young warrior. No matter what his skill was he would not have the strength to defeat a younger opponent and so it is with this sword."

I took out Ragnar's Spirit and held it aloft. "I need no other sword with which to fight so long as I have this one. I need the sword to be a symbol. It rallied the people of Rheged once and I am hoping it will do so again."

He smiled and said, confidently, "Then it can be repaired. I can make the sword that was broken whole again but I cannot make it look as it once did." He looked pointedly at Aiden.

"Could you do that for me Aiden? Could you make it look as it once did? You remember, as we saw in the cave?"

Even though I knew he was desperate to say 'yes' he had grown much of late and reflected. If he gave his word then it would have to be with the knowledge that he could deliver on his promises. He reached down and picked up the weapon. He touched it, tenderly, as though it was a living thing. Finally he said, "I can do so."

We all smiled. "When I return, after the winter I will expect you to have done your work, Bjorn, and then Aiden here can begin his magic."

The next day flew by in a flurry of activity. '*Wolf*' and '*Bear*' were fitted out and their spaces filled with the weapons and supplies which we would need for a winter on the mainland. We would, largely, take what we needed but there were some vital items which we had to have; arrows, sails, and salted fish. Winter was a hard time to be without some sort of food. It was as well to be prepared.

We needed new ship's boys to be trained. Erik Short Toe had joined the young warriors being trained and he would remain with Dargh. Arturus would be one and we also took Magnus Larsson who was a little older than Arturus and had sailed with us once before.

We were ready to sail on the evening tide and we would make the journey across the water in the dark. There had been a time when sailors such as us would have feared to sail in the dark. We had learned that, if you were careful, then you could sail in the dark. We used the stars and we used our memories. This voyage would be a short one. We could leave after dark and sail the short way to the mainland in a few hours of hard rowing. That way we would arrive unannounced before dawn. Our ships could be hidden and my wolves would emerge like wraiths from the sea. It was our way and it worked.

Chapter 2

The Ulfheonar occupied the front benches and faced me. Our helmets and weapons were stored for the voyage. Our shields, lining the sides, were the only sign that we were prepared for war. As I steered with Magnus and Arturus watching my every move I too was watching. I was looking at the warriors behind the Ulfheonar. I was watching the way they rowed and how they sat close to their new companions. Although friends sat with friends if there was an odd number then, inevitably, some warriors would sit with a neighbour they did not know well. They were the ones I scrutinised. I did so to detect any tension and I began to relax a little when I saw that there was, apparently, none.

Glancing up at the mast head I saw that the Allfather favoured us for the wind was blowing us east. The oars were not even necessary but there was a ritual about going on a raid. We always rowed the first day. I knew, without even looking, that Rolf would be on station behind me. We had sailed and fought together enough times now to be confident of the other's moves and actions. In a skirmish that could be the deciding factor.

I heard Magnus and Arturus whispering. "If you must speak then speak so that we can all hear. We are brothers on this boat and we have no secrets." Even as I spoke I knew that was not the truth. I had secrets deep within me. Only Erika knew some of my innermost thoughts and I kept one or two from her.

Arturus looked at me guiltily. "Magnus and I wondered when we would get to steer the boat."

Haaken laughed, "He is as keen as his father used to be."

I scowled at Haaken. "When I think that you can do so without putting us on rocks." I pointed at the cloudy sky which hid the moon. "Do either of you think that you could land us successfully with no moon to guide you?"

They shook their heads and Arturus asked, "How do you know you are travelling true?"

"I watch the rowers. If they keep time then we move straight. I watch the waves at the prow of the ship. I watch Rolf and see that he is in the same position. When we reach land we will see how well I have done. If the Allfather smiles upon us then we will see the estuary ahead of us and if not then we will have more rowing for my strong warriors."

In my mind there was no doubt that we would hit the estuary where I predicted. The winds were coming from the right quarter and the journey was short enough to minimise the chance of error.

The warrior we had questioned had told us where Harald One-Eye had set up his camp. He had occupied and rebuilt the wooden monastery and nunnery we had attacked some years earlier. It would not be made of stone. There would possibly be a ditch and a wooden wall surrounding his hall and huts. He would have guards on the walls watching for enemies. All of that would make him feel secure but he did not know how good my Ulfheonar were. His warriors we had slain when he tried to take my home had taken that knowledge to their graves. Had they survived then they might have told Harald that the men in the wolf skins were able to hide in plain sight; rise from the ground like the ghosts of the dead and kill silently and swiftly no matter how great a number of warriors faced them.

I would be with my Ulfheonar when we attacked and Rolf would command the rest. Our task would be to find the stronghold and eliminate the guards; Rolf and the others would capture it. It sounded easy when you said it quickly but it would be hard. These were neither Saxons nor Hibernians we fought. They were our people. More than that they were people we knew. I had grown up amongst many of them. I did not make the mistake of underestimating what Harald One Eye and his warriors would be capable of.

I sent Magnus up the mast to get an early view of the land. I could have sent Arturus but I did not want to risk him yet. Magnus was a little older and stronger. Magnus shinned up the mast using the ropes to help him. He scrambled to sit across the cross tree with his legs dangling down the sail. I had told him what to look for; a darker line across the horizon. If he saw breakers then he was ordered to shout a warning immediately. "Arturus, keep your eye on Magnus. When he signals you need to tell me. Do you understand?"

"Yes father."

I shook my head, "No, on this ship I am jarl. Address me as the others do. You are one of them now; you are a ship's boy. You are one who serves me. When we return home then you will be my son again."

He nodded. The darkness hid his expression. I was in uncharted territory here. I had had no father when I was his age. I had been a slave and treated as such. I had to learn how to be a father now; no-one had showed me what to do.

Suddenly he said, "Jarl!"

I looked up and saw Magnus waving. The land was close. "Half oars, get the sail down." I turned and waved my arm. After a few moments I saw a wave from Rolf's ship. With the sail down we slowed perceptibly. When the rowers began to row once more we edged closer to the land. "Arturus, go to the bow and watch for danger. Wave if you see any. I will be watching."

I leaned on the steering board and flicked my glance from Magnus to Arturus. Dawn was still some time away. I detected a change in the motion of my drekar. We were closer to land. "Haaken go and help Arturus watch for the river."

Haaken left his oar and one of the rowers on the opposite side let go of the oar. We had to maintain our balance and our rhythm. A few moments after he had reached Arturus I saw Haaken's arm go to the left. I leaned on the steering board until Haaken's arm dropped. He had seen the estuary or the signs of it, at any rate.

"Cnut, slow the rate down."

Cnut was the oar master when we rowed. When he could he sang to keep the rhythm but at night, this close to land, he used his body to keep the beat. The drekar slowed. Haaken raised both arms above his head. We were on the right course. I noticed more movement in the ship as we hit the fresh water from the river. We were almost there. When Haaken's left arm came out I knew that we were ready to beach. I saw Arturus scamper down the walkway to get Haaken's weapons and cloak. He gave me a grin as he picked them up. He would be joining Haaken ashore.

"Aiden of to Magnus. Tell him to get down and prepare the ropes."

As soon as my message was communicated the young sailor slid down the rope and was at my side in a moment. I pointed to Arturus and Haaken. "Secure the ship to the land when we touch." As he ran off I said, "Half oars."

We were barely making way now against the river but, in the dark, our lack of movement would make us invisible. I did not want any guard alert enough, to see us. Haaken's arms came out at either side. "Up oars."

I did not need to worry about Rolf. He knew what he was doing and his ship's boys were more experienced than mine. He would land further upstream from me. I saw Haaken and Arturus leap from the prow of the ship and disappear from view. I centred the steering board and then donned my helmet. Aiden fitted my wolf cloak and handed me my shield. By the time I had reached the bow of the ship most of my warriors were on the beach in a defensive circle. Magnus had found a large tree some fifty paces from the water and he had tied '*Wolf*' to it.

We had arrived at the perfect time. Dawn was just about to break and I could make out Arturus standing at the top of a small ridge. I knew that Haaken would be scouting the immediate vicinity. We did not expect any warriors this close to the water but it paid to be careful.

Rolf and his warriors joined us. '*Bear*' was just fifty paces from our drekar. "Leave eight of our warriors to stay with the ship's boys and guard the ship.

"Eight? Are you sure Jarl? It will leave us shorthanded."

"If we lose our ships then it will be even worse. I have been stranded on this shore before now, Rolf. We have more than fifty of the finest warriors I have ever led. Harald One-Eye left his oathsworn to die on Man. Who will be left to defend his home?" I shrugged. "If we cannot do this with the warriors I take then it was not meant to be."

Arturus and Haaken jogged back to us. "The land appears to be clear. I smelled wood smoke from the east."

I nodded, "As I recall that is where the monks of the White Christ lived." I turned to Arturus. "Join Magnus and guard '*Wolf*'. Rolf is leaving warriors to help you."

He looked at me defiantly, "We do not need help!"

"And if I say you need help then you need it. Learn to obey, Arturus, or this could be your first and your last raid!" My voice was laden with the threat I would carry out. He quaked, nodded and scurried aboard the ship.

"Are you not being a little hard on him?"

I whipped my head around to face Haaken. "When you are a father and you lead warriors on a raid then tell me how to do things. Until then keep silent."

His mouth opened and closed like a fish. Cnut chuckled, "He is right ,Haaken. Let us worry about our job and let Dragon Heart do the thinking as well as being the father."

Haaken nodded and then smiled, "You are right and I am sorry."

I turned to Rolf. "We will find this settlement. Give us a start and then bring the others. Watch for our signs."

We had devised signs; trees we would mark, arranged piles of rocks. Rolf would follow in a straight line unless he saw a sign.

The eight of us set off. Snorri, as the youngest, left first with Beorn, who was the most experienced of our scouts. They were a good team. Both had the ability to sniff out danger and to move without leaving a trace. We jogged along behind. This was when my wolf helmet did not help me. It muffled sound and restricted my vision. I was happy to stay towards the rear. Even with the helmet I was able to smell the wood smoke. I knew we were nearing a settlement and the odds were it would be Harald's. He would not countenance anyone else living this close to him.

Beorn hissed, "It is close."

We had climbed up from the river and there was a low ridge. It continued to rise but was very gentle; it was almost a plateau. I recognised the site. The trees and bushes had not been cleared very well and we were able to secret ourselves some fifty paces from one of the gates. As I recalled, there were two.

I waved Snorri and Beorn over. "Find somewhere to the east for Rolf's warriors to hide. Return when you have found somewhere."

They ghosted away almost without disturbing the leaves. I took off my helmet to examine the walls more closely. The sun was coming up and soon the gates would open as the settlement came to life. We had a short time to inspect the defences. I risked wolf helmet being seen.

They had repaired rather than renewed the walls. That was a mistake. We had broken through in a couple of places but we had damaged other parts of the walls that they had not repaired. The buildings inside were hidden by the wooden stockade but I that they too would be made of timber and lath. They would offer no defence to an axe. All that we needed now was to identify the numbers.

I counted two guards on the gate. Both had a helmet and a spear. I could not see any light reflecting from armour. If we had to we could use arrows to eliminate the guards. There did not appear to be any others patrolling the walls. Either that was over confidence or they did not have the manpower. Just then I heard movement behind and turned. I saw Rolf and the rest of the warriors arrive. He waved to them and they hunkered down below the ridge to await orders.

Snorri appeared from the ambush site. I signalled to Rolf to follow him and they disappeared along the trail. I looked at where they had been. The ground was heavily disturbed. Harald would soon know that there had been a large number of warriors there.

I led the Ulfheonar directly down to the river. If I could persuade the hunters that we had gone down to the river it might allay their fears. None of my men questioned my movements. When we reached the river I headed up stream. I deliberately broke the branches of the overhanging bushes and trees. "Make them think that we headed upstream."

Soon it looked as though an army had tramped up the river. I found part of the river where there was a shallow beach covered with pebbles and shingle. I led the Ulfheonar into the water. It was icy. We waded upstream along the river. After a hundred paces or so I spied some rocks leading to the shore. I jumped from rock to rock until we were back on firm earth. I did not need to tell them to follow my exact footsteps, they knew what to do. We made our way up the steep slope and I heard a low whistle. I headed towards it and found a grinning Snorri.

"I had a bet with Beorn that you would come this way!"

I growled, "If Rolf and his men had been more sensible then we would not have had to do so. They left a trail that Kara could follow!"

Rolf heard, as I had intended him to and he looked contrite, "Sorry Jarl Dragon Heart."

I nodded, "Set sentries. I want to know how many men we face. We all eat and then half the men sleep." I took off my helmet and cloak. I was tempted to take off my mail shirt but if we were surprised it would take too long to don. We were few in numbers but we were well armoured. I would not jeopardise our safety for comfort. "Rolf, wake me at noon or when something happens."

I was not hungry, I was ready for war. After the battle I would eat as much as any man but I knew that at that moment I needed sleep. I slept fitfully. Dreams came and disappeared rapidly. I could remember nothing. In many ways that was reassuring. The spirit world had nothing to tell me. I was woken by Rolf who spoke quietly.

"Jarl, there are hunters heading this way."

I was awake in an instant. I saw that all of my men had hidden themselves. There was neither track nor trail in the woods where we hid. There were no animal tracks and so, in theory, the hunters should not come anywhere near us. I drew my sword just in case.

I saw that my archers had arrows notched. Beorn and Snorri were nowhere to be seen. They would be stalking the hunters. I heard the voice of one of the men from Harald One-Eye's village, "Are you sure you saw a deer here Karl? I can't see any tracks?"

I heard the answer shouted, as though from some distance, "I am sure I saw movements. It looked like a deer."

"Well there are no tracks and this is too close to the walls anyway. We'll head down to the river. You normally find a few down there."

I looked at Rolf and nodded. They would have to pass by us to reach the river. There was no trail but Karl's mistake had meant that they would travel through our hiding place. The three sisters were playing with us once more. We could not take a chance and I drew my finger across my throat. The hunters would die.

They moved noisily through the undergrowth as they converged on their leader. We could not see anyone yet, the undergrowth hid all. We had to prevent them making a noise and ensure that none escaped to warn Harald. That was where Beorn and Snorri came in. They would be behind the last hunter.

I was next to Haaken and Cnut. Rolf had left to hide with the bulk of the men. I had not had time to don my helmet and I saw that the others were without helmets too. As these were hunters approaching us it was unlikely that they would have either shields or armour. They would, however, be armed and ready to loose their arrows and their spears in an instant.

It was Haaken who killed their leader. He suddenly appeared before us with a bow in his hand. Haaken's sword sliced towards him. It smashed the bow in two and then Haaken ripped it across the hunter's stomach. He fell to the ground clutching at his entrails which were spilling out like bloody eels. There was a warrior close behind the dying leader and he thrust his spear at Haaken. Even as Haaken's sword deflected the spear head I thrust forward with Ragnar's Spirit. I stabbed upwards and the man died silently as the tip entered his heart. I heard a flurry of noise and a few groans and then all was silent.

Snorri appeared. "They are all dead. There were seven of them."

"Rolf, take their arms and have their bodies thrown into the river. Beorn, find us somewhere else to hide."

Haaken smiled, "Thank you, Dragon Heart; that was a timely blow."

I smiled back at him. We were old friends and our harsh words were now forgotten. "You are welcome." I nodded to the bodies as they were carried down the slope. "They will be missed but not until evening." I noticed the blood on the trail and on the leaves of the bushes. Any scout worth his salt would know that someone or something had been hurt here. I just hoped they would believe it was an animal and that the hunters had pursued it.

I shaded my eyes and looked up through the canopy of leaves. It looked to be about noon. The hunters would not be missed until late afternoon or even early evening. I would have to change our plans.

Beorn returned. "There is a good place on the other side of the settlement. There is a rocky knoll which overlooks the other gate. There are fewer trees and bushes but we can hide."

Rolf rubbed his beard thoughtfully. "That will put the settlement between us and our ships. I like it not."

In truth neither did I. As the other men returned I made my mind up. "Rolf, you take the men with Beorn to this new hiding place. I will take the Ulfheonar to the other gate. Instead of waiting until dark we will attack later this afternoon. You will have seven of our warriors dress as the hunters and head towards the north gate. We will attack the southern gate at the same time."

Cnut shook his head, "I can see a number of things wrong with that, Dragon Heart. How will we know when to attack and what is to stop them killing the men dressed as hunters before they make the gate?"

He was right of course. "Then we must make them think that the hunters are in danger. Rolf, you and the other warriors will chase the men who are dressed as the hunters. Make noise and we will hear it. Our approach will be silent. Attack when they bring the animals in from the pastures." The village would have shepherds and cowherds with the cows, goats and sheep. They would make sure that they were safely within the walls before dark. It was as good a signal as any.

"Suppose they bar the northern gate?"

"Then we will fight our way there and open it."

Rolf's mouth dropped open a little. "But there are so few of you and we know not how many warriors he has within."

"True Rolf but we know his walls are weak. If he bars the gate then use your axes to break through the walls and we will distract him from within."

"I like it not."

I smiled as I donned my helmet. "You do not need to like it. You just have to follow my orders. If we fail then take my body back to the Lady Erika."

Cnut growled, "We will not fail. It is a snake we seek and we just need to be careful but by nightfall he will be ours."

Rolf nodded, "Beorn, when you have taken them to the new hiding place find us by the southern gate."

We headed down the slope to the river. We clambered back over the rocks until we were below the bluffs which rose to the gate. Surefooted Snorri led the way. He halted frequently to sniff the air. He was like a human hound. He was seeking our enemies. Satisfied that there were none he moved forward until he reached the place he had chosen from which to watch the gate. He waved us to the ground. We were close to the place we had first landed, hours ago now. There was a scruffy stand of elderberry bushes mixed with hawthorns. It gave a screen through which we could peer.

There were just eight of us and we would be easier to hide than the whole band of warriors. The spot Snorri had found was a good one. We spread out and lay beneath the tangle of thorns and berries, our armour and helmets preventing injury. I could see the gate just eighty paces from us. We were not directly in line with the gate. It meant that the guard's attention would be to their front and we would only be a blur in the corner of their eyes. When we moved we would be like the shadows of clouds flitting across the ground. We would not shout a war cry or try to intimidate our enemies. We would wait until we were sword to sword for that. They would know who we were by our wolf cloaks, black helmets and the red eyed wolves painted on our shields.

Suddenly Beorn the Silent was by our side. He lay next to me and whispered, "They are in place. They are only a hundred paces from the gate. I think that the decoys should be able to make the gate before it is shut. The rest will be up to us."

"You have done well. Now we wait for the animals to be brought back."

Of course there would be no animals on the river side. It was too steep to risk valuable animals such as cows. We would have to be on our toes and judge our move. We had to be moving before we heard the cries of danger from the northern wall.

Chapter 3

It was the sound of a cow moaning which alerted us. It lowed and mooed as it was driven back towards the wooden walls. It wanted milking. They were coming! We all slipped from beneath the hedge which had protected us and moved towards the open ground to our right. With Snorri and Beorn leading the way we moved towards the walls. We did so slowly. Each of us paused at a different time so that only two would move at any one time. A larger number of movements attracted attention. We were inconspicuous.

Suddenly we heard a loud shout from the walls. I glanced up and saw the two guards looking towards the north gate. I ran towards the walls. The rest of the Ulfheonar quickly followed me. We were pressed against the wooden walls before we were seen. Had they had guards on the walls above us then we would have been seen but there were none there.

I led the way and headed towards the gate. We reached it just in time. Two guards had descended from the walls and were closing them. Their hands were holding the gates and Haaken and I killed the two men before they even knew we were there. All attention appeared to be on the northern gate. We pushed the bodies to one side and my men opened the gates. We could see warriors rushing from huts while hurriedly donning helmets and armour. The warrior hall and Harald One-Eye's hall were at the northern end of the village and we raced, like an armoured arrow, through the huts. We left any women and children alone but as we spied a warrior he was cut down. Three had died before the inevitable happened and I heard the shouts, "It is the wolves from the sea!"

"It is Dragon Heart!"

Whatever was going on at the north gate those within would now know we were amongst them. The space before us emptied as those who were there fled from our bloody blades.

As much as I hated Harald One-Eye, I knew him to be a good warrior. Prince Butar had told me that. He was cunning and he had a strong sense of self preservation. He had shown that when he callously abandoned his oathsworn at Hrams-a. Now, however, he had nowhere to run. Now he was like a wounded wild boar backed up against a wall. Now he would be at his most dangerous.

I stopped. The Ulfheonar stopped too. I tightened the grip on my shield and slipped a seax into my left hand. I turned to Haaken and Cnut who were on my right. "Now we end what was started across the icy seas. Now we avenge Prince Butar!"

With a roar of, "Ulfheonar!" we raced towards the hall of Harald. He was there with a shield wall of warriors before him. He looked to have twenty warriors. I knew that there would be others but they would be fighting Rolf and his men. The nine of us would have to take these on until help came.

We formed an improvised wedge with me at the fore. I saw that Harald stood on the steps of his hall with two of his warriors. The other eighteen or so were spread out with shields locked before him. That was his first mistake. I would have had a double wall of warriors. I hurled myself and my shield at the warrior in the middle. He stabbed at me with his spear but I angled my shield and the tip slid and scraped along the metal studs of my shield. The force of my blow and the weight of me and my armour thrust him to the ground. I stabbed him in the throat as he lay wriggling beneath my feet.

I pointed my sword at Harald. "Harald One-Eye! Face me as a man and save the lives of your men!"

Suddenly everyone stopped at my words. It was as though the gods had frozen all movement. I had issued a challenge. Our rules meant that Harald should take up the challenge and fight me. He was however cunning and he had not lived this long without knowing when to fight and when to back off; he laughed. "I should fear a boy and eight men in animal skins? Others may fear you, thrall, but I do not. Thorir and Finni, kill him!"

As his two largest warriors stepped forwards the clamour of battle resumed. Both men were armoured from head to toe. Both had helmets with nasals. One wielded a sword while the other had a skeggox. They grinned as they descended.

"Now I will have the sword touched by the gods." The warrior with the axe whirled it as he spoke and swept it towards my head.

I knew that he expected me to use my shield to defend myself and then his sword wielding companion would strike at me. "First you need to kill me!" I spun around away from the blow and the second warrior. The axe hit fresh air and I continued the swing with Ragnar's Spirit. He was above me and had his shield protecting his left side. His mail shirt went down to his knees and Ragnar's Spirit sliced through the flesh and the bone below that to sever his left leg. Knocking his companion over, he crashed to the ground. I raised my sword and with one mighty blow severed his head.

The one with the sword scrambled to his feet but the sight of his dead companion and his blood which had showered his face had unsettled him. All that he saw was my black wolf helmet and my red painted eyes peering from within. I lowered my voice and growled. "And now you will die. You will taste Ragnar's Spirit!"

He was brave although he had already lost the bout in his head. He swung at my shield and I deflected it. I swung overhand and he put his shield up to protect himself. When I struck the wood I felt my arm shiver and saw a huge crack appear in the shield. It was not as well made as mine. He took a step back towards the hall and I swung again. I hit the same place and the shield split in two. The edge of my sword continued down and bit through his mail and into his arm. He tried to retreat again and I saw fear in his eyes. As I stabbed forward to end his life I heard Snorri shout, "My lord! Watch out!"

Harald One-Eye had suddenly launched an attack at me. Had Snorri not shouted I would have died there and then but his warning allowed me to spin. The sword sliced down as I staggered backwards, its tip severed four or five mail links in my mail shirt and then was stopped by my leather byrnie. I managed to keep my feet.

I saw Haaken begin to move to attack One-Eye. "No, Haaken. I will scotch the snake."

Harald One-Eye laughed, "I should have thrown you overboard when I first saw you. I should have known that the witch that was your mother was a volva. I could see it in her eyes. I will remedy that now!"

"You have shown that you have no honour One-Eye. You had the chance to face me like a man but instead you tried a treacherous attack when I was fighting men who were brave. You will not die with a sword in your hand." There was conviction in my voice and I saw fear flicker across his face.

I stepped down so that we were fighting on the flattened area before his hall. Rolf and his warriors had joined with the Ulfheonar and a battle raged around us.

Harald came at me cautiously. His shield was, as mine, covered in leather and metal. It would not shatter as his oathsworn's had. His sword was a Frankish blade and it would neither bend nor break. We were evenly matched and this would be decided by my skill and the gods. I was sure that the gods were on my side and I knew that I was a skilled warrior. I just needed patience.

When I had first met Harald, all those years ago he had seemed to be a giant. Now, as we circled each other I saw that I was as tall but, more importantly, I was broader. I had more strength in my arms. I feinted at his shield. He raised it and I changed the angle of my attack so that I struck his sword. He had not been expecting that. I had put my entire strength into the blow and drove him back a little. I smiled as I feinted again. This time he anticipated the sword but the blade did not strike. Instead I punched with my shield and the metal boss struck his right arm. It would have stung and, I hoped, numbed it.

He took two steps back and shook his head to clear it although I not gone near to his head. He was working out how to defeat me. He went on to the offensive as I had hoped. He brought his sword over his head as he took two steps forward. He sliced down at my helmet. He hoped to split my head open. Had I been tired or slow I would not have been able to bring up my shield. I was neither and the blade cracked against the metal of my shield. The red eyes of my wolf on the shield were pieces of iron painted with beetles' blood. When his sword struck them sparks flew and fear filled his face.

"Are you a gladramenn?"

I laughed as I swung my sword at his head. "No, just a better warrior than you."

His shield came up but it was a little slower than it should have been and the edge of my sword caught the top of his helmet. It would have made his ears ring.

I did not give him time to recover and I swung my body around to attack his sword side. The swing took him by surprise and he was slow to lower his sword and meet the blow. Ragnar's Spirit sliced through his mail and into his leg. His whole right side lowered to compensate and I spun around the other way and brought my blade across his back. The whole force of my body was behind it. I heard something crack and then the blade bit through the mail, his byrnie and into his back. His sword dropped to the ground and he fell at my feet.

He lay unmoving. I think I had broken his back. He looked up at me with hate in his eyes. "Go on then give me my sword and finish me off!"

In answer I walked to his sword and picked it up. It was a fine sword and had been the best one in the village in which I had become a warrior. "No, Harald One-Eye. You will not go to Valhalla. Nor will I kill this sword. I have another purpose for it. And I will not end your suffering. You have hurt me and my family for the last time." I turned to those around me. All fighting had stopped and they were watching me. "No one ends this man's suffering. I will kill anyone who does so. Hel will come for him and drag him to Niflheim where he will be tortured until the end of time."

"I curse…" They were all the words he managed for Haaken walked up to him, grabbed his tongue and sliced it from his mouth.

"You will curse no one."

I turned to those warriors of Harald's band who still lived. "You who fought against me; I know that you defended your jarl, treacherous though he was. You can now be given a warrior's death or swear allegiance to me. It is your choice. If you swear allegiance then drop your weapons."

There were twenty warriors remaining and they all dropped their swords. I held Ragnar's Spirit by the blade. "Swear on the spirit of Ragnar that you will defend this land for Dragon Heart."

They chorused, "We swear!"

"As for the rest of you I will not enslave you. You are all free to stay here." I saw the relief on the faces of the women as they gripped their children tightly. "The only one who has to die is the witch who changed Harald One-Eye. Where is his wife? The Saxon princess?"

They all looked to the hall. I waved Haaken forward. He knew who she was. She had been the one who had lied about my mother and Prince Butar to have us driven from our homes and I would never forgive her. A few moments later Haaken brought out her body. "She killed herself, with poison."

I heard the gasp of horror from all of the women of the village. I nodded, "Then it is over. The past is another country. The witch is dead and the evil that was Harald One-Eye is ended. Today we begin again."

Rolf and his men had suffered casualties. There were ten warriors who travelled to Valhalla but it was a small price to pay. The arms and treasures of the dead enemies were divided amongst our remaining warriors while Harald's treasure was given to me. We sent the treasure back with *'Bear'*. She was to return with more warriors to replace the dead. I left Rolf and his men to sleep in the camp while I took the Ulfheonar to my son and *'Wolf'* where we would sleep. I wanted nothing more to do with the settlement of Harald One-Eye. It was now mine but I would not visit it again.

When Aiden and Arturus heard, from Haaken of the battle, they were both disappointed to have missed it. I smiled. I understood their feelings. I took out Harald's sword. "I had a mind to give this to you Arturus but then I realised that you will inherit Ragnar's Spirit when I die."

Arturus' face went from disappointment to elation in the blink of an eye. "You would not have the sword killed when you die?"

"No for this sword is the guardian of our people. I give the sword to you Aiden. You have done me great services already and when you have finished with the sword of Rheged you will have done more than I can repay. Take this sword for the love I bear you."

He was grateful beyond words. His eyes began to fill and he dropped to his knees as he took the blade. When I looked at my son I saw the nod of approval. My boy was growing into a man.

We had just eaten when Rolf came down to report to us. "Harald One-Eye is dead."

I nodded. "Have his men strip his body and then throw it into the sea."

"That is how it should be." Rolf nodded his approval. "His men seem to be happy that he is gone. He was not a good jarl."

"Is there one who can command?"

"Audun Thin-Hair seems to be a good warrior and well liked. He killed two of our men before we took him."

"Then tell him he commands for me. This will be Audun'ston. If he displeases me I will find another." I remembered Audun and he was a dull boy, when I knew him, but he was dependable. He would stand in a shield wall and never falter. He would make a good leader for my first settlement in Northumbria.

I sent Snorri back with *'Bear'*. He was a sound sailor and a good captain. We spent three days tending to the wounds our warriors have suffered, hunting and exploring up the river. It was good land. Harald One-Eye's presence had driven the Saxons further east and I knew that Audun'ston would prosper. In time more people could settle here. Perhaps one day, when he had consolidated his power then Eanred might try to retake the land but I doubted it. We would only grow stronger.

Snorri arrived back earlier than I had expected. He came with *'Serpent'* in close company. His face told me of bad news. My heart sank to my boots. Had something happened to my wife or my family?

He leapt ashore as soon as the boat touched the sandy shore. "Jarl, disaster has befallen Anglesey. The Welsh under Cynan have retaken the island. The people there all chose to follow him as their king. Our warriors were slain."

I nodded, "I understand. Raibeart and the others were closely related to the Welsh. What of Thorkell and the men of Wyddfa?"

He shook his head, "They are no longer there. It is now a Welsh domain once more."

I led Snorri and the others to our camp. This needed questions, debate and thought. Rolf and the Ulfheonar sat close by me as Snorri told his tale.

"Alf had taken *'Serpent'* to Anglesey and he was attacked from the fort there. He sailed to the straits and Wyddfa but he saw that it too was in Welsh hands. As he sailed back to Man he came across a Hibernian trader who told him that Cynan had sent emissaries to the island without the knowledge of the warriors there. They arranged for the Welsh to gain access to the fort and slaughter the garrison. Of Thorkell he knew nothing save that the Welsh ruled."

My dream of a land ruled by us close to Wyddfa and the cave of my ancestors was gone. I saw Arturus looking up at me with questions in his eyes. Haaken, Rolf and Cnut also waited for me to speak. I closed my eyes. I need the spirits to speak with me. I had felt closer to my past in the cave and in the land of the Welsh than at any other time. Should we return and fight for it? If I took every warrior who had sworn allegiance to me then I would have, possibly, two hundred warriors. My island home would be defenceless. Could we retake those impressive forts? I doubted it. And what was there for me in the cave and in that land? I had taken the gold and the blue stones I had coveted. I had discovered the sword and my ancestors had been buried beneath Wyddfa's rocks. It was clear to me that the spirits had led me there for a purpose and that purpose had now been served.

I opened my eyes. "We need to sail south and see what became of Thorkell. I owe him and his men that much. If he can be rescued then we shall do it and if he needs to be buried we will give him a funeral worthy of a fine warrior."

Cnut, who knew me as well as any man, said, "Will you try to retake what the Welsh have stolen?" There was no judgement in his words. He was an honest man and the question needed an honest answer.

"No. The land we held briefly is now lost to us. I am not a gambler. I could risk all to regain it and lose all. If I did regain it then it would take men's blood to keep it. I will not do that."

"You do not need the land, Jarl Dragon Heart, for you have all that was precious within it."

I looked around at Aiden. It was as though he was reading my mind. Those had been my thoughts too. "You are right Aiden. We have the sword and the treasures. The only other things of value are my men and we will seek them."

The question came from Rolf. "Where will they be?"

"I will throw that back to you Rolf. If you were Thorkell and you lost your home where would you go?"

He stroked his beard, "Not south. That would just trap me. The mountain blocks the route east and the sea, west. I would have to go north."

"Aye and head for Caerlleon."

Haaken nodded, "And that is where Ragnar Hairy-Breeches is."

I smiled, "*Wyrd.*"

Chapter 4

The three ships headed down the coast toward the Maeresea and the Dee. I did not wish to risk the Dee. The river had many sandbanks and I did not know if Ragnar would be friendly. He was a man who sought power. I knew that he wished to be a king. I would use that to my advantage. He would need my support to become king. My warriors might be few in number but all knew that they had never been beaten so long as I led them.

We landed close to the village where Scanlan and his family had lived before we took them. The village had long been abandoned but the huts and walls could be repaired and would give us a base. We left just the boys and Alf to watch the three ships. Aiden and Arturus were visibly disappointed to be left behind but there were no arguments this time. Arturus had learned his lesson.

After we had repaired the village I left for the Dee with the Ulfheonar and thirty of Rolf's best warriors. The rest I left with Rolf to scour the river bound peninsula for slaves and booty.

"I am curious, Dragon Heart, why we did not bring all of our men?" Cnut queried as we marched south.

"I do not come to fight Ragnar. Not yet anyway. I want to know what happened to Thorkell. If there is no word of him then we will cross into Wales and look for him."

"Thorkell is no fool. According to Alf the heads of the garrison adorned the walls of St.Cybi. There were none at Wyddfa's fort."

"There is a puzzle here. Thorkell would not have given up without a fight."

"Unless he had no other choice."

Thorkell and the others had chosen to settle where they had because they loved the land and thought that they would be able to defend it. If they could not then there was no point in dying for it. None had families. That would have come when they had tamed the land. Obviously that would not happen now.

The old Roman fort had formed the centre of the town which grew up by the river. A sprawl of huts and smoking buildings tumbled from the old stone walls. There was no wooden wall; they needed none. If enemies came then they could flee to the safety of the fort.

We marched with shields at our backs and helmets by our side. We were here in peace but I saw a flurry of activity as we marched down the cobbled road built by Roman soldiers hundreds of years earlier. Many of those in the huts were taking no chances and they fled to the fort.

I wondered if the gates would slam shut in our face when we reached them. If they did then that would be a message from Ragnar. The gates remained open although I noticed that the guards there were wary and fingered their weapons as we approached.

A warrior in mail came forward. "I am Thorir Leather Neck. I command the jarl's guards." He was a big man and he pointedly stood in the middle of the gate with two of his men just behind him. He spoke as though I should have known his name. I did not.

"I am Dragon Heart and I would speak with your jarl."

If this Thorir thought he could intimidate me then he was mistaken. I would speak with Ragnar or no-one. Thorir stared at me. I inclined my head slightly and he nodded and stood aside, "You are welcome, Jarl Dragon Heart." His tone and his expression belied his words.

Ragnar had grown even bigger since the last time I had seen him. He was, indeed, a bear of a man but he had the cunning of a fox. He strode up to me and threw his arms around me to embrace me. "Good to see you Dragon Heart and your famous Ulfheonar." They all nodded and gave a slight bow. It barely acknowledged his title. "Thorir, take the jarl's men to the warrior hall and give them food and ale."

Haaken, Cnut and the others looked to me. I gave a slight nod and they followed Thorir. Ragnar frowned as he led me to his table. "Your warriors looked as though they did not trust me, Dragon Heart."

I shrugged, "They remember being betrayed by Jarl Harold the False and they are very protective of me. They meant no offence."

He grunted. I wondered if he would make something of it but then he smiled and poured me a horn of ale. "I never thanked you properly for telling me of this fort. Once we drove the Saxons from it we have a base which cannot be taken." The smile on his face was not matched with the look in his eyes.

I drank the ale and commented, "This is good ale."

"Aye, I have some fine ale wives who brew it for us." He wiped his mouth with the back of his hand. "I hear the Welsh have taken back their forts."

His eyes were constantly assessing me as he spoke. "I had heard that." I shrugged. "We have other places and it is not worth going to war over." I had to take the bull by the horns for he knew more than he was saying. I could dance around him all day and not find out that which I needed. "Have you heard of any of my men passing through your land?"

His impassive face gave nothing away. "Your warriors? No. None of our people have come through." He smiled, "Saxons and the Welsh fear us now and they avoid us."

I nodded. That made sense. Thorkell and the survivors would have had to come north using the secret ways. There had never been many warriors in the fort. No more than twenty. It might only be a handful who survived the war. "Then I must, with your permission, Jarl Ragnar, take my men south to seek my warriors."

There was the pause of a heartbeat. I wondered if he might refuse. It would not stop me but it might cause problems. He smiled, "Of course but you will stay the night with my warriors? We will hold a feast in your honour. The men would like to see the sword touched by the gods."

I shook my head, "We will have a feast when we have found our men. Time is passing and they may need our help. If we leave now then we can cover another fifteen miles before dark."

"Of course, besides the only way north is across the bridge which my men hold."

I ignored the veiled threat in his words. He would not risk war with me yet. He would hold this favour on account. At some time in the future he would try to reclaim my help. I would cross that bridge when I came to it.

We were cheerfully waved off and we smiled our thanks. Once we were in Saxon territory I walked with Haaken, Cnut and Rolf. Snorri and Beorn scouted far ahead. We would not be ambushed.

"What did you learn?"

"That Ragnar Hairy-Breeches is ambitious. He sees himself as king of this land."

"Northumbria?"

"Aye. Eanred has proved to be a little weaker than his predecessor and Ragnar thinks to exploit that. Coenwulf the King of Mercia is a more dangerous enemy. I suspect that is why the Welsh have expanded west. With the grain from Anglesey they are in a better position to resist the Saxon advances. It is said that their king seeks to claim land which is west of the dyke." The dyke was Offa's Dyke and had been built to mark the edge of Mercia and the start of Wales. It seems there were many ambitious men around.

We had enjoyed the fruits of Anglesey for a couple of years or so. We would now have to resort to raiding to get what we wanted.

"I thought Ragnar seemed over confident." I told them of the jarl's words and my interpretation of them. I think we were right to come east. Who knows what would have happened had Ragnar been given a free rein.

Snorri and Beorn found a dell where we could camp. There was a nearby knoll and we placed two men there as sentries. The hunters brought back some deer and we ate well that night. It was as we lay around our fire looking up at the stars that we heard, in the distance the sound of shouting and metal on metal. Beorn had the best ears. He climbed to the top of the knoll and listened. When he returned he said, grimly, "It is some miles away but there are warriors fighting."

From his look he thought it was Thorkell and his men. "You think it is our warriors?" He nodded. "Could we find them in the dark?"

"If they continue fighting then, yes we could find them."

"Rolf, I will take twenty of your men and the Ulfheonar. We will try to reach this combat."

"But Jarl, we can come with you."

"I need you fresh for tomorrow. Come at first light. We will leave signs for you." I was being sensible and planning to extricate all of us from this land. Others had hunted and I had been resting. I would be tired the next day but if we could save just a few of my men it would be worth it. I owed it to them as much as they owed loyalty to me.

Snorri and Beorn set off to lead us and Sven White Hair brought up the rear. He would mark the trees. We had our own signs and Rolf would catch up to us sooner rather than later.

We trotted behind our two scouts who chose an obstacle free route. Every mile or so the two of them would halt, and we would wait and listen in silence. We thought that the sounds of combat had ended but then we heard it again; much closer this time. It spurred us on. The next time we stopped the sounds were so close that we could hear the voices of those fighting. I swung my hand in a circle and the band spread out. Drawing my sword and swinging my shield around, we advanced.

Suddenly we came upon three of my warriors. Ulf Gunnersson was lying on the ground; he was wounded in the leg. The other two, Eystein Carlson and Thord the Grim were standing over him and trying to defend against eight warriors who were jabbing at them with spears.

We wasted no time. I leapt towards them. The first Welshman half turned as he heard my feet. Eystein shouted, "Dragon Heart!" and another two turned. I pushed the spear head away with my shield and skewered the first with my sword. Haaken and Cnut finished off the other two. Two more lay dead and the last couple tried to run.

"Snorri. Beorn! Stop them!" My two hunters leapt off into the dark to pursue the two Welshmen. I took off my helmet and turned to speak with my warriors.

Haaken dropped to his knees and began to bind Ulf's leg. I could see that the other two had taken slight wounds. There was blood everywhere. I gave Eystein my water skin as Cnut and Einar dressed the two men's wounds.

"Tell me what is important. I will get the detail later."

He swallowed some of the stale water and nodded. "Jarl Thorkell and the rest of the men are holed up a few miles deeper into the forest. There is an old stone circle and palisade. We were surrounded by a large warband. Five of us were charged with escaping and bringing help. We heard that our people were at Caerlleon."

"Aye, Ragnar Hairy-Breeches. Good. You three stay here." I pointed to two of Rolf's men. You two stay with them until Rolf comes."

"But, my lord, we can fight."

I smiled, "You have no need to prove it to me. Now obey me for we shall need your strength before too long." Snorri and Beorn returned. They both nodded. The last of the Welshmen were dead. "Thorkell is holed up not far ahead. There are Welshmen trying to kill him."

"We will find them."

The two of them turned around and disappeared into the forest. I donned my helmet, slung my shield and sheathed my sword. We ran once more. The Welsh we had killed had not worn armour. They had had spears, short swords and small shields. That was how my handful of warriors had defeated them. The trail to Thorkell was well signed. We followed the corpses of the Welsh. We also found the bodies of Lars and Olaf. Both had sacrificed themselves for their comrades. There were bodies surrounding them. They would be in Valhalla now.

We saw the first hint of dawn in the eastern skies over the mountains and Beorn signalled for silence. He put his head close to mine and whispered. "They are up ahead. There are over a hundred of them. They have some horses but most are like the ones we slew."

I had a dilemma. I really needed Rolf and his men. I had twenty five warriors and we would be outnumbered four to one. If we delayed then the enemy might be reinforced too.

"Take me to their camp. I need to see myself."

I signalled for Haaken to take charge and slipped away with Beorn. He ordered me to lie on the ground and to slither along. Suddenly I felt Snorri's foot. I had had no idea he was there. He was featureless, as I was, in his black helmet and wolf cloak. He tapped my helmet and pointed. I could see, through the thin branches of the bushes before us, their guards. There were four of them around a fire. Their comrades were sleeping. Snorri tapped again and pointed to the left. There were twenty men and they were facing away from the camp and towards a shadow which I assumed was the knoll. The horses were tethered well away from the camp and the sleeping warriors were between us and the horses. They would not give us away. I had seen enough and slithered backwards with Beorn. Snorri would remain on guard. He would need no instructions.

When I reached our men I gathered them around me. "Cnut, take the other warriors and attack the twenty men guarding the knoll. They are along the left fork of the trail. I will take the Ulfheonar and we will attack the camp. Attack when you hear the noise from the camp."

He nodded and led his men away. "I want us to kill silently. There are four guards. Use your arrows. Then we go amongst the sleeping men. Kill them silently if you can, but kill as many as you can."

They nodded and we followed Beorn. When we neared Snorri, Beorn and four of the others took out their bows. Without speaking the five arrows flew straight and true, At only thirty paces range they could not miss and each of the guards was struck in the throat and fell to the ground. Even as they fell we were racing towards those who were asleep. I saw a warrior in mail who would be a leader and I ran to him. The noise of the falling guards must have roused him for, as my sword swung down, he rolled away. He scrambled to his feet and began to shout. I ripped the sword across the man's throat and he fell dead in a sea of blood. The damage was, however, done and the camp was awake.

My companions had been more successful or luckier than I was and six other warriors lay dead. The remaining warriors began to struggle to their feet. I still had my shield around my back and I used a short seax in my left hand. I thrust the tip of Ragnar's Spirit at a swordsman who tried to take my head. At the same time an unarmed warrior hurled himself at me. It was pure instinct that made me move my left arm and the luckless warrior impaled himself upon my seax.

The rest had now awoken and were organising themselves. All that they saw were a handful of warriors and they circled us with spears making a hedgehog of blades and iron. We formed our own circle. I was shoulder to shoulder with Einar and Snorri. I knew that, like me, none of my companions feared these men of Cymru. We had fought them before now and we had defeated them.

They rushed at us and that was their first mistake. They got in each other's way. I parried a spear aside with Ragnar's Spirit and sank my seax into the eye and brain of the spearman. He dropped to the ground in an instant. I continued the swing of my sword and brought it down on the leather helmet of a second Welshman. It sliced through the leather and his skull.

Suddenly it felt as though someone had punched me in the side. When I looked a spearman had stabbed at me. The head had penetrated the mail links and then been stopped by the leather byrnie. The warrior thought he had killed me and he had a surprised look upon his face. I slashed my seax across his throat. And then I heard two roars: one from our left and one from our fore. Cnut and his warriors had dealt with the guards and they fell upon the spearmen. Thorkell had led his beleaguered men from their hill fort and wreaked revenge on their tormentors. It was soon over. The Welsh had been shaken by our night time attack and their leaders had fallen. The survivors fled.

When we checked we had lost but two warriors although Sven and Einar both had wounds to their arms and some of those who had attacked the guards had suffered knocks. I knew that I would have a bruise the size of a turnip from the spear thrust but it would not slow me down. As dawn broke we surveyed the carnage we had caused.

"Cnut, get the warriors to strip the bodies of anything valuable. Have it loaded on the horses. Snorri and Beorn, see if we are going to be surprised by any more Cymri. Haaken, have a look for food."

By the time Rolf reached us we had eaten and the horses had been loaded. The sun was rising in the sky. We would have to move soon. We were in enemy land and some distance from safety. I would not wish to be caught here by other Welsh warriors.

I had not questioned Thorkell. He and his men looked exhausted. All of them bore wounds which were testament to their courage and resilience. Haaken's food helped and, as Rolf and his warriors arrived I took the Jarl of Wyddfa to one side to discover what had happened.

He looked at me with sad eyes as he said, "You know we lost Anglesey?"

"I was told."

We would have suffered the same fate had it not been for Raibeart. He was torn; he felt he owed you a warning as a descendant of the Warlord of Rheged but he was happy to be part of Gwynedd. He did not manage to warn the garrison at St.Cybi but he sought us out and told us that the Welsh were going to launch a surprise attack." He shrugged, "We did not have enough warriors to defend against an army. We had always planned on using the locals to help us. We all thought it would be the Saxons or the Irish who would come. We never dreamed it would be Cymri."

"I was as complacent as you were and men have paid the price with their lives."

"We barely made it out of the fort before the Welsh arrived. We used our secret trails to hide from them. We thought we had evaded them until yesterday when we began to move towards the River Dee. They had laid an ambush not far from here. They had over two hundred men and we numbered less than thirty. Had Erik the Tall not remembered this old hill fort then we would have perished. I sent five men to reach our people at the river. We had heard that Ragnar was there."

I pointed to where Rolf now stood with the three survivors. "They found us and that led us to you. If we had not come during the night and surprised them then I think it might have gone ill for us."

"*Wyrd*. Wyddfa watches over you still, Dragon Heart."

"And now what will you do? You and your companions thought that this land was perfect. How say you now?"

He shook his head, "We will serve you again, my lord. My decisions have gone awry. I am not meant to lead your men."

"No, it was the Weird Sisters. They have been spinning their webs and you can now join us on a new quest here on the mainland."

Just then Snorri and Beorn came racing in. Their shortness of breath told me that these fit young warriors had both run hard to reach us. "It is the Welsh my lord. They are about five miles behind us."

"They outnumber us."

"Put the badly wounded on the horses with the weapons. Get them moving. Rolf, you and the fresher men will be the rearguard."

"We will protect you, my lord." He and his warriors formed a defensive half circle as we drove the horses and our tired bodies back towards the north and what we hoped would be safety.

And so we began a race to the river.

Chapter 5

The ache in my side from the spear thrust proved a blessing. The pain and the ache kept nagging at me. Had I wanted to rest the blow would have prevented me. Snorri and Beorn were our greyhounds leading us on but how they did so I had no idea. As they had passed me they had given me the estimation of numbers. There were almost a hundred warriors including ten on horses. We had captured ten horses and I sorted that information in my head. They used a mixed force. I remembered the horses we had found on Anglesey. It must have been a tradition of Rheged.

The horses looked to be a cross breed between the smaller hill horses and the larger horses used against us. They were tough little beasts and hardy but they had neither weight nor bulk. They were for bringing warriors to war and not for fighting.

Thorkell and his warriors had negotiated the difficult terrain when they had first evaded their pursuers. We now had flat land dotted with strange knolls and hills. Once the Welsh found their dead companions then they would hurry. I hoped that we would either have somewhere to make a stand or have reached the river by then. If we were caught, strung out as we were, by fresher men then we would be slaughtered.

It was noon when we heard the clamour of battle behind us. There was a clatter of weapons and then shouts. Although we kept running I sought shelter and defence. There was one of the smaller knolls just ahead. I could see a ring of trees poking above the hedge ahead.

"Head for the knoll. We will need to rest the beasts and it seems they have caught us." The trail we were following was old and, in places, was cobbled. It appeared to lead us where I wished to go.

There was silence behind and I wondered why. Snorri appeared before us. "My lord, the river is just five miles ahead."

"Good. You have done well. Lead Thorkell and the horses there and cross. We will wait at the knoll for Rolf."

He looked at me, "My lord there are just seven of you!"

"Snorri!"

"Sorry, Jarl Dragon Heart. I will obey." The knoll had a few rocks and trees which afforded shelter. As the horses passed with their cargo my Ulfheonar peeled off.

"Get your bows and we will hide among the rocks."

Four of my warriors had bows. Cnut, Haaken and I would have to use our swords.

"What do you think happened back there, Jarl?"

"I think that Rolf ambushed our pursuers and bought us time."

We waited and a few minutes later we heard the clamour of battle again. This time it was much closer.

"Ready!"

I saw the backs of my men as they retreated down the trail. Rolf was using a shield wall to retreat before the Welsh. He had one line with their shields protecting the first line from the Welsh arrows.

As they drew close I readied my men. "Send over three arrows each and then we charge them in their flank."

Cnut laughed, "They will think we are an army!"

"I hope so Cnut."

"Well it will make a good song for me to sing should I survive!" Haaken added wryly.

I could see that my men had lost warriors and some of those in the rear were wounded but Rolf was in the centre with his two oathsworn, Ham the Silent and Erik the Redhead. Even as I watched they lunged forward to kill the two Welshmen, braver than the rest, who had closed with them. The ten warriors on the ponies were to the rear. They were waiting to exploit any weakness in the shield wall.

"Aim for the men on the horses! Now!"

The twelve arrows soared into the sky in three rapid flights. Haaken, Cnut and I had started down the slope towards their side even as the first arrow rose. We all yelled "Ulfheonar!"

The effect was astounding. The Welsh had been pushing forward one minute and suddenly they found their rear and their sides attacked. I took in the fact that three warriors were knocked from their horses and three others skittered away. The warriors who were closest to them looked around nervously and one or two began to move backwards.

Fear is infectious. As my other Ulfheonar joined us I saw the panic set in. They saw seven black cloaked phantoms with full helmets and armour. They saw the red eyed wolves hurtling towards them. At the same time Rolf and his men lurched forward and the inevitable happened, they ran. The handful of warriors, who were engaged at the front, fell as they were deserted by those behind them. I did not even wet Ragnar's Spirit for they ran too fast.

I held up my sword to halt us. I clasped Rolf's forearm. "Well done Jarl Rolf. The river is five miles away. Let us run before they regain their courage and work out there were just seven of us."

As we ran down the road Rolf chuckled, "I thought that there were more than seven of you. I wondered if you had hidden the rest up the hill."

"No, I sent Thorkell and the others to the river. It was the surprise which aided us."

I say we ran to the river but it was more of a fast walk for we were all exhausted. I saw the Roman Bridge ahead and felt relief that we had made it. Snorri and Beorn stood guard at one side and I saw the horses, Thorkell and the wounded on the other.

Once we crossed I said, "We make camp here. We can run no further."

We ate the dried meat we had brought with us and we drank the river water. We were exhausted. Had anyone found us, even a party of the monks of the White Christ, we could not have fought them. We had just two men on watch and they woke the next two after a short time. We all needed sleep.

I was woken by Einar and took my place with Cnut.

"What do we do on the morrow Dragon Heart? Do we all spend time with Ragnar?"

I shook my head. "I do not trust that snake. No, we will send Rolf and the others directly to the ships. My Ulfheonar will visit with the Jarl." He gave me a strange look. "I do not wish to give him grievances. If we snub him completely then he may take offence. I do not want him to raid our home. We will visit with him and give him a version of the truth. We will tell him we fought the Welsh and lost warriors. Our band was picked up by our boats."

"Will he not be suspicious?"

"Of course but he will worry where Rolf and our other men are and we should be safe. He thinks all men are as treacherous as him and that they will be up to no good."

Rolf and Thorkell were as unhappy as Cnut when I told them of my idea. The advantage of being Jarl is that you cannot be gainsaid. They obeyed. The Ulfheonar, in contrast, were happy to be going to Ragnar's stronghold. They feared no man, least of all Ragnar.

As we approached his gates I said, "Remember, we lost many men to the Welsh and the remnants of our band are now heading to our ships. Do not look victorious."

Haaken laughed, "That is difficult, Dragon Heart, for we have yet to taste defeat."

Ragnar must have been watching for us. He greeted us himself as we came through his gate.

"Jarl Dragon Heart; where are the rest of your men?"

"The Welsh ambushed us."

"Did you find those you sought?"

"We found the survivors." I pointed vaguely to the west. "We have sent them to our ships but I came directly here as a courtesy. My warriors have passed through your land."

He nodded, "You had my permission but it shows respect and I appreciate it."

He led us to his hall. I noticed that this time my Ulfheonar were not taken to the warrior hall. He sent for food and drink. We needed it but we all needed sleep more. I hoped that he would offer us his hospitality. He did not did disappoint. "I insist that you stay for a feast tonight in your honour. As I said before my men would like to see the sword touched by the gods." I saw the avarice in his eyes. He was desperate to own the magical blade. He was not renowned as a warrior. He led men and he conquered but he had no name. If he could own Ragnar's Spirit then it might give him that elusive trait. They were stepping stones to a kingdom.

We washed up and removed our armour. I knew that my men were less than happy to do so but it would have been seen as disrespectful had we remained armoured. It felt good to be without armour, however briefly. I felt lighter even though I also felt vulnerable. We all retained our swords. That was to be expected.

I sat next to Ragnar and his wife. I had not met her before but Hallgerd was not what I expected. She was much younger than Ragnar and although she was with child her cheeks showed that she ran to fat. I thought of my Erika whose body was as slim as a swan's neck; each to his own. Hallgerd was also less of a hostess than Erika. She just sat, listened and ate. In truth she looked bored. Ragnar ignored her. I smiled to myself. I would do such a thing at the risk of the sharp edge of my wife's tongue.

"Tell me of the Welsh. So far they have not bothered us."

"I think that their new king is flexing his muscles. The Mercians are pressing from the east and the land to his north would seem to be ripe for plucking." I saw a frown on Ragnar's face. "He may not know you are here yet, jarl, and he may think it is Eanred."

Mollified he said, "That makes sense. How are they as warriors?"

"The ones who ambushed us had few men with armour but they use horses and have many archers. They outnumbered us and we were in a strange land." I added by way of explanation for our apparent defeat. They pursued us to within five miles of the river."

He looked concerned at that. "I thank you for that information. I will have to send scouts out to seek them." He stood and raised his horn. "Everybody drink to my friend, Jarl Dragon Heart!"

Everyone toasted me and we all drank. I made sure I took just one swallow whilst Ragnar drained his mighty cup.

As we sat down he asked, innocently, "Where are your ships? I sent my men to offer your guards some food but they could not find them."

I kept my face as impassive as I could, "We had them sail back to Man to bring more men in case we needed them. We arranged to meet them in a few days."

The frown reappeared and then vanished almost as quickly. "You have many warriors who follow you then?"

"Aye. I was not sure if I would need them to rescue my men."

He waggled a finger at me, "I hope you left enough men to guard that pretty little wife of yours."

Had I been drunk then that would have sobered me up. "Do not worry Jarl Ragnar Hairy-Breeches, after Harald One-Eye's treacherous attack I have taken precautions. No man will harm my family every again." I put enough venom in my voice to make him recoil a little.

"And I believe you. Good. And when will you meet with your ships?"

"We will leave on the morrow and go to the place we arranged." I shrugged, "They will return when they can."

"Would you like my men to come as guards for you?"

I laughed, "I have the Ulfheonar. If there are any Saxons here who would threaten us then we are more than enough for them."

He smiled but it was hollow.

I slept in the warrior hall with the Ulfheonar. I did not sleep soundly as I still expected a blade in the night. Ragnar must have worried that it would prevent his ambitions from coming to fruition for we had an undisturbed night. The next day he tried to press his men upon me once more but I declined.

"No Jarl Ragnar Hairy-Breeches, for you will need to watch for the men of Cymru. I will be safe but I thank you for your consideration."

When we left I had Snorri lag behind while Beorn tracked ahead. When we crossed a stream and halted to drink some water Snorri said, quietly, "We are being followed. There are scouts and, I think, a warband."

Einar growled, "Let us teach this dog a lesson Jarl."

"No, Einar, we will let him believe that we trust him. Do you fear the whelps which follow us?"

He laughed, "Do I fear the fleas in Ragnar's halls? No!"

"Then ignore them. Snorri you and Beorn can find our ships."

We spotted their masts even as the two scouts returned to say they had discovered them. I felt relieved. I was not worried, Alf was too clever a sailor to be caught but I knew that I had left him shorthanded. Rolf's guards found us and led us towards the river. One of the more sharp eyed amongst them, Thord the Left-Handed said, "Jarl Dragon Heart, you are being followed."

"I know. Pretend we are Saxons and cannot see them eh?"

"Yes my lord."

Arturus ran to meet me with Aiden trying to catch him. He suddenly seemed to remember that he was now part of the crew and not my son. He stopped abruptly. I hid my smile, "How goes it Arturus?"

He was bursting to tell me something. Aiden came next to him and said, "Later, Arturus, when the jarl is aboard the ship." There was warning in his voice.

Arturus replied, meekly, "Yes, Aiden."

Alf had not left his ship and he waved cheerfully, "We had exciting times Jarl. I will let your boys tell you about it. They did well."

I looked at the two of them and they had both adopted innocent looks. "Good. We sail for Audun'ston."

"We are all ready when you and your warriors are aboard."

The Ulfheonar were the last to board and as soon as they were at the benches and ready I ordered Magnus and Arturus to cast off. I had to concentrate until we left the estuary. As soon as the sea caught us and the wind filled our sail I was able to relax more.

"Arturus, come and take a turn at the steering board while I take off my mail."

His face split by a beaming smile he raced to the stern and he moved the steering board until I nodded my satisfaction. Aiden had helped me with my armour, cloak and helmet before now and I was soon feeling lighter as it was carried to the box at the stern.

"So Arturus, can you sail and speak or will Aiden tell me of your adventure?"

Happy that he was steering he said, cheerfully, "Aiden can tell you. He has the words."

I sat on the chest with my armour. I could listen and watch the masthead to see that Arturus was following '*Bear*'. "Go on then Aiden. I am intrigued."

"Captain Alf said he was unhappy with where the ships were moored. He decided to move them down stream and across the river where a stand of willows would afford some protection. Once there we waited." Aiden sighed, "Some of the boys became a little restless." From his shamefaced look I knew that it was Arturus. "Captain Alf sent Arturus and me to hunt for some small game. Magnus and one of the other boys rowed us in the boat to the shore close to where we found you. We managed to bag a hare and two ducks. On the way back we heard a noise and we hid. It was Ragnar Hairy-Breeches' men."

I stiffened, "How did you know?"

"We were hiding underneath some bushes and they stopped above us and spoke. I heard them say his name. They thought that they would be in trouble if they went back without discovering our ships." Aiden sighed. I knew that he was going to tell me something he did not think I would want to hear. "When they left we followed them. They travelled up stream. We were quite worried when they neared our hiding place but they saw nothing. We hid until they had left. We waited until we were sure that they had gone and then we signalled Captain Alf."

He hesitated as though he was afraid to say more. Arturus looked at me expectantly. I nodded, "You have done well. I am pleased that I brought two such resourceful boys to be part of my crew. Well done."

The relief was clear on both their faces. Aiden rushed on. "And when we reported we decided to keep two men on the opposite shore to watch for you and Ragnar's men in case they returned."

"Excellent. And now I will have the steering board Arturus. Relieve Magnus at the masthead and he can watch at the prow."

I had much to think on. Aiden began to move away. "No Aiden, I would speak with you." He returned and leaned on the stern. "You have been with my son more than most what are his strengths and his weaknesses?"

"Jarl Dragon Heart, I am little more than a thrall I cannot speak."

"You are no thrall. You are one of my warriors and a free man. You now have a mighty sword. You have an opinion and I value it. You may never stand in a shield wall but you are intelligent, resolute and brave. Use that courage now and speak the truth to your Jarl." As I spoke I suddenly realised that I sounded like Olaf the Toothless when he would chastise me. I smiled to make it easier.

"He has courage. He was not afraid of the warriors and I saw him with his hand on the hilt of his seax. He is quick thinking. He has skills which could make him an Ulfheonar."

He was silent. "I need the truth Aiden. What are his weaknesses? How can he be made better than he is?"

Aiden seemed satisfied, "He can be a little reckless at times and he takes chances."

"That can be useful in a warrior when tempered with a mind. Can he plan? Can he reason? Can he think?"

"Yes," he said slowly, "but his mind needs training."

I had finally managed to have Aiden arrive at the place I wanted. "Good. Can you train his mind?" He looked at me. "I know that the sisters of the White Christ taught you to read and to play the game they call chess. That helps the mind does it not?" He nodded. "Then teach him that game. The two of you will be spending much time together guarding the boat. Use the time well. I know he will not enjoy reading but you are a clever youth. You can make games which will improve him."

"I will do so, Jarl Dragon Heart."

"Good."

I could barely keep my eyes open as we headed the forty or so miles up the coast. The estuary was almost in darkness. The thought came to me that I ought to have a tower built where men could keep watch and have a light lit to guide our ships to safety. Even as I thought it I realised that we would have to make the town better defended. If we could take it then so could our enemies.

Chapter 6

We remained at my new settlement for a week. We helped Audun and his men to improve the defences and sent out, each day, patrols to hunt and investigate the land around. We found that the river could be sailed for a few more miles upstream. After that our passage was barred by an old Roman Bridge. We found farms and isolated hamlets but the ones who were Saxons fled when they recognised us. We discovered some of the people who were descended from the people of Rheged. When they spoke their Saxon was accented and a little like the Welsh. Once they found we meant them no harm we were welcomed.

I sent '*Serpent*' back to Hrams-a with the weapons and treasures we had liberated from the Welsh. When they returned we heard the news that Sihtric was now controlling parts of the Irish coast. He extracted money from the Hibernians in return for letting them live. As soon as I received the news I knew that it would only be a matter of time before he began to cast covetous glances at my island.

We sent Alf to try to get some more Frankish blades. There had been an edict banning their sale to Danes or the Norse. However, Alf was certain he knew places where he could go. "Besides, my lord, we are using an Irish ship. We may get away with it."

Alf was resourceful and clever. We would not need him now as I did not intend using my ships for transport. We would travel north towards what had been Rheged, on foot. I intended to find what was there before we headed deeper into Northumbria. We had expected more opposition from the Saxons but Eanred seemed to be preoccupied. I would take advantage of that.

Some of the men who had been wounded during the flight from Cymru had not recovered and we left them to guard the boats. Audun had impressed me as a leader and I knew that the two ships would be in safe hands. We still had the tough Welsh horses and we took those with us as we headed north into the land which was still a mystery to us. I had been along the part where the Romans had built their wall but that was many leagues to the north. None of us had any idea what lay between.

We let the boys tend the horses. It gave them something to keep them occupied and safe at the same time. We had just sixty warriors this time. We had lost some and left some with the ships but there were now twelve Ulfheonar. The three who had left us, albeit briefly, had come back stronger. They had tasted defeat and did not like the bitter taste.

Snorri and Beorn had recovered well from their exertions and ranged far ahead of us. It was they who found the monastery and hill fort. We later found out it was called Cherestanc. At the time we just knew that there were Saxons who were still there. There was a hill and behind the hill rose the mountains which marked the middle of the land. The hill fort and the monastery were on a small promontory which stuck out from the hill side. As soon as we knew of its existence I sent Rolf and twenty men to get to the other side. They would wait until we had launched our attack.

"Be patient, Rolf. We know that there is always much treasure at these places where they worship the White Christ. Better to take our time and get it all than rush in and risk losing the best." He nodded. "Position yourselves so that you can cover an escape to the north and the east. We will find the best way to gain entrance to this treasure trove."

I glanced at the sun; it had passed its peak and that meant it was early afternoon. It was not yet high summer and so we had plenty of time to spy and even assault this Saxon home.

I left the warriors, horses and boys under the command of Olaf the Witch-Breaker. He had recently joined us from Orkneyjar and had shown himself to be a good warrior when we fought the Welsh. Rolf had praised him and that was enough for me.

I led the Ulfheonar up the slope towards the walls. I could see that the monks had terraced the hill and were tending their fields. They had built dry stone walls to afford protection from the westerly winds. We were able to find a location which gave us an excellent view across their terraces and their gate. By spreading my warriors out we were able to get a better picture of the settlement.

There looked to be about fifteen monks working the fields. They had no armed men with them which showed me that they were not expecting trouble. There were two men with spears lounging at the gate. I wondered what was within.

I gestured for Beorn to join me. "Can you get a closer look at the inside for me?" His answer was to slither away up the slope. He looked like a dark shadow. I had seen him do this before. When someone neared he tucked his legs beneath his wolf cloak and looked, for all the world, like a black sheep asleep on the fells.

Whilst he was away I observed the work of the monks. They tended bees as well as fields with vegetables. As we waited I heard the noise of sheep. We could not see them and I assumed they were higher up. This was a prosperous community. It seemed that they wanted for nothing; it should be well endowed. They had built a path which wound between the dry stone walls up the hill to the gate. It would provide some protection from attackers such as us.

Beorn returned and he led us a little way down the slope so that we could speak. "They have built well. There is a building within which looks like a hall. I saw a mailed warrior and what looked like his family. They had horses and were about to ride somewhere. They had three children with them. There look to be fifteen armed men within. Some were practising with weapons. They have a gate to the east as well as this one to the west. They have a ditch but they have one flaw. There is a rock which is the same height as the walls and is but four paces from it. Archers could send arrows into the fort and not be seen."

That decided me. I led the men down to the others. "Beorn, you say archers could send arrows into the fort?"

"Easily."

"Could warriors get into the fort from the rock?"

"Not all warriors. They would have to be skilful climbers."

"Like Ulfheonar?"

He smiled and looking at Sven White Hair, who was one of the older Ulfheonar, said, "The younger, fitter ones, yes they could."

Sven cuffed him about the head, "I can still whip a young whelp like you."

"Then I will give you five archers from the warriors and you take the Ulfheonar who can scale the walls. I will bring the rest of the warriors through the fields. Be ready to climb the walls and have the archers keep the warriors from the gates. We will drive the monks from the fields. If you can prevent them from closing the gates then we might be able to capture this monastery easily." Beorn nodded. "You can see the fields from the rock?"

"We can see the path which leads up to it and that is enough."

"Good. Choose your men. I will speak with the others."

I gathered the warriors around me. "We are going to attack this monastery." I paused, "We will drive the monks up the hill. They will be sheep and we will be the wolves. We need to make as much noise as we can. The monks are unarmed. They can be easily subdued. You do not need to kill them. There is no honour in that and besides, they are valuable as slaves. There are not many warriors within the walls. I want as much treasure as this place has and as many slaves to sell." I looked around their faces and saw that they were keen and ready. "Olaf, choose the best six archers and send them to Beorn."

I noticed Sven and Tostig returning from Beorn. I smiled; both of them would have struggled to make the leap Beorn had described. There would be a time, soon when both would be leaving the Ulfheonar. All of us knew that the demands of the Ulfheonar were high.

"You two are on my shoulder." I turned to Aiden. "Take charge of the horses and the boys. I saw the disappointment on the face of my son. "Not yet, Arturus. Not yet."

When we were all ready, with our war faces on, I led them down the slope to the lowest terrace. We kept low beneath the walls. I spread the men out on both sides and I took Sven and Tostig with me to the path which wound between them. I slid Ragnar's Spirit from my scabbard and yelled, "Attack!"

My warriors took me at my word. As the three of us ran up the path they leapt over the dry stone walls screaming blood curdling shouts. I saw the monks hesitate for a moment and then flee up the slope. They shouted, "Vikings!" in terror. I saw one brave or foolish monk wield his rake at one of my warriors and watched as he was cut down. The others who had contemplated using their tools thought better and joined the flood.

We ran up the path which twisted and turned around the stone walls. At each turn the gate was a little closer. I saw that it was still open but that mattered not. We could easily force it with our axes. I saw the monks who reached there first, milling in the doorway. My warriors had formed up behind me as the fields were cleared and I was almost on the heels of the last monks. One of them fell. I leapt over him and heard a sharp crack as one of my men stunned him with the haft of his spear. The two guards lay dead both pierced by arrows. Once we were inside I saw that it was chaos. Their dead littered the gate and the inside of the fort. Some had been killed by arrows and others by Ulfheonar. I saw Thorkell and Snorri with bloodied blades.

I stopped and yelled, first in Norse and then in Saxon. "Stop!" My men all stopped. The survivors of our attack began to look for an escape.

"I am Jarl Dragon Heart. If you do not resist then you will live. I give my word that you will not be harmed." There was a pause and then I saw the monks nearest me slump to the ground in resignation. Those with weapons threw them down

"Olaf, secure the gate. Snorri, fetch Rolf and the others. Haaken, Cnut, secure the prisoners. Einar, fetch the horses."

I looked around and saw that there were just three warriors left alive. There were ten of the monks who had been working in the fields and another two who were dressed in finer clothes. From my experience I knew that one would be the Abbot. I nodded to Erik, "Watch the two monks in the fine clothes." Erik wandered over to them and drew his sword. He could speak Saxon. Of the man Beorn had seen on the horse and his family, there was no sign.

I waited until all my men were within the walls. It was coming on to evening and I wanted secure walls around us and food. We still had the buildings to search. That would be better on a full stomach.

When Snorri returned with Rolf I could see from Rolf's face that he was not happy. I waited patiently for him to report. Something had gone awry. That much was obvious.

"The ones on the horses escaped." I waited. He pointed to a shamefaced warrior. "Thorgill, here, could not wait to take a leak. The horses came and he still had his breeks around his ankles. Jorgen and Carl the Lame were both killed." Jorgen and Carl were young warriors from Duboglassio. They were not as experienced as Thorgill who was one of my oathsworn.

"You will pay the families, Thorgill." He nodded. My word was law. He would recompense the mothers of the two boys who had died because of his mistake. The result might have been the same and Thorgill dead too but he lived and he had to live with and pay for his mistake.

"How many were there, Rolf?"

"A mailed warrior with two other warriors, a boy and a woman." He looked shocked, "The woman rode like a man."

Beorn joined us having heard the end of the conversation, "They fled when they heard the noise of your attack and the guards were slain. We tried to reach them but the warriors held us up."

"Bring me the surviving warriors."

The three who had managed to live through our attack were dragged to me. Their hands were bound. Had they not been followers of the White Christ I might have left their hands unfettered and offered them a warrior's death. As it was they were not to be trusted. Their word meant nothing. There were two younger warriors, one was little older than Arturus and an older greybeard. I spoke with the greybeard. I saw that he bore battle scars on his arms and face.

"What is this?"

He remained silent.

"Who is lord here?"

He obstinately refused to speak.

"You know you will die if I do not find out what I wish to know?"

He nodded, "And I will die if I tell you so why should I help you?"

"You will live if you tell me."

"As a slave?"

"As a slave."

"Then kill me now for death is preferable to slavery."

I shook my head, "I was taken as a slave on the Dunum and look at me."

He nodded, unsurprised, although his two companions looked shocked. "I thought you spoke our language well for a Viking. You must be the one they call Dragon Heart."

"I am."

"I have heard of you. They say that you are not as bad as the rest and that you keep your word."

"I do. So tell me."

He shook his head, "I am too old to learn to be a slave. I would have died defending the church had I not been struck a blow from behind."

"You follow the White Christ then?"

"I do." He took out the cross from beneath his kyrtle. It was a small one made from metal. "I shun the old ways."

"You do not wish a sword then?"

He shook his head. "This is my sword." He kissed his cross. "Do it swiftly, one warrior to another."

I nodded, "Thorgill."

Thorgill was keen to regain my favour and he took out his sword and took the old warrior's head off in one blow.

I looked at the other two. They had been splashed with the greybeard's blood and looked shocked. "He was a brave man and I can understand him. He was too old to learn new ways. I make the same offer to you two. Tell me what I wish to know and you shall live as slaves. You will be treated well and may attain your freedom as I did."

They looked at each other. The younger of the two looked terrified and I felt sorry for him. The other warrior put his arm around his shoulder. "I am Aelle and this is Aethelfrith my brother. I promised our mother I would look after him. She died of the fever last year." I nodded. "We served Eorl Osbald. He ruled here for King Eanred."

"Good. You shall live. And he left with his wife, son and oathsworn?"

"Yes my lord."

"And where would he go to?" There was hesitation. "It cannot hurt him but I need to know."

"Dunelm; his brother and the king are there."

I was satisfied. It would take many days to reach Dunelm. They could not give chase. Aiden and the others had arrived, "Aiden, you and the boys watch over these two. They are to be taken to Man. Treat them well but keep them secure."

Aiden nodded seriously. He would not let me down.

"And now let us see the priests. Rolf, find some food. The monks may be able to help."

I went to the two monks who were dressed well. I took the Ulfheonar with me. I wished to intimidate the priests and my men looked fierce. We all wore red paint beneath our helmets and I know that the followers of the White Christ thought we looked like devils. They were creatures from their religion that they feared.

The two men tried to rise as we approached. I drew Ragnar's Spirit and, resting it on the shoulder of one, forced him back to the ground.

"I am Jarl Dragon Heart. I do not fear your White Christ so curse me all you will, I do not fear him. Nor am I afraid to spill the blood of monks. I will sleep easily after doing so. I tell you this because I want you to know the truth. I hide behind no man and no god." The older monk nodded. "You are the abbot?"

"I am. I am Abbot Kernhelm. What happens to us?" He swept his arm around his monks all of whom were looking very sorry for themselves.

"You will be taken back to my island and you will be slaves. Some will be sold and some will work on the island." I smiled, "Your monks will find it no different from here but you will."

"It will not be the same. They will not be able to worship our God, Jesus Christ."

I laughed, "We do not impose our gods on you. We have others such as you, women too and they are allowed to worship whom they choose. I think it will be the hard work which you will not like Abbot Kernhelm."

"I am not afraid of hard work."

"Good for you shall have plenty. Now tell me where your treasures are." He hesitated. "This is not a large place and we could tear it apart in less time than it takes to make a blood eagle." I saw that they both touched their crosses when I mentioned the blood eagle. It was a thinly veiled threat and they knew it.

"There is a room beneath the altar and two chests within. They contain our treasures."

"And your books?"

He looked at me in surprise. "You can read?"

"I can but I don't." I smiled, "We can sell them in Frankia. Thank you Abbot. You have just saved many lives."

We went to the church. I pointed to the candlesticks, lace and other objects they used in their rituals. "Tostig and Ragnar Siggison collect those and keep them safe." We opened the door to the cellar and Snorri descended.

"It is only small. There are two chests." He handed the first one which was reassuringly large. We pulled it to one side. The other was disappointingly small and light.

We opened the larger one first. In it were some bones, two rings which looked to be seals and two bags of coins. The larger bag contained silver and the smaller, gold. I took some coins out. They had heads imprinted on them and the names of rulers. I would get Aiden to find out who they were later. "The bones are obviously saints' bones. Cnut, take them outside and ask the Abbot which saints." He looked at me curiously. "That will affect the price we can get."

I carried the other chest outside. It was a finely made chest and it was locked. I was tempted to break it open but it looked too fine to be destroyed. I walked over to the Abbot. "The key."

He shook his head, "The Eorl has it. This was his. It has nothing to do with the church."

I believed him. Haaken said, "I can break it open."

Aiden was still nearby and he shouted, "No! I can get it open." I handed it to him. He looked at Haaken apologetically, "It is too good to destroy and all it takes is some skill." He took out a thin dagger and some thin metal. I smiled as I saw Haaken peering over his shoulder. After a few moments' exertion a grin appeared on the Irish boy's face and he opened the box.

He had handed it to me after closing it again. "You should be the one to see what is within Jarl."

Haaken ruffled Aiden's head, "Every day I see you become more of a gladramenn!"

I opened it and, at first, I was disappointed, it was just a piece of calfskin. I took the calfskin out and underneath was a large gold coin. I saw writing along it which looked like Latin to me. I handed it to Aiden while I unfolded the calfskin. Once again it was Latin.

"It says '*Corona Aurea*'.

The Abbot stood. He held out his hand, "May I?" Aiden looked at me. I narrowed my eyes. The Abbot said, "I have never seen inside the box but I have studied Roman coins and this seems to be a Roman coin." I nodded to Aiden who gave it to him. He turned it over in his hands and then handed it to me. "It is a Roman medal awarded to soldiers for incredible acts of bravery. This one was awarded in the reign of Antonius Pius. He built a wall further north of the one built by Hadrian." I could see that he was desperate to read the calfskin.

"Well Aiden?"

"This is a letter written to someone called Dux Britannicus…"

"He was the military ruler of Britannia after the Romans left." I flashed a look at the Abbot and he was silent.

"It says that this is all that remains of a family called Aurelius. According to this the head of the family was an equite?"

The abbot looked at me and I nodded, "A knight or horseman."

"He was an equite who guarded the land close to the wall. Oh I can see a name for the Dux Britannicus, it is Coel."

This time the abbot could not contain himself. "He was the King who founded Rheged. He lived north of here. I had thought he was a legend. He was real!"

I took the letter and looked at the writing. I recognised some of the words but Aiden had done a good job. I fingered the medal. I could feel that they were connected to me. I did not know how but the hairs on the back of my neck tingled. Once again I had been meant to find something: the box. I replaced the treasures in the wooden casket. "Thank you Aiden, thank you Abbot."

The Abbot looked disappointed. I think he wanted to examine them in a little more detail.

I turned to Rolf. "Tomorrow you can take the slaves and the treasure back to Audun'ston. Take them home and return with your ship." I looked at the Abbot. "Is there another estuary north of here?" I saw him debating whether to tell me or not. "Your slavery can be with a good family or a pig farmer so choose your words carefully."

"The River Lune is not far north of here but ships can only travel a short way up it."

"Good, then Rolf, you will meet us at this river. We go north, we go to Rheged."

As the others went about their business I sat with Aiden and examined the small casket. I saw that the lid had been well decorated. It looked Roman rather than Saxon. I had not noticed it before but now it was clear. I could see that there was a horseman and he held a lance with something fluttering from it. I peered closely at it. It could not be! I was making something out of nothing.

"Aiden. Examine the box and look at the lance. Tell me what you think it is that flutters there."

He looked at and then his mouth dropped open and he started at me. "It looks like a dragon's head, Jarl."

I nodded slowly, "And that is what I thought too. '*Wyrd*'."

Chapter 7

We set off in the hours just after dawn. Two of the horses were used to take back the treasures and weapons. We also divided the food we found so that some would augment Audun's store. It was somehow easier walking knowing that we would be close to a river soon. A river meant safety for we had an escape on one of our ships should we become trapped.

We walked along an old Roman Road. Many of the cobbles were missing used, I imagined, by people living locally to improve their homes. We saw few of these people as we trudged north under the hot summer sun. I wondered why for the land look to be bountiful. Aiden and the boys still led the horses. I knew that both of them were desperate to speak with me about the casket. I did not expect for one moment that Aiden would not have told Arturus what he had seen. I had been awake half the night trying to make sense of it.

My mother had said her people came from Rheged and her father had been Warlord and yet from what the Abbot had said and the letter had implied, Rheged only came about when the Romans left. Where did my heart come from? Whose blood coursed through my body? I thought I had discovered much in the two caves but now it seemed that the more I found out the less I knew and the more there was to discover.

I had been silent for some time and Haaken and Cnut joined me. "What troubles you Dragon Heart? Did you discover something in the box which was evil?"

"No, just the opposite. I found another link to my past."

I explained to them all that I had discovered. Haaken was fascinated. "A horseman with a dragon's head on a lance? Why?"

"I have no idea but the horseman on the box looked much like those horsemen who pursued us on Anglesey. If Raibeart was correct then that is how the men of Rheged fought; fully encased in mail, riding big horses and carrying lances. Now we know that they had some connection with a dragon."

Cnut shook his head, "There is something greater here than we can fathom." He clutched his wolf amulet, "This is the work of the sisters."

"Aye and that worries me for we all know how precocious they are. I will make a sacrifice when we reach the river."

I saw that the land to the east was steep and hilly. Woods covered its sides and, I assumed, would be teeming with game. It seems that those who lived here, the people of Rheged, were not farmers. If they were then there was little evidence of them having cleared the land.

We reached the river and I saw that the priest had spoken true. We could almost walk across it. "We will head down stream and watch for Rolf."

It was only mid afternoon when we made camp. Some of the men set up nets across the river to catch fish which would come and go with the tide. Those who prepared our food began to make the fires. I sought Haaken and Cnut.

"I intend to make a blood sacrifice before we cross this river. I should have done so earlier." Their expressions told me that they understood. "I will go into the woods and find an animal worthy of a sacrifice."

"You will go on your own?"

"I need to make the blót a special sacrifice for the gods."

"Aye but we will come with you. Not to hunt but to watch over you. We are your oathsworn."

I could not gainsay them and so the three of us left. We deigned armour and helmets. We needed to be able to move swiftly and silently. I took a good spear and my bow. Thorkell was less than happy for me to be going but he obeyed orders and promised to watch over Arturus for me. I left the casket with Aiden. "See what else you can discover while I am away. There may be secrets we cannot yet divine."

The nearest forest was a mere six miles away. Without shield, armour and helmet we almost ran the whole way. It was good to feel the wind in my hair and my beard. I do not know about the other two but I felt years younger. It was like being a boy again and hunting in the forests high above our village.

Once we struck the forest we looked for the animal trails. They would all head for water and so when we found a deer trail we followed the one which led down through the forest to the stream we knew would be there. There seemed to be an understanding amongst animals that they would all use the same water at sunset. Once they left the water then there would be danger. The only danger to animals at water would be man.

We found the spoor of some deer. I would not sacrifice just any deer. It had to be a kill worthy of a sacrifice. It would need to be a fine stag; a leader as I was. In a perfect world we would capture the beast and kill it at the river. However we had neither the time nor the means for that. We would kill it and use its heart and its blood.

We moved silently and carefully through the darkening forest. We had little time before sunset. When we saw the lightening of the forest ahead we knew that there was a clearing; it had to be water. I waved my two companions away. They were there to protect me and not to kill for me.

I saw that it was a small mere, a patch of water bigger than a pond. I could smell the deer. That meant the wind was in my favour. Soon, I could see three does drinking. They would not do. Then I saw the antlers of a fine red deer. He was on the far side of the mere. He would be a worthy sacrifice for the gods and the sisters. I looked over and saw that the other two had seen him. I laid my spear against a tree trunk and strung my bow. I drew a hunting arrow and notched it. I was going to descend to the side of the mere when I saw him enter the water and begin to wade across. The gods wished me to make this sacrifice and were bringing my victim to me. I knelt down and took aim. When he emerged from the water I would have a clear shot of his chest. It would only be forty paces distance and I could not miss.

I pulled back on the bow and began to let out my breath. Suddenly I heard the sound of leaves rustling and a roar of anger. I spun round and saw a wild boar hurtling towards me. I loosed the arrow which pierced his eye. It served merely to enrage it. I had almost no time to think. It was less than ten paces away and coming towards me roaring its pain and its anger. I grabbed my spear and, jamming the end against the tree pointed the head at the beast. Its mouth was open and was covered in the blood dripping from its eye. Its tusks looked ready to rip me apart. As the spear entered the boar's mouth I realised that it was not a boar spear. I would die when the spear went down the boar's insides and its teeth and tusks found my soft flesh.

With a crack and a tearing sound I saw the spear head emerge between the boar's ears. It stopped dead, quite literally. I watched the life go from its eyes. Its teeth and tusks were just a hand span from my fingers. I had been saved by luck once more.

Cnut and Haaken appeared, white faced by my side. "I was convinced you were dead. I could not see how you would stop such a beast." Cnut's eyes widened as he took in the size of the animal.

"The spear must have entered its brain and killed it instantly. That is why there is so little blood."

"Then it will be a worthy sacrifice."

I looked down at the mere. The stag and its does were edging away from the noise. "Farewell king of the forest. It was not your day to die."

We tied the boar's feet around the spear and hauled the enormous animal out of the forest. It was dark by the time we reached the camp. We saw the flames from the fires and they helped to guide us. Arturus, Aiden and Thorkell rushed to meet us as we laboured along the old Roman Road.

All of them were impressed by the size of the beast. We rigged up a frame to keep the body from the ground while I prepared the sacrifice. I washed and cleansed myself in the river. I dressed in clean clothes. Haaken and Cnut put one of the cooking pots beneath the dead boar. When all was ready the men formed a circle around the animal. I whetted my seax until I could have shaved with it. I began to slice and saw through the underside of the wild pig. I did it carefully for I did not wish to waste any of the blood. When the entrails began to pour forth I dragged them out of the way and the, putting my hands deep within the animal I sought its heart. Even though it had been a couple of hours since it had been killed the heart was still warm. I ripped it down and suddenly blood poured into the pot. I placed the heart in the bottom and waited until every drop had drained.

Haaken and Cnut carried the pot towards the river. We had a procession of warriors behind. Every warrior was armed to honour the dead beast and each carried a lighted torch. When we reached the river Haaken and Cnut placed the pot in the water and stepped back. I reached in and took out the heart. Holding it before me I sang,

> *"Odin the Allfather,*
> *Take this heart,*
> *Odin the Allfather*
> *Grant us strength."*

I laid it in the river.

> *"Odin the Allfather,*
> *Take this blood,*
> *Let it flow to the sea,*
> *Let it keep us safe"*

I tipped the blood into the water. There were eddies which made the blood swirl around my feet.

I knelt down in the bloody water.

> *"Odin the Allfather,*
> *Hear my plea,*
> *Protect the Dragon Heart*
> *and all of his people."*

I knelt down to touch the water. As I did so the light from the torches around showed the dark red eddies disappearing and the blood flowing to the sea. I stood and raised my hands. "We thank you Allfather!"

The warriors erupted. It had been a good sacrifice. The river had drunk the blood, consumed the heart and take both to the sea and Odin.

We skinned the boar and buried it in a fire pit. We covered it with grasses, bushes and branches and then earth. While we slept it would slowly cook.

I felt much happier when I awoke the next day. It had been a good blót. Had the blood and the heart remained at my feet it would have been a bad sign but the fact that it had gone to the sea was perfect. The heart of the boar had been enormous and the blood had almost filled the cooking pot.

The men dug up the boar and we ate well on succulent, slowly cooked meat. We spent the morning salting the fish which had been caught the previous day. The boys went, under Aiden's supervision, and collected wild berries. We foraged when we could for we were going into an unknown land.

The sentry we had placed downstream ran to us, "The '**Bear**' is here!"

Rolf had made a swift passage; another sign that the blót had worked. He tied the ship to a rock and strode over. His face split into a grin when he smelled the meat. "You have feasted well Jarl Dragon Heart."

"Aye and we had a good blót. This place shall be known as Blood Pool from now on. Have your men enjoy the meat."

He did so. We all knew that to eat the meat of the animal which was sacrificed enhanced the powers of that sacrifice. As they ate, Rolf, who had travelled more widely than any of us, said, "I know some Jarls who would have sacrificed a prisoner or even one of their own men to ensure a good voyage."

Aiden looked up from the berries he and the boys were cleaning, "Did they eat of the flesh?" I knew that the Hibernians had different customs.

Rolf looked at Aiden and said, darkly, "Aye they did."

There was a pause as Aiden took it in. "And did that work?"

Rolf looked thoughtful for a moment, "You know I never found out. I did not sail with the jarls who did that."

Aiden was a thoughtful youth. He asked questions which had not been asked before. This was my first blót. I had made sacrifices myself before but they were for me and my family. I had sacrificed this time as jarl and that was much more serious.

I looked ahead at the hills. "Aiden fetch the map we have."

When I had first begun sailing with Olaf and Prince Butar we had started to draw a map with the places that we knew. At first there was more that was empty than was filled in. Now, however, we had lines showing the coast and there were few gaps, at least on the western side of the island. The older marks were now faded but the red of Audun'ston stood out.

Aiden laid it on the ground and took out the feather he used to make the lines. "I will add the new places, jarl."

While we examined it he went to last night's fire and took some of the charcoal which he mixed with water. Then he went amongst the rocks and lifted them. He collected a couple of black beetles and crushed them. He returned to the map and drew the line of the coast from Audun'ston and then the river then he carefully put a red dot and marked it with some letters.

Cnut asked, "What is that Aiden?"

"That is where we are, the Blood Pool."

I took out my seax and used it as a pointer. "Rolf, we know that up here there is a mighty river." I jabbed at the river which ran close to the Roman Wall. He nodded. "What I need to know is what is between these two rivers. This one we cannot sail up. Is there one further north?"

"When we sailed in, this morning, I saw a river to the north for the bay seems to sweep around. I do not know if there are any others."

"Then we make for there. Load the boat with as much as we can. We will take the horses. It will take us longer to reach there but you can have a camp ready on the banks of this new river."

"Aye my lord."

We swam the horses across the river, which was lower than it had been, the tide was on its way out, and then Rolf ferried us across. It was easy going as we headed north. The land was undulating and we found that the beach grew ever closer. With our ship carrying the heavy items we made good time. Snorri said, "Jarl Dragon Heart, look!"

He pointed to the sea and I could see that it was retreating before my very eyes. I had seen the tide go out before on flat places but never like this. We stopped and watched as the blue grey water changed to yellowy mud and sand.

" Look at '*Bear*'! She is stuck!"

We all looked to where Beorn of the sharp eyes pointed. Rolf had been sailing towards the northern shore and had been caught out by a rapidly retreating tide. He was going to be stranded on the sticky muddy patch of sand until the next high tide.

"We can do little to help him. We will push on to the river and hope that he is refloated on the next tide." Perhaps the sacrifice had not been a good one or perhaps the sisters were toying with us once more. All of our food and shelter was on board our ship. We just had the weapons and clothes we stood in. There was little that we could do about our ship. We pushed on.

Summer had been good but that day the sisters decided to be particularly precocious and sent a sharp summer storm complete with black clouds and torrential rain which made seeing further than a few hundred paces ahead impossible. The men's spirits sank and we trudged on, heads down watching each footstep as the only marker of our progress.

And then, as suddenly as it had sprung up, the storm stopped. The clouds fled towards Man as rapidly as they had come from the east and the sun began to dry our sodden clothes. I saw that we had reached the point where the bay headed west. Out to sea there was no sign of the *'Bear'* and I began to fear for her safety. Then I remembered that Rolf was a good captain and that it had been a good blót. I had to have faith in the gods. So far we had not lost a man and I had no reason to believe that the Allfather had fallen out with us.

"Come we will push on. The river cannot be far ahead."

Suddenly, just half a mile ahead Snorri shouted, "A river!" However when we found it we realised it was not the river of which Rolf had spoken. It was shallow enough to wade. We trudged on as the sun began to sink towards the west. We found Rolf's River just when the sun began to dip slowly beyond the horizon. We could see that this was a bigger river. We could have moored six or seven boats in its mouth.

"Make camp!"

The men threw down their shields and began to build shelters. If the rains came again we would need them. The food we had last eaten at noon was now just a memory and I knew that the pangs of hunger would be gnawing at the insides of the others as it was with me.

I sent the boys to the sands to dig up shellfish. We could, at least, make a fire and bake them. They would not satisfy us but they would, perhaps, make us feel as though we had eaten. The chewy cockles and limpets did not lift our spirits much but the fires which dried our clothes and the presence of something warm inside, did, at least help us to sleep.

Chapter 8

When we awoke there was no sign of the ship and I sent the scouts out to see what the land around was like. Haaken and Cnut led men to go hunting.

Beorn and Snorri arrived back before the hunters and they brought disturbing news. "Jarl Dragon Heart, there is a fortified settlement on the other side of the river. It is just on the opposite bank. They have armed warriors there."

"How many warriors?"

"It looks to be a warband of over fifty."

"Are they Saxon?"

"I do not think so. If I was to take a guess then I would say Hibernians."

Snorri nodded his agreement. "Aye, there were bare chested men with tattoos and lime in their hair."

I needed my ship. I needed to be able to cross this river. When Haaken and Cnut returned I set the men to cooking while I took the Ulfheonar to investigate this Hibernian fort.

We found a low rise on the eastern bank of the river. We chose a place where the river narrowed from the wide estuary to just a few hundred paces. The village was a mile or so away from the water. There was a small hill which gave us some cover and we watched the settlement. The wooden wall around the huts was not intended to keep out man. It was intended to keep animals in and wild animals out. It would not prove an obstacle. They had one gate and it looked to be the type that you dropped into place. It would be broken easily but it would stop the Hibernians fleeing once the wolves were in the hen house. "You are right, they are Hibernians. But look, in the fields beyond. What are they doing?"

Beorn's eyes came to our aid again, "There are thralls working in the fields. They have yokes about their necks. There look to be over sixty of them."

I led the Ulfheonar down the bank so that we would not be seen. "Well that explains the Hibernians. They have taken the village and enslaved the people."

"Then why not take them and sell them?"

"I think, Haaken, that they might well do that when they have harvested the crops which are growing. The Hibernians are clever people. They know how to make a profit."

Tostig nodded, "Then we can travel up this side of the river and when we return they will be gone."

I shook my head. "No, we will destroy these Hibernians and free these people."

Most of the Ulfheonar, with the exception of Haaken and Cnut, stared at me as though I had the moon madness. "But why Jarl? They are not our people!"

"You are right Einar but I am not of your people. I am half Saxon and half something else. I told you before we left Man that I was seeking answers. I wish to find out about my past. The box I found in the monastery was another pointer. We are being led here." I looked at them. "You are Ulfheonar and you have all sworn an oath to me but I will have no man bound to me when he does not wish to follow. Any who chose to leave may do so. I release you from your oath."

There was a stunned silence and then Tostig and the others began to clamour. Haaken held up his hand, "Do we want adventure? Do we want riches?" No one said a word. "Then we follow Dragon Heart. I, for one, wish to see where this path we tread, leads. It may be to death but at least there will be great glory and we will be seated close to the Allfather in Valhalla."

They all nodded their agreement. I was riding the storm clouds and my wolves were with me. We feared no-one.

It was noon when a battered '*Bear*' limped towards us. Rolf edged her close to our camp and the boys raced to tie her securely to the shore. "Get the mast down, Rolf."

Rolf knew better than to question my orders and the mast was quickly taken down. He came over to me. "What is the matter Jarl Dragon Heart?"

"There are Hibernians across the river. We are going to attack them tonight. I do not want them to know there is a dragon ship on the river." He nodded. "What happened?"

"It was my fault. I thought to take the short route across the bay and the outgoing tide caught us out. It took some time to refloat her and when we did the storm drove us away from the shore. But we are here now."

I could see that he was both annoyed and angry with the events. He hated letting me down but it was not of his doing. Had he sailed successfully to the shore then the Hibernians would have spotted him and would know that we were in the vicinity. The sisters had been spinning and they had approved of the sacrifice.

"Will she float?"

"Of course Jarl but I would not like her on the open sea."

"All I want is for you to transport the warriors across the river after dark so that we can attack when they do not know we are here. The longer we delay the more chances there are of them seeing us."

"Then I will take us across."

We chose ten warriors to row the ship back. We attached ropes so the boys could use the horses to help pull the damaged drekar back. The last thing we needed was for us to be stranded. We had the rest of the afternoon to prepare. We sharpened weapons. We used seal oil to protect our amour. My Ulfheonar donned their red paint and chose their weapons. We would take just shields and swords. The bows could be used by the others.

My plan was simple. The Ulfheonar would go to the far side, the side nearer to the sea and scale the small wall. We would infiltrate the village and kill the guards. As soon as the alarm was raised then Rolf would lead the others from the river side. It was a variation of the plan we had used the last time.

Having made sure we had all eaten well we left as soon as the light left the sky. We moved swiftly across the water on the overloaded drekar. We had three men to an oar. After scrambling ashore we watched as the dragon ship was hauled and rowed back to the other bank. When it reached safety I was relieved. I led the

Ulfheonar along the river and left Rolf and the rest to secrete themselves along the bank and to wait. There were no discernible trails but the ground was relatively flat and without obstacles. We could smell the smoke from the stockaded town and we could see the glow from their fires. It was easy to find the far side.

We hid behind some low bushes and stunted trees. I knew that we were as hard to see as it was imaginable. Dressed from head to toe in black there was no flesh to be seen. Even our hands were blackened. Our eyes were darkened within our helmets and our bright swords remained sheathed until we needed them.

We could see beyond the low wall and we saw the Hibernians moving around. We heard a scream; it was a woman and she was in trouble. I hoped that Rolf would realise that this was not our attack. The screams reached a crescendo and I heard the rough cruel laughter of drunken men carrying across to us. This was the time to attack; they were preoccupied. I waved my line of eleven warriors forward.

I drew my sword as we moved slowly across the rough ground. It was littered with small stones and the rubbish discarded by the village. It meant we had to be careful to avoid making the noise of a slipped footfall. We reached the ditch which surrounded the wall. It was mercifully dry. Pausing to listen for noise I lifted my head to look over the top of the rough wooden wall. There was a large fire in the middle around which sat some of the Hibernian warriors drinking. Just to one side was the woman who was being assaulted by the drunken Hibernians. She was lying still. I could not see any armed guards but I knew, from Snorri, that there were at least another thirty, in addition to the twenty, I could see. I raised my sword and slipped over the wall.

There was barely a sound made by the twelve of us. Any slight noise was covered by the noise from the men close to the fire. We ran in a wide circle. I wanted our attack to have an instantaneous effect. It did. One of the warriors on the far side of the fire must have seen us for he stood and shouted, "Wolf!" I had almost reached the line of warriors whose backs were to us. They turned. I sliced the head from the nearest warrior and backhanded the one next to him. Ragnar's Spirit sliced his ribs open. A warrior stood and tried to grab me. I punched him in the face with my shield and he tumbled backwards into the fire. He ran, like a spectre with the lime in his hair on fire.

The ones near the fire had been easy to kill. They were drunk and they were surprised. The ones who emerged armed from the huts were prepared and would not be easy to kill. I sensed movement behind me and turned just in time. A huge warrior swinging a two handed long axe aimed at my head. I ducked beneath the blow and stabbed forward. My sword stuck him high in his thigh. He gave an angry roar and reversed the swing. He had quick hands and I stepped backwards to avoid it. I was holding my shield high and did not see the dead Hibernian over whom I tripped. Although the axe missed me he screamed in triumph and lifted the axe high to split me in two. I kicked hard at his good leg and he fell, I rolled to avoid his body and, leaping to my feet, fixed his body to the ground with my sword.

I took the opportunity to regain my breath and I stared around. I could see many dead Hibernians but my Ulfheonar all stood. I saw Rolf and the other warriors fighting on the far side of the fire and they were being forced back to the wooden wall.

I hefted my shield around and slipped my seax into my left hand. I ran to the aid of my men screaming, "Ulfheonar!" I knew that any of my warriors, who could, would come to our aid.

I hurled myself at the back of a heavily tattooed warrior wielding two swords. He was quick. He must have heard me coming for he swung around and both swords sliced towards my head. I saw his grinning face and noticed that it too, was heavily tattooed. I held my shield and sword up. They took the blows of the two swords and I head butted him. I heard the crack from his nose and his forehead. He slumped to the ground and I stabbed him through his throat.

The Hibernians are a wild people who will fight amongst themselves if there are no enemies for them to kill. They fought ferociously. We were better armed, better protected and better prepared and yet they continued to fight long past hope. I had to admire their courage; futile though it was. They fought to the last. None asked for quarter and none was given.

The ground was awash with blood, bodies and discarded weapons. We had not managed to avoid losses. Eight warriors were dead and four others would never fight again. Six warriors, including Tostig and Einar had wounds which needed stitching. I hoped that the sacrifice had been worth it.

"Snorri, find the villagers and bring them here."

My warriors went around ending the suffering of the dying. Already Rolf had the men taking the weapons and the treasures from the Hibernians. Some of them had metal torcs around their necks. One looked to have gold and silver inlaid into the iron. These raiders were wealthy.

I heard a wail as the villagers were led out. They cowered. I could see that mothers gripped their children as though they expected them to be torn away from them. Their yokes made this difficult. They look thin and emaciated. They had not eaten well.

One man, a little younger than me, stood proudly and stared at me. I realised that we all had our helmets on and we must have looked intimidating. I laid down my shield, sheathed my sword and, taking off my helmet, smiled. I was not certain what language they spoke and so I began with Saxon.

"Who is your headman?"

The proud looking man said, "I am Pasgen son of Urien and I am the headman." He paused and then, before I could speak, said, "If you think we fear you Viking, you are wrong. We did not fear the Irish and we will not bow the knee to you."

I turned to my men, "Take their fetters from them." I spoke in Norse and when my men approached them I saw that they bunched their fists and looked ready to fight. I held up my hands and said, in Saxon, "We mean you no harm. My men will take your yokes from you. We come not to enslave you but to free you."

I could see the doubt on their faces but, once the first wooden yoke had been taken it was replaced by joy. Pasgen dropped to his knees when he had his yoke taken from him. He spoke in his own language. "Forgive me wolf man. I thought you came as they did to enslave and abuse us."

I lifted him to his feet. "Do not believe all the stories you hear of the Norse. They are not all evil although there are some, I must admit, that I would not turn my back upon." I pointed to the pots of food. "You all look as though you need food. My men will remove these bodies while you eat and then we will talk."

I understood much of what he said. "Rolf, remove the bodies. We will make a pyre by the river else the carrion will come and feast. See to the wounded."

Haaken joined me, "They have been cruelly treated. It was a good thing we did here today."

"I know. It is *wyrd* is it not? We were meant to come here. It was a good blót. Have some guards placed outside. I do not think that any escaped but it is better to be safe than sorry." He left and I waved Cnut over. "Have the Ulfheonar collect the treasure and take it to the river. Signal the camp and then they know we are safe. When it is dawn we will get the drekar and bring it over."

Cnut nodded and then said, "I thought that huge warrior with the two swords might have had you Dragon Heart."

"Once I realised that his hands were full I just used my head. Fighting without a helmet and armour may look heroic but it is foolish."

Pasgen joined me, "I cannot tell you how grateful we are." He suddenly looked worried. "Will we be beholden to you now? Owe you fealty?"

We sat on one of the logs by the fire. "You owe me nothing." I took a deep breath, "I am not Norse. I was born of a Saxon father and a mother who was the daughter of the last Warlord of Rheged."

If I had conjured something out of the air he could not have been more amazed. "You speak true?"

I laughed, "I am Dragon Heart and known to be a man of my word. I found the tomb of Myrddyn and a Warlord I believe to be my ancestor. I also found a sword. I have been told by some priest of the White Christ that my ancestors came from around here."

He nodded, "I am descended, through my father, from the Royal family. We kept the names but for time immemorial we have just been farmers and fishermen. When the Warlord took our warriors south we were forced to fend for ourselves. Your coming gives us hope."

"Good. I look forward to exploring this land that gave birth to my mother's father."

He looked fearful, "You cannot leave yet!"

"Why not? We have killed the raiders."

He shook his head, "There are others who brought them. They are due back with the new moon."

I looked up in the sky. That would be less than seven nights away. "Then we will stay."

He relaxed, "Good. My father resisted them and they killed him and my mother. They are heartless and evil."

"We will stop them."

He suddenly seemed to see my shield and how we were dressed. "You look like wolves."

I nodded, "We are the Ulfheonar. The wolf warriors."

His eyes widened. "Then you are indeed descended from the Warlord for he was called the Wolf Warrior."

I felt a shiver down my spine and the presence of Ragnar. "*Wyrd*."

He nodded, "*Wyrd*! What is wolf warrior in your language?"

"Úlfarr."

"Then we shall rename our town as Úlfarrston in your honour. We will be the town of the wolf warrior. You did not ask me for fealty and I shall give it of my own free will. I am your man and all my people will follow you."

"But I may not stay. I have my family on Man."

"It matters not. We will follow you. It was meant to be."

Most of the people and many of my warriors had returned to the huts or lay down around the fire to sleep. I could not. My mind was a maelstrom of thoughts and dreams.

"Tell me Pasgen what you know of this." I took out my seax and drew the dragon we had seen on the box.

He smiled, "That was the device and the banner carried by my ancestors. It came from the Roman Army and was a piece of cloth fashioned to look like a dragon. When the horsemen rode the wind blowing through the head made it wail. It frightened our enemies."

Suddenly it all made sense; the sword, the banner, the cave and my involvement. Now I knew that my destiny lay not on Man but here, in Rheged.

Chapter 9

I awoke and felt the stiffness in my body. Although I was not old, the fact that I had aches and pains after a battle such as the one the previous day showed me that time was passing and I still had much to do. Had my ancestor, the one buried with the wizard beneath Wyddfa's rocks, managed to achieve all that he intended? I doubted that for Rheged had been conquered. I had to work harder before it was too late.

I went to the river. Rolf had had some of his men swim across the river and I could see them loading the ship. He was still trying to make up for his delay with the storm. Pasgen walked behind me. "What do we call you?"

"My people gave me the name Dragon Heart and I am a Jarl."

He nodded, "Then we will call you the same. Jarl Dragon Heart." He looked to the west. "When the Hibernians come what will do you, Jarl Dragon Heart?"

"I have fought them before. They are a cunning race of warriors. They are disorganised and wild but they are clever too. If they see my ship then they will know that something is wrong and will return to their homeland for more men. There are many young warriors on their island who seek adventure and battle." I pointed to the river. "How far up the river can we take my drekar?"

"There is a bend not far up there. I would say a Roman mile or so."

"Good. Then when we have repaired my ship I will moor it beyond the bend where it can be hidden." I looked to the north of the small settlement. The land rose gently. There appeared to be dips and hollows for I could see the tops of some trees. "My men will build a camp up there where we can hide from view and we will watch for the Hibernians. When they return what do you expect them to do?"

A frown passed across Pasgen's face. "They will take the children who have grown since their last visit and sell them. They will find the young girls who are now women, take them and sell them." I saw him stiffen, "Any women who are not with child will be taken."

"This village is a valuable source of income to them?"

He nodded. "In the spring they take most of the new animals born over the winter."

"And that is why you are all hungry."

"We could not hunt with the yokes and when they hunted they kept it for themselves. We were forced to live off the fish in the river. But their numbers have declined."

I led him to his gate. "We will make the Hibernians fear this place but there are others who will come. There will be Saxons and Vikings who see you as something to be devoured. We need to make them fear you. I want each one of your men and young men to take one of the weapons we captured. Practise until you can use them. Then we will show you, when they have been defeated, how to make a better gate, a deeper ditch and higher wall. I am afraid you made it too easy for them."

"I know but that was my father. We had had peace in his lifetime and that of his father. No-one bothered us and he thought it would stay that way." He shook his head. "He kept dreaming of the day that the Warlord would come back and men in armour would ride to our rescue with the Dragon Banner."

"That will not happen. There are no such men now."

He looked at me curiously, "But he was right about one thing. He said that one day the Wolf Warrior would return and here you are. He will be happy now, in the Otherworld. We will do as you say. I hope your warriors can show us how to use the weapons."

"Oh they can do that all right."

When I reached the river they were unloading the drekar. I saw the relief on the face of Arturus. Aiden gave me a slight nod. My son had come through the ordeal well. It was all part of becoming a warrior. This voyage would see my son take the last steps as a boy before he became a man. The winter would bring many changes.

"Rolf, when we have repaired her we can moor her up river beyond the bend. Without the mast she will not be seen."

He rubbed his hands. "Good. I will get the horses unloaded and then," he grinned, "the boys can get rid of the horseshit from the bottom."

I saw Arturus' face fall. As the son of the jarl he had not expected to be doing such menial tasks. I had begun life doing just that. Strangely it was good for a warrior to experience that kind of job. You realised that it had to be done and that everyone in your community was as valuable as everyone else.

I gathered my Ulfheonar around me. Rolf and the rest of the men would need all of their energies to repair '*Bear*'. We had other things to do. "Come with me." I led them up the slope to the low ridge which overlooked the river. As I had expected there was a depression, it looked like a bowl, which would serve as our camp. "We are going to build a hidden camp here. I will use the boys to watch for the Hibernians and I am hiding the drekar beyond the bend."

"When do you expect them?" Haaken was the one who liked to plan. He was the natural leader when I was not around.

"They came in the spring to harvest the animals and the children. I would imagine that they will come towards the end of summer. The headman thinks they will come with the next moon."

"We do not have long then."

"No, Haaken, we do not. I am going to give them some of the weapons we captured. I want you to train them to use them. We will not be staying here. I intend to move on and winter elsewhere."

That surprised them. "Why? There is shelter here and we are close to the river and our ship."

"Because, Cnut, I would explore this land. I have a mind to bring my family here. From what Pasgen told me there is little danger here save from Hibernians and they like to strike close to the coast. I intend to find somewhere safe deep behind those mountains. They are not as steep as Wyddfa but these have no Welshmen lurking behind rocks."

I saw Thorkell nodding. "Snorri and Beorn; I want you to explore the land north of here. Follow this river. See where it leads and how far along we can take a drekar. You have six days and nights. Do you want Aiden to go with you and draw a map?"

Snorri laughed and shook his head, "He will slow us down and I think, Jarl, that we too can draw a map. We may be just warriors and we cannot read but we can make marks on calfskin."

"I am sorry Snorri. I was not trying to make light of your skills. I just wished you to be able to give me the information I required. If you are both happy with my instructions?" they nodded, "then waste no more time here."

They raced back to the boat to collect what they would need. "The rest of you can spend the day hunting. These people have little food and the woods around here must be filled with animals."

As we walked back to the town which would now be Úlfarrston Haaken walked with me. "Where is the youth who happily cleaned out the bottom of the drekar and cared for an old man?" I looked at him with a puzzled expression on my face. "Now you are so decisive and know your own mind."

I laughed. "He is still within but now he wears the skin of a jarl."

"You know the men think of you as a prince?"

"I would not have Prince Butar's title. I can never be the leader he was."

Haaken shook his head, "You could be greater. There is nothing to stop you from becoming king."

"King? King of what?"

He swept his hand around the land and the sea. "This is not Northumbria and it is not Hibernia. Pasgen said as much. This is the land of Rheged or what remains of it. He is descended from the last kings but he does not claim the title."

"Enough. I am happy to be jarl and watch over my family."

He nodded, "Then we will continue to serve you."

The next five days passed quickly. The ship was soon repaired and I took Pasgen aboard as we rowed up the river. I saw smaller rivers which entered the large one. I realised that I could have saved my scouts much work had I spoken with Pasgen first.

"Where does this river lead? And how far along could we sail this drekar?"

"It ends at a large water. There is an old Roman fort at the head of it and my people used to live there. As for sailing?" He shrugged. "It is wide enough for this boat all the way to the water but I do not know about how deep it is. It becomes almost dry in the summer. In winter, when we have had the rains and snow, then it would not be a problem."

That sounded promising. Once the problem of the raiders had been solved I would take my men up the river and see what we could find.

In the evenings I spoke with Pasgen and learned all that I could about this Warlord. They had many stories which had been passed down from father to son and I was sure that they were not all true. There was one story about how the Warlord flew with his wizard into the castle of a treacherous king and killed him before walking out through the walls. I did not believe that. However I learned that he too wore a wolf skin and fought under a wolf banner. The mounted men fought under an old Roman standard. The Dux Britannicus was called King Coel by Pasgen and was revered. He was keen to tell me all the tales he could. The Warlord appeared to have come from the east. The night he told me I felt shivers down my spine. "He came from a place close to the river the Romans called the Dunum."

Could it be that I had been taken from the very place that my ancestor had grown up?

On the sixth day, late in the afternoon, Snorri and Beorn arrived back. Although I had spoken at length with Pasgen he had only given me a second hand account of the land to the north. He had never been there himself. It seems the community had kept to themselves. Had the Hibernians not visited them they would have remained isolated for all time.

They took off their weapons and slumped by the fire which was cooking our evening meal; the hunting had gone well. "This is good land, Jarl Dragon Heart; far better than that around Wyddfa." I saw Thorkell exchanged a glance with Harald Green Eye. It was they who had liked the land around the high mountain. This was, perhaps, some compensation for them. They had lost one dream and now another came their way.

"Yes, Beorn is right, Jarl. This river twists and turns and ends in a long and wide water. The water of the river was quite high but I do not think we could get *'Bear'* into the water. Perhaps when the rains come…"

"That is what their headman told me."

"The water teems with fish and is surrounded by mountains. We headed west after that and found a most disappointing place. It was filled with biting insects and flies." Snorri showed me his arms which were covered in tiny red bites.

"Aye, we thought to turn around and come back down the river but we kept on and we were glad that we did. We found another water, longer and narrower than the first. This was closely surrounded by mountains. We only found two passes to it from the north. We followed the river south and it brought us out just a mile or so up this river."

"Both places would make good settlements but Beorn and I preferred the second one."

They exchanged a look with each other which made me curious. "Why?"

"The air was cleaner and there were fewer flies."

That did not convince me, "And…?"

They both looked a little sheepish and embarrassed. "And there is a mountain which looks like old Olaf the Toothless bent over. We saw it as the sun set behind it. It was *wyrd*."

"Then when we have dealt with these raiders we will visit the old man and pay our respects."

We had another few days training Pasgen's warriors. They were not very good. They had not been trained with weapons from a young age. Arturus had used a wooden sword as soon as he could walk. It was funny watching my son, who was little more than a boy, showing men twice his age how to use the swords we had procured for them. They were better with their bows and javelins, having used them for hunting but we had to show them how to make arrows which could kill a man. We made them better spears which they could not throw as far but which penetrated flesh better.

Their blacksmith was the only one we did not have to train. He had a mighty hammer which he wielded like an axe. He would fell any foe who came within his swinging weapon.

Magnus brought us the news of the arrival of ships. He raced in, out of breath and panting. "Calm down, Magnus, and regain your voice." He went to open his mouth and I held up my hand. "Gather your breath and your wits. I want a report that I can understand. Someone give him a drink." Arturus handed him a water skin.

He drank, wiped his mouth and then nodded to show that he could speak. I waved my arm. "There are two ships a mile or so off shore. They are not drekar and they look like '*Serpent*'.

"But they are not?"

"No, Jarl Dragon Heart."

"Do they have oars?"

"Some but not as many as '*Wolf*'."

"Good, you have done well." I ruffled his head. "They will be the Hibernians." I turned to Pasgen. "You know what you and your people have to do?"

He nodded. "Don the yokes and go into the fields."

"Good. Do not worry. They will not get to you. You have my word."

"But there are two ships. That is what they brought the first time. They will outnumber you."

"I know but e'en so we will prevail. Now go and prepare. Hide your weapons where you can get at them. You will know when the time comes to shed the yokes and wreak revenge on your tormentors."

I turned to Rolf and my Ulfheonar. "Our plans are made; we just need to carry them out. Put the warriors in the village who are to play the Hibernians. Have the ones who will secure the boat hide close to the river bank and then put the rest close enough to get to the centre of the village quickly."

"I still do not like you putting yourself and the Ulfheonar at risk again."

"We are the bait. Our name is known. There are too many dead Irishmen for that. I want them to think that we are on our own and an easy target. They will seek glory by killing Dragon Heart."

Chapter 10

We went into Pasgen's hut. It was the one the pirate leaders had occupied until our arrival. It would be where these new Hibernians would go. I was not worried. I was more concerned for the twenty men who would lounge around the village pretending to be drunken raiders. They would have no mail. They would be in danger until we emerged. I stuck my head out of the door. "Keep your faces hidden and play drunk. Have you your weapons handy?"

The leader of this group of volunteers was a doughty warrior called Windar. He had a great sense of humour as well as being a natural leader of men. "Aye my lord but I thought we had to get drunk, not play drunk."

"When they are dead then you can get drunk."

"Good. Then they will die quickly."

That was my men all over; even the warriors without mail, the ones who had a sword, shield and helmet, all thought that they could beat anybody. Success breeds confidence.

Inside the hut it was stifling. The fire was burning and there were twelve sweating warriors within. We had all drawn our swords ready for the moment we made our exit. Pasgen had told us that the Hibernians kept the gate open and we had done so. It faced the entrance of our hut and I sat, in the darkness watching. I noticed that the men who were playing the Irish were doing a good job. They were all moving and lolling together much as the real ones had done when we had arrived.

I saw, beyond the fence, the masts of the ships as they came up the river. "It will not be long now."

I stood ready to step out. We had talked over our strategy and I knew that it was the right one. I did not know who the leader would be; I suspected one of the many kings they had in Hibernia. That was another reason why I did not want such a title. What did it mean? This king would enter the village and see what he expected to see; his men lolling around while the villagers worked in the fields and the meadows. We had a few of the villagers armed and looking like the raiders to convince them of that. I needed their leader and some of his better warriors to enter into the killing zone of the walled village. Windar and some of the other warriors were charged with closing the gate and trapping the leader and his best warriors within. Those outside would be like a beast without a head.

I heard them before I saw them. The village was on a higher level than the river. The first thing I saw was a pole from which hung four dried skulls then I saw a helmet which looked to have bird's wings sticking from the side. It was not an effective means of decoration. It might look good but it afforded too many opportunities for a sword to knock it off. The leader was a tall man and the upper half of his body appeared before his men. He had a metal corselet on. It looked to be the type worn by Romans long ago. I had seen some rotted examples. When he reached the gate I saw that he carried a very long sword, almost as long as a man. His arms had many tattoos. I was fifty paces away and could not make them out. All I saw was the ugly blue scarring. He also had things dangling from his ears. I did not know exactly what they were but I suspected that they would be human bones from some rival he had killed.

He was flanked by four warriors who were dressed in a similar fashion but their helmets were not adorned with bird's wings. The two had tattoos and bones as decoration. Like the ones we had killed I could see their hair beneath their helmets; they had used lime to give it a hard appearance.

I waited until ten warriors had entered and then I stepped out and walked towards them. Behind me were Haaken and Cnut, behind them Snorri, Beorn and Thorkell and so on. We were already a wedge but it looked to be a casual formation and they would not be suspicious. The warrior with the winged helmet was non-plussed. He stared at me. He did not notice his drunken raiders rising and slipping away. He only had eyes for me. I said not a word until I was five paces from him. I had but a few words in his language. I had learned them over the last few days.

"Your time here is over!" Then I resorted to Norse as I raised my sword into the air, "I am Dragon Heart! I have the sword touched by the gods!"

He seemed lost for words. I watched, out of the corner of my eye as Windar and the others silently slipped the gate into position. This Hibernian had twenty warriors with him. Suddenly one of his oathsworn leapt at me swinging his own double handed sword. Instead of stepping back as he expected I stepped into the blow. Ducking my head I thrust forward with Ragnar's Spirit. The deadly blade came out of his back and I felt the wind from his blow as his sword struck empty air..

It was as though the sound of his death, a low gurgle followed by his body slumping to the ground was the signal for battle to commence. The winged leader swung his sword. He was a life too late and a few paces too close. Haaken took the blow on his shield and stabbed into the thigh of the Hibernian. They had allowed us to close with them and our wedge was like a giant armoured arrow. Blades protruded from every angle. The Hibernians hurled themselves at us and did not realise that there were twenty other warriors hacking at their backs. On the other side of the gate and the wall I heard the roar as Rolf and his men and Pasgen and the villagers fell upon the leaderless Irish outside.

I stabbed at the man trying to chop off Cnut's head with his axe. I skewered him as one would a choice piece of meat at a feast. I punched the next warrior with my shield and Haaken finished him. We were fighting as a wedge, as one force. The Irish were trying to show their courage by attacking blindly to defend their wounded leader. It was not an even contest. With Windar and the others hacking at their backs the twenty, became ten, became five, and became none.

I turned to Haaken, "You and Cnut guard their leader. Windar open the gate. Let us end this!"

With the gate lifted open we roared out and fell upon the disorganised rabble that was the Hibernian warband. They fought bravely but they were faced by two or three warriors fighting together. It might have made a great song but it did not make a great death. It became a slaughter as they were hacked to pieces by villagers angry at the way they had been treated and warriors who wish to gain the treasure of the dead. Soon it was over and Rolf and his men went around finishing off the dying.

I went to the wounded leader. Haaken had wrapped a bandage around the thigh but I could see, from the puddle that he was bleeding to death. He would live an hour at most.

"Who are you?" He croaked.

"I told you I am Jarl Dragon Heart of Man."

"Why help these sheep? Wolves like you devour them."

"Not true." I said as I stood over him, sword in hand. "I devour those who are cruel and lazy. I kill those who think they can milk these people and give nothing in return. I am the Hibernian's Bane!"

He nodded and coughed up frothy blood. "I had heard of you and avoided Man for fear of falling foul of your blade."

I held it up, "And yet it is here and you are dying. *Wyrd*!"

He nodded, "Give me my sword and end it." I nodded to Haaken who kicked his sword over. The Irishman grasped it with one hand. It was all that he could manage and he lowered his head. "I go to my ancestors."

I swung Ragnar's Spirit and his head left his body.

Cnut said, "He died well."

"Aye he did. A shame he did not live well."

We had lost villagers and I had lost warriors but all had died well. The threat was gone. We had the bonus of two ships and the arms and armour of a petty king of the Irish. I gave one of the ships to Pasgen but kept the treasure and the other for me. It had been my warriors who had taken the risks.

Although he was grateful for the gift he knew not what to do with it. "But Jarl Dragon Heart. What will we do with a ship?"

"Begin to trade. Stop hiding here, hoping that the world will pass you by. You are descended from a proud people. You fought against the Saxons; fight again." I saw from the looks on Haaken and Rolf's faces that they thought I had been harsh but I had not. Pasgen could be a good leader. He just needed to decide to be one.

After we had burned the bodies I sent one ship back to Man with the treasure. I also sent those warriors who were too wounded to continue in a winter campaign. I knew that it would be a hard winter and I needed my hardest and toughest warriors. While we waited for the ship, now named *'Butar'* to return we set about improving the defences. We had eager volunteers from the village. They had seen that they could be better protected for just a little effort. A deep double ditch was dug all around the wooden walls and we used wood from the nearby forest to raise the wall to twice the height of a man. Aiden drew a gate and we told them how to build it. "When you have built one then build a second so that you have another way out should you need it."

Pasgen looked disappointed, "You will not be here to help us?"

"No, my men and I will explore the land further north. We wish to explore this land. When we return we will see how successful you have been."

I hoped that we would not need as many men as we had when we landed. I sent some back with our newly acquired ship along with the treasures. We left most of the boys and four warriors to watch the *'Bear'*. If winter struck early they were to take her to Úlfarrston for shelter. We headed north with my Ulfheonar, Rolf and twenty chosen men. Windar was amongst them. He had impressed me when we had trapped the Hibernians. He had rallied his men and stopped those outside from interfering. He was a leader and had those qualities which were rare amongst most warriors.

Of course I could not leave Arturus behind. When I informed the boys that they were to stay with the ship I saw the crestfallen look on his face. I could not do that to him and, besides, he and Aiden were able to look after our ten horses. We could carry our armour on the captured beasts.

The first leaves were beginning to change as we headed up the river towards the north. Snorri and Beorn led. We were going to the water which was close to Olaf's mountain. In our minds, even before we had seen it, we had named it thus. We always called it the Old Man. Olaf had been a popular warrior, irascible though he was. He had not suffered fools gladly but he had taught us all well. I could see immediately what Beorn and Snorri had meant about the river not being navigable. The tributary soon narrowed so that a good horse could have leapt over it.

The ground gradually rose but not as much as the mountains which we saw rising to our east and our west. The land was heavily forested and the trail almost indiscernible. Haaken commented on it as we marched north. "We are almost breaking trail here."

"I noticed. That means that few men use this path."

"This is good timber. There looks to be more here than on Man."

Timber for our ships and for building was always needed. We tended to trade for it but this forest would mean that we could trade it with others and become even richer. Each step confirmed my view that I should move here.

Four hours after leaving the village the sky suddenly opened and we saw the long water for the first time. It was narrow and twisted north. On its eastern side was a thick forest rising a few hundred paces into the sky. To the west we saw, above the tree line the mountain which looked like a gnarled old man. Haaken laughed. "Snorri was right, it is Olaf."

The sight of the mountain seemed to lift our spirits and we soon found ourselves on a flat area at the northern end of the water. It had remained about the same width all the way along but we had seen no one. It was late afternoon and we camped. Although the land appeared to be deserted we posted guards but it was one of the most pleasant places I had ever seen. It was so peaceful. The mountain to the east reminded me of a smaller version of Wyddfa and just as comforting. Both mountains took me back to the hut where I had grown up with Ragnar.

When we awoke it was to a chilly morning. The water was wreathed in mist. What struck me was the silence. I was the first awake and I strode down to the water's side. It was so quiet that I could hear the creak of the leather on the sentry at the far side of the camp. Each moment I was here confirmed my original thoughts. This land was where I was meant to be.

After we had eaten the men looked to me expectantly. "Snorri and Beorn. You travelled here from the east. Is there somewhere which you think would make a good place to build homes?"

Cnut said, "What about here? The land is flat and there is plenty of wood for building."

"I know there are no enemies that we can see but that does not mean that they will not come. I want somewhere that we can defend if we have to." When we did move here we found how prophetic my words were.

Beorn looked to the other side of the misty covered water. "There is, at the northern end of the water a knoll. The land is almost as flat below it as here. It is not far."

I trusted my scouts. "Then let us visit there. I would use this part of the land as a base and we can explore the country hereabouts."

We reached the potential site within a very short time and Beorn was right. It was perfect. The slope down to the water was gentle but on the eastern and northern sides it was steep, almost precipitous in places. I smiled and nodded. "Rolf, get the men to build a hall for us. If we are to spend some time here then we should be comfortable. Aiden, you and Arturus set up some nets and see what fish there are." I turned to the Ulfheonar, "I will take Haaken, Cnut, Snorri and Beorn. We will investigate to the north. Thorkell, take the others and hunt. There should be much game in these woods."

As we went north I had not felt as happy or free since, ironically, I had been a slave and hunted with Ragnar in the forests above our home. I had the same sense of freedom. It was as though I owned the world. It was made even better by the fact that I had my friends with me. We were comfortable with each other. We came across a small patch of shallow water less than a mile from our new home. I saw deer drinking there. We had a readymade larder.

Snorri smiled as we passed, "You are safe for now brother deer but the wolf will hunt soon."

Beorn had explored a little of this land before and he led us to the west. The ground dropped gently to a small stream and a boggy patch of land. Keeping to the high ground we moved up the slope to the col that we could see ahead. It was as Beorn had told us, a narrow pass. We had a back door to my new land and we could stop an army with a few warriors. The mountains rose sheer to the east and the west. The path which led south, to our water, was steep.

I clapped both of my scouts on the back. "You have done well. This is perfect country. We will travel towards Olaf. I would get closer to the Old Man and view the land from the west. We found an old Roman Road which was well overgrown but showed that the land had been used at one time by many people. To the north was another small patch of water. It was bigger than a pond and looked to be teeming with wildfowl.

We had travelled for an hour or so when Snorri held up his hand. "Wood smoke!"

We all had bows with us and we notched arrows. There was no need for words and Snorri and Beorn disappeared ahead. The three of us hurried down the trail. I suddenly realised that the trail we were on was well worn. This had been used more than the trail from the south we had used the previous day. There were people ahead. Snorri and Beorn were crouched next to a low dry stone wall which ran around a clearing. Beyond it we saw a large hut next to some smaller animal shelters. The low wall ran all the way around and I could see what looked like a ditch in front of the hut. Hens and ducks noisily fought for food around the clearing and in the ditch. The smoke we had smelled spiralled from a hole in the middle of the round house.

We waited patiently. Eventually we were rewarded by a woman coming from behind the hut with a wooden pail in her hand. Two small children skipped along behind. Beorn's head snapped around and he pointed to the south. Someone was coming along the trail we had used. We disappeared into the woods and bushes. As Beorn and Snorri retreated they removed all signs of our presence.

I heard the swish of branches being moved and then I saw the hunter striding along with a brace of birds and a hare over his shoulder. He was whistling and obviously oblivious to our existence. When he had passed Snorri I stood. He dropped his animals and he reached for his bow. Snorri's dagger appeared at his throat.

I held out my hands in the sign for peace. I now had a few words in the language of the people of Rheged and I said, "Friend." He looked at me blankly. He did not speak the language. Either that or I had spoken it badly. I repeated it in Saxon and he lowered his bow.

"Friends do not put a dagger at another friend's throat."

I nodded to Snorri who removed the dagger. "You are Saxon?"

He shook his head. "I am Lang and I am my own man."

"And yet you speak Saxon."

He nodded. I was taken as a slave when I was a child." He shook his head, "I do not know where I was taken from. When I was older I met Morwenna, my wife. She too was a slave. I did not like the way my master treated her. I killed him and his family and we fled here. No one had bothered us until you came."

This was an interesting development. "We will not bother you."

"But you are Vikings. Your people raided the monastery close to where we lived in the east and killed the priests."

"I know but I have said I will not harm you and you are safe."

He looked surprised. "I can go?"

"You can but we would speak with you."

"I have your word that you mean us no harm?"

I took out my sword. "I swear!"

"Come we will go to my home but, please, keep your weapons sheathed. My wife is nervous."

He led us along the wall until we came to an opening. I saw that he had fashioned a gate with which he could close the gap. His wife looked fearful as we approached and she grabbed her children about her.

"Fear not. They mean us no harm."

I noticed, as we approached, that there were two large logs outside the hut; they looked to be seats of some kind. They faced west. Lang gestured at them and we sat down. He looked at me expectantly, "You say you fled here. Why did you choose here to live? We have seen no villages close by."

"That is because there are none. We travelled over the high mountain and saw no one. Once we dropped towards this fertile place we saw few villages and farms. We walked for a whole day and half and did not see anyone. When we found this valley we settled here." I nodded. It made sense. "And you?"

"My warriors and I are at the long water just south of here."

"Close to the animal water?"

"Where the haughs are close to the tarns?" He nodded. "Yes that is a good place to hunt animals."

"It keeps us in food." Even though there were five armed warriors Lang was not intimidated. "Do you come here to rule?"

I laughed, "No but we may come here to live. We may be neighbours. Does that bother you?"

"Not so long as we are left alone."

"That is not always a good thing." I told him about the Hibernians and the raid.

"That is why we chose here. No one passes. You are the first visitors we have ever seen."

"But there is a Roman Road."

"It travels to the coast and there are a couple of villages there but the pass to reach the coast is high. You know that in the winter you cannot get out of this land? The passes are blocked by snow. From the time a month before Yule until the first flowers peer through we are isolated." He smiled, "I like that."

"We will leave you alone but when we return to live by the long water I hope that you will visit. We have children and it might do your children good to visit with others and our wives are gentle too. Women like to talk do they not?"

"They do and I will consider your words."

We left and his words had helped me to make up my mind. We would visit the other water and then travel back to Úlfarrston. I did not wish to be trapped in this land over winter.

The skeleton of the house was almost finished when we returned. Thorkell and the others had plenty of game although when we told them of the tarns and the animals he was rueful. We went east and not west." He showed me his arms. They were covered in bites. "We caught the animals but the insects fought us all the way. I would sooner face a Welsh army than those creatures."

As we ate, we watched the sun slowly set over Olaf's mountain. I told them of my decision. "Tomorrow we will all finish the house. The day after half of the warriors will explore to the west, the mountain of Olaf and I will take the other half to visit this other mere. We will risk the biting insects."

Chapter 11

Surprisingly Aiden did not wish to travel to the other mere with me; he wanted to go with Rolf to the mountain. He said, "I have seen the light reflecting from rocks." He shrugged, "There may be metals there that we can use."

Arturus was now torn but, in the end he came with me. The Ulfheonar all went north east to explore the land there. We would be leaving in a few days and I wanted as clear a picture of the land before I returned to Man.

It was the first time I had travelled in close proximity to Windar and I found him interesting. I had always thought him to be older than me; he always had a confident manner about him. I found that he was the same age as I was and he, too, had been briefly enslaved. It made the journey interesting as I found out about this warrior who was now a leader.

He showed his confidence within a mile of leaving the house. "My lord, Snorri and Thorkell said there were biting insects in the forests to the east. We also have to climb the ridge to reach the other side. Would it not be better to follow the water course we see?"

He had spotted a small stream heading north east. "As you will, Windar; we will try that way. According to Beorn it is not far to the other water anyway."

It was a wise decision. In a couple of hours we spied the large mere on our right and we had travelled along the stream without the onslaught of insects. We saw a similar aspect to that of the other water except that this one was, as we had been told, bigger. The mountains to the east looked as high as the ones near to our pass.

Windar was particularly impressed. "This is, for me, Jarl Dragon Heart, a better place. I would like to live here."

I was noncommittal but I stored his words. He sounded much as Thorkell had done when we had first seen the land around the Clwyd. We travelled around the northern edge of the water and saw the remains of a Roman fort and the huts of the village which surrounded it. I saw, in the distance, tendrils of smoke which bespoke isolated farms such as the one occupied by Lang. As we headed back I had an argument with myself in my head. I needed to sort out my thoughts before I spoke with my men and then faced my wife.

Aiden, when we returned, was almost beside himself with excitement. "Look, Jarl Dragon Heart. It is copper!" He held in his hands pieces of rock. "The mountain is full of it. I brought back as much as I could carry."

Rolf smiled, "When he told us it was metal I had my men collect it too. If it is worth anything then I can take the horses on the morrow and we can collect much more."

I looked at Aiden who nodded. "It is valuable my lord. It is not iron but we can mix it with iron."

Rolf said, "And from the top of the Old Man you can see Man. It is a sign."

"Good. Then we have two days to explore and gather and head south." The warriors who were there looked disappointed. I realised that they did not know about the winters as I did. "I am pleased that you like this land for I am taken with it too but you need to know that if we stay beyond the first snows we would be here all winter. I, for one, would like to be with my wife when the snow falls. We have come ill prepared to winter here. I had thought we would have to fight to claim the land but that is not so. When the Ulfheonar return then we will hold a *thing* tonight."

Back on Man, Prince Butar had begun to hold a thing for the jarls to discuss laws and to pass judgement. It worked and we had no blood feuds. We would do that this night.

After we had eaten we wandered down to the shore. Water fowl were swimming up and down, their calls giving a background to our words.

"When I came here I wished to find out more about the place my family originated many lifetimes ago. I now see that it was meant to be for I feel happy in this land. I thought I would never find anywhere which would surpass Man but, here, I do. We have trees, we have animals and we have metals. Man has few of those. I also believe we have security. The passes in and out of this land are easy to defend. We would not be prey to raiders from the sea."

I stopped.

Haaken said, "You wish to come here and live?"

"I do." I knew I had made it clear but Haaken knew me well and he was giving the question for those who might not have followed. "What do you think?"

Windar could not keep silent any longer. "I think it is a good idea. We visited the other mere today and it is a place I would like to call my home."

Everyone laughed. Haaken said, "In that case we shall name it after you. It will be Windar's Mere." The name stuck and long after we had moved to the land we still called it that.

Rolf stood and rubbed his beard, "It is a fine place and I can see why we would want to live here but if you wish us to give our opinion I say what about women? There are few settlements. Where would we find the women and girls we would need to make more warriors?"

It was a point well made and was a setback. He was right, of course. It had been a slightly smaller problem on Man as there were the Saxons who chose to stay there but many of my warriors were now looking for a wife. They were ready to become fathers.

It was Thorkell who gave us the answer. "We had the same problem and we decided to use the slaves we captured. Most slaves would choose to be a wife rather than a slave. We have never had any problem finding slaves have we?"

"Aye but remember the last raid; we found only men."

"You are right Cnut; we must raid further afield." I pointed to the east. "I was born to the east and there are many villages there. We can raid in the spring. Before that we have the winter for those who wish to choose brides from Man."

Aiden put up his hand. "You do not need to ask permission, Aiden. You are not a thrall and we value your opinion."

"From what I have heard all who are assembled here would wish to move." He paused and heads nodded. It was as though it needed someone else to voice the thought for it to become reality. "But what of those at home, on Man, who do not wish to leave the island? There are many who fled there for security."

Aiden was a bright youth and he was right. All faces turned to me. "Then they can stay. As can any of you. I will do as Prince Butar did when we left Norway. Only those who wish to come should come."

We talked around it for quite a while but everyone knew that we would come in the spring and we would be leaving behind some of those who wished the life on Man to the uncertainty of life here in this watery paradise.

We finished the hall and a second building before we left. They were crude affairs and would need improving when we returned but we would have some shelter when we came back. We decided to go back the way that Snorri and Beorn had arrived. We left by Windar's Mere. There was a good deal of banter as we passed that huge patch of water. Windar took it all in good part.

"Just because it is named after me does not mean you may not look at it. Of course you may. Later I may charge but for now it is free!"

When we reached the river which led to Úlfarrston we stopped to examine the sections that would be too shallow. Ketil Flat-Nose had sailed with the Rus. "The Rus travel down rivers like this on their way to the spice markets of the east. When they reach somewhere like this they cut down trees as rollers and carry the drekar to the next patch of water. I have heard that they take them over mountains. Here it is just a few hundred paces."

Windar nodded, "And we could deepen the channel easily." He pointed to the vast water. We could not drain that.

We made the rest of the journey before nightfall and reached the crew of the *'Bear'* and then Pasgen and Úlfarrston. As we sat in the headman's hut we heard the first of the autumn storms crashed against the walls we realised how lucky we had been to have reached the houses when we had. Pasgen was pleased that we would be his new neighbours. His people allowed many of the men to sleep in their huts and only a few of my men had to suffer the rain aboard the *'Butar'* and the *'Bear'*.

The next day Pasgen allowed us to use his ship the *'Úlfarr'* so that we could transport all of my warriors down to Audun'ston. A week later and we arrived back in Hrams-a. We had not been away as long as I had expected and yet we had accomplished far more than I could possibly have imagined. I believed that, for once, the Norns were being kind. I realised, when the spring came, that I was wrong. They were merely playing with us as a cat might toy with a wounded mouse.

My first task, when I reached home was to speak with Erika. I was never one of those warriors who just expected their wife to go along with whatever idea he had. My mother would never have stood for that and the only marriage I had witnessed was that of Butar and my mother. I told her all the reasons why I wished to make the move.

She listened and then said, "So you wish me to leave my comfortable home and take just that which we can carry on a ship. We will travel to a land which is perilously close to the Saxons and where there is not even a house for us to use."

"That is about it. Are you unhappy?"

She smiled, "No, you goose, but I wanted to make sure that you had given me the truth. It will be hard but, from what you say it will be even better than Hrams-a, eventually."

I told her of the *thing* and how I intended to bring it up at the Yule festival when the jarls would visit me.

"Then I will need to prepare well for it may be the last such feast we hold. This might be the last time we see many of our people."

As I said, she was sensible but thoughtful too. How lucky I had been on that midsummer all those years ago.

I made one exception I went to see Bjorn the blacksmith and confided in him. "Bjorn, would you walk with me and Aiden." I had brought Aiden, not for moral support but for his knowledge of the metals. We walked by the sea. "Bjorn I will ask that you keep what I am to tell you in confidence."

"I will, of course, but this sounds serious."

"It is a decision I had not taken lightly." He looked up at me with concern etched across his rugged face. He was worried and I could not keep him that way. "I intend to take my family and any others who wish to come with me to the mainland. We have found a place due east of here which I think is perfect."

He nodded, almost relieved and asked, "The Ulfheonar will go with you?"

"They wish to as do most of Rolf's men."

"I am happy here and it is the place where my father died. I feel close to him here."

"I know and I feel the same way about my mother." I cast a glance at the spot where she had fallen. "If it is any consolation I always feel close to my mother and her spirit guides me still."

He smiled, "As my father's spirit does when I am working the forge. I can almost hear him when I make a mistake." He looked at me, "You wish me to come?"

"With the exception of Haaken and Cnut there is no one closer to me than you. Every time I go to war I carry a piece of you with me. Your skill has saved my life and I am loath to lose that skill. Your brother Harald is now one of my warriors and he has already said he wishes to come with us."

"I see." He looked over to the west. "He has a young wife and two sons. It would be good for him."

Aiden said, "You see that place you are looking at in the distance?"

"Aye."

"That is the place we would go. Rolf and I climbed there and we saw Man." Bjorn stared at the tiny spot of land as though he could see every valley and gully. Aiden held out his hand, "See what I found there."

"Copper!" Bjorn picked it up and smelled it then held it up so that he could see it better. "This is high quality. Did you have to mine it?"

"No, for it lies on the ground."

"With this we could make even better weapons, armour and jewellery." I smiled. He was convincing himself. He looked at me and I could see the sincerity in his eyes. "I have a family." I went to speak. "I will not mention this but if I come with you and they like it not I will return and I mean no disrespect to you."

"And I will take none. Thank you for that."

He put his arm around Aiden. Bjorn was so big that it went all the way. "And you and I have much work to do. We need to repair the sword of Rheged before it is returned there."

As it was to be the last Yule on Man I had gifts made for the jarls. I used some of the gold we had acquired to have wolf brooches made for their cloaks. Bjorn and Aiden even managed to incorporate some of the copper into the design. It seemed to make them look even better.

The hall was packed and all were seated as close as it was possible to do. Erika had made sure that we had plenty of food and ale. Since her mother had died two years earlier it had been my wife who was seen as the island's matriarch and she wanted no-one to suffer. When we went it would be Erik's wife who would fulfil that function. Erika and I could not see him leaving the island. His wife was far too comfortable for that and besides she had always slightly resented Erika. This would be her opportunity to be Queen of the island.

When all had eaten and Haaken had sung his latest saga I stood and silence descended. All knew there was to be an announcement and there was much speculation. I had even heard the rumour that I was to name myself King of Man; as if that would ever happen. Prince Butar had been the only one entitled to a title on Man.

"Friends, for I feel that we are friends, this will be the last Yule my family and I spend on Man. When the winter storms are over we will travel to our new home across the water in Rheged."

There was an audible gasp although one or two nudged their neighbours as much as to say, "I told you so." I knew that despite my wishes the secret was no longer a secret.

"I invite any who wish to follow me to do so but if you do not then I wish you well." It was interesting to watch the reactions of the people before me. I confess I only looked at the men but I knew that my wife would be observing the female reaction too. I saw Dargh nod and knew that he would come. At the same time I saw Jarl Erik and his wife with superior smiles. It suited them.

The looks were replaced by words as a babble of noise broke out. I saw Haaken and the Ulfheonar. They stood and all went silent. "We have seen this land and the Ulfheonar follow Dragon Heart."

A flash of annoyance flickered over Jarl Erik's face.

Rolf and the rest of my men all stood, "We too are going. The Jarl offered to release us from our oath." He smiled, "We will follow across the poisoned sea if he asks!" My men all banged the table and cheered.

Dargh stood, "I owe everything to you Jarl Dragon Heart. I will follow you."

One by one the men who guarded my fort stood and repeated, "And I."

I was genuinely touched. I now had enough people to make this venture work. The rest of the evening was spent in people trying to persuade others to their position. Erik sought me out and led me outside. "I will be staying here, brother. I love the place too much and too much blood has been shed to relinquish our hold on it."

"I know and I wish you well." I clasped his hand.

He looked a little worried as he added, "I have spoken with those jarls who will not be following you and they seem to think that they would like me as leader."

"That is expected. When I leave I do not expect to have any say in how the island and the Tynwald are run."

He seemed relieved, "And as such they wish to confer on me the title of Prince."

I was not shocked but I was mildly surprised. Such an announcement would never have happened like that when Butar ruled. We had a long *thing* and we heard all the arguments before he became Prince.

I nodded, "As I say, when I leave then do as you will. Until then…" There was a veiled threat there. He would not take the title whilst I was on the island.

"No, of course, that would be wrong. And if we can help in any way."

"I will expect you to care for those who choose not to come."

There was a slight hesitation and then he smiled and said, "Of course."

I was not convinced but I would make it clear to those who were still loyal to me that if they remained then they would be under the over lordship of Erik.

Later that night, as the thralls were clearing the hall, I lay in bed with Erika and I told her what her brother had said. She laughed, "He is ruled by that one. Well he is welcome to her. Prince indeed! He might be my brother but he is a mere shadow of the man he wants to be."

"And who is that?"

"Why you, you goose!" And she kissed me.

Chapter 12

The freemen such as Scanlan had not been at the feast but over the next few days they all came to say they wished to serve me still. Surprisingly the thralls, even though they had no say in the matter, were equally happy to be leaving. The abbot and the monks had not been sold yet and seemed to want to return to the mainland. The cold winter passed by in a blur as we planned and packed ready to leave.

We had, almost, a fleet. We had four drekar and two Hibernian ships. Many of the fishermen, when they heard of the waters chose to travel with us. Even so we would not be able to fit all on board our six ships. Prince Erik did not offer any of his ships and kept away from us during that time. It did not upset me but Erika had words to say about her brother. We decided to take all of the warriors and the men first. Then the two Hibernian ships could return for the women and the equipment. That would give us time to send a party ahead to prepare our settlement and expand the houses.

Already Windar had asked to make his home on Windar's Mere. I was happy for that. It would protect our passage down the river. He would be the leader along with Rolf and his men. It was a large mere and could accommodate two jarls.

The day that we sailed felt strange. Hrams-a looked deserted and empty. Only a few of the people had wished to stay. I knew that as soon as the women left then Erik would descend and occupy it. I was just grateful that he had waited until I had sailed. I wondered if Erika was disappointed that her brother was not saying goodbye but I think she had realised how shallow he was. Since Prince Butar's death he had changed. He was not becoming like Harold the False but he was not the warrior who had sailed with me years earlier.

It was a brisk late winter morning when we left. The thin spring sun peered warily over the eastern horizon. We had the wind behind and I hoped for a fast voyage. The gods were with us and we reached Úlfarrston within a few hours. Pasgen came to greet us and make us welcome. We quickly unloaded and then sent the two slower ships back to Hrams-a. We were keen for our families to join us. The slower ships would take more time but they much more room than our faster drekar.

"I wondered if you would come back Jarl Dragon Heart."

"I said that I would."

"I know but I was not certain that you would wish the wicked winters we have here in Rheged." He looked at all of the warriors and the men I had brought. "This is an army."

I nodded, "Now you see what it means to have my protection. I am sending two ships up to Windar's Mere. They have many of the animals and my warriors who are to build the new homes."

He looked at me, "Windar's Mere?"

I laughed, "It is what we have named the large water from which this river flows." I shrugged, "It is how we are." I pointed to the warriors who would remain with me at Úlfarrston. "The rest will wait here for our families."

Rolf and Windar took '*Bear*' and '*Man*' up the river. We hoped that the recent rains would have made the river navigable but we did not mind it we had to port the ships to the water.

"We will camp where we stayed the last time and journey tomorrow."

"Your women cannot sleep in a cold field. We will accommodate them." He hurried off to arrange it.

The two slower cargo ships seemed to take forever to arrive and I was quite worried. It was almost dark when they were seen on the southern horizon and I saw many of the men with a look of relief as their families arrived.

The Ulfheonar and twenty other warriors left at first light to walk to the house we had built. We left much of our supplies, the anvil, the spinning wheels, the bulky items, with Pasgen. We would need all the space for our people. We hoisted sail and manned the oars and began the journey up the river. It was not a long journey but it was one which demanded care. It was a narrow river and, in paces both rocky and shallow. I used the ship's boys to run along the bank and warn us of problems. Arturus and Magnus, in particular, enjoyed that responsibility. When we reached the section of the river I was worried about I was relieved to see that the water level was high.

As soon as the women saw the land and the water they were happy. I had worried that we had built it up too much but, even at the end of winter, it still looked magnificent. I saw the two drekar at the head of the mere and we headed in that direction. As we approached on the placid waters I saw that the men were hard at work cutting down trees for building. They were wasting no time.

Time was of the essence. We needed shelters quickly. Everything would have to be built. Windar and Rolf were both stripped to the waist despite the chilly air and they were sweating profusely. "We will have houses up before dark, Jarl Dragon Heart."

I smiled, "And we will be sleeping under a roof too, for I will take my people to our new home. I will return tomorrow and take '*Wolf*' down to Úlfarrston to bring the rest of our goods. Then '*Serpent*' and '*Butar*' will need to sail back to the sea. We will need their trade more than ever now."

The march to our new home was a cold one but I noticed the spring in the step of all. We had five of the horses with us and many of the women took turns to ride on those. I noticed that our two nuns of the White Christ were looking particularly happy. I remembered that they had lived not far from here. It must have been like coming home for them. The Ulfheonar had worked hard and the skeleton of a third building was taking shape. The men would not have a roof but they would have shelter from the winds.

I led Erika across the threshold of our new hall. "Here is your new home."

She looked down towards the mere and over to the mountain which looked like Old Olaf. There were tears in her eyes as she said, "It is good. You are right. We were meant to be here."

I left early the next morning. The Ulfheonar would protect my family and the warriors we had brought would build the homes. Bjorn claimed a site by the water for his smithy. He was big enough so that no one argued with his decision. Besides it was a good choice. He could use the water and the smoke from the smith would blow down the valley. I took one of the horses to ride back. I was alone and I rode hard. It was exhilarating and not a little frightening. In the short time I had been away Windar and Rolf had built a jetty for the ships and more houses.

Rolf said, proudly, "Today we begin our ditch and wall." He pointed to the Roman fort. "We can use some of the stone from the old fort."

"Good. I will take '*Wolf*' and escort Captain Alf and the two cargo ships. I will be back before nightfall. Have lights ready."

"We will."

My crew were ready. They were not Ulfheonar but they were young warriors who wished to be. They would try to impress me. Magnus was the only ship's boy. Arturus was with Aiden. As we had more rowers we led the way. If my drekar could ride the shallow sections then the other, lighter ships would fly over them. I was amazed at the speeds we managed. I even had the sail shortened for we were leaving the other two behind. When I saw Úlfarrston on the starboard side I was almost disappointed. I had hoped to ride the river a little longer.

The tide was on the turn when we reached the mouth of the river and we waved to Captain Alf and his two ships as they took advantage of the conditions and headed for Man and then Frankia. We would need the trade more than ever now. I had the men load the last of the goods that we had left here at the mouth of the river and I went to speak with Pasgen to explain to him how our trade worked. I knew that we could sail all the way to our new home for half of the year but the other half would mean we would have to offload at Úlfarrston. When I explained he did not mind.

He had just offered me a horn of ale when I heard a shout from Magnus. "Jarl Dragon Heart. The far shore!"

I ran to the river and looked at the eastern bank. There was a huddle of people there. I saw their arms imploring us for help. I suspected a trap but Magnus suddenly shouted, "They are from Audun'ston, Jarl, I recognise them."

It was not a trap. "Get on your oars and row across the river."

It was not easy fighting the tide but we managed to turn the ship and head across the short stretch of water. I could see now that Magnus was right. There were many women and children, probably fifteen or so, three youths and a warrior who looked to be wounded.

"Up oars! Magnus, secure us and get these people on board." There was something about the way that they kept looking over their shoulder that had me worried. I drew my sword and pointed to the first four rowers. "Grab a weapon and come with me."

I ignored the thanks from the women as they were helped on board and I ran down the trail. I heard the bark of dogs. "On me!"

The four warriors closed ranks and we stood in a line ready to face whatever came at us. The dogs came first. They were the kind the Irish use to hunt wolves. As big as a small pony they seemed to have a head filled with teeth. There were four of them and they leapt at us snarling and snapping. I slashed with Ragnar's Spirit and two of them died with my first mighty blow. A third fastened its teeth on my leg until the warrior next to me took off its head. The last one was despatched by two of my men. We waited then for the hunters who would follow. They were Saxons! There were ten of them. All had a spear but none were mailed. I glanced over my shoulder and saw that most of the refugees had been boarded.

I said quietly, "Be ready to move back to the ship when I give the command!" With just a sword, no helmet, no armour and no shield we were in no position to fight off ten well armed Saxons. We just had to buy time. I said loudly, "Look boys, more dogs. These have two legs!"

As I had expected my words, in Saxon, enraged them. Without my shield and my helmet they would not know who I was. Had they known, they might have been more cautious. As it was they raced at us. I ran forward, flicked the spear head which was heading for my chest away and sliced my sword across the stomach of the first warrior. I spun around and brought Ragnar's Spirit through the backbone of a second and, grabbing the spear head of a third I rammed the crosspiece into the eye of a third.

I heard Magnus shout, "We are boarded, my lord!"

It was time for a retreat. I had surprised them once and they would be more wary when next they attacked. I also saw another ten warriors heading up the trail towards us. I shouted, in Norse, "Back to the ship!" I then roared and feinted at the men in front of me. They recoiled and I turned and ran back along the river. I heard a whoosh and looked up as a flight of arrows soared above my head. As I clambered aboard, *'Wolf'* I turned to see the Saxons preparing to advance behind their shields.

"Push off!"

We rowed back to the western bank where Pasgen had his men armed and ready should they be needed. They would not. The Saxons had no means of crossing the river, they were afoot and there looked to be just a band of them. Not enough to worry us, yet.

I concentrated on steering the ship against a receding tide. I would have to wait some time before venturing upstream to Windar's Mere. As we bumped into the bank Magnus threw the rope and we were tied up. I went to the wounded warrior. It was Thrand the Silent. I could see that he was badly wounded. He had a stomach wound and they were slow to kill but impossible to heal.

He nodded as I approached, "Thank you Jarl Dragon Heart. That was bravely done." He coughed up a little blood as he chuckled, "When I get to Valhalla I will tell old Ragnar of the way you slew those three Saxons with just a sword."

I nodded, "Tell the old man he taught me well." There were no lies between warriors. We both knew he was dying. His hand still gripped his sword. "What happened?"

"The Saxons came. They appeared to come in peace and Audun opened the gates to them. I was out with the boys and we were hunting. We saw them enter from the hill where we were standing. They fell upon our people and slaughtered them. Audun fought well but he knew they were doomed and he ordered the women to flee through the northern gate. We found them. Audun and the men died to buy them time and I brought them north. I knew you had gone north and you were our only hope." His body was suddenly wracked with pain and he closed his eyes.

One of the youths who now had a long scar running down his face took up the story. "Our men held them a long time and it was a whole day before they found us. They had dogs. We had to rest because of the women and the children." He held his head proudly. "Else we could have outrun them."

Thrand patted the boy as he opened his eyes, "You are right, my son. When I am dead do not kill my sword but use it to kill others. Jarl Dragon Heart, I am going now. Will you watch over my son and the others?"

"I so swear!"

"Then I die happy! I come my …"

The last effort was too much and the last warrior from Audun'ston died. The last of the warriors who had followed Jarl Harald One-Eye joined the others in Valhalla. It was a good death for he had saved lives.

I took the sword from his dead fingers and handed it to his son. "Here is your father's sword. Use it well."

He nodded and, holding it, said, "I swear to serve you Jarl Dragon Heart."

The other two also swore. "I will take you into my band and I will watch over you as though you were my sons."

I looked at them expectantly. Thrand's son said, "I am Sigtrygg Thrandson."

"I am Gunnstein son of Olvir."

The last youth was a giant. He was taller and broader than I was and yet much younger. "I am Thorir the Tall."

I smiled. "I can see where you got your name from. You are all my oathsworn now. When we have loaded this ship we will row to your new home."

Sigtrygg asked, "This is not your home?"

"No, but these are good people and I needs must speak with them."

Gunnstein said, "The other warriors died so that we could get here. The Saxons killed them this morning after Thrand was wounded." He pointed across the river to the south. "What of their bodies, Jarl Dragon Heart?"

These were no longer youths, these were now warriors and they deserved the truth. "Their bodies will be despoiled by the Saxons and their weapons taken." I could see the upset that caused. "But they died with their swords in their hands and they are greeting Thrand even now. That is the best that a warrior can hope for." I wanted them to know the truth and I was pleased when they set their faces and nodded. "See to the women while I go and speak with the headman."

Pasgen was waiting patiently. "This is not good Pasgen. The Saxons may come back. I have brought danger to you."

"No, you have not for you rescued us from a worse danger. We now have a better place to defend and we have weapons. We will keep watch and we will be ready."

I pointed north. "They will cross the river higher up and come at you from that direction."

"How do you know?"

I smiled, grimly, "I too am a raider and it is what I would do. You need to have men watching from the hill where we made our camp. When they do come then send word. You will only have to hold them for a day and then my wolves will fall upon them."

"We will not let you down."

It was dark by the time we had loaded the drekar and we were tightly packed. We also had three new rowers who were keen to prove themselves to their new jarl. We had Thrand's body by the prow. We would bury him amongst his own people. His grave would be revered. He would be the first to be buried in our new land. The gods favoured us for, as we passed the shallow section our extra weight made us scrape along the rocks but the warriors pulled even harder and we were soon in deeper water and the dark depths of the mere were ahead. I saw the lights in the distance and knew that soon we would be home.

I saw the line of warriors waiting for us at the newly built wooden and stone jetty. There was clear concern on their faces for I knew we were much later than they had expected us. Their questions were silenced as the women and children were led from the boat by my warriors. They saw a story unravelling before their eyes.

I was the last to descend after Thrand's body had been carried by my three new warriors and young Magnus who was growing in stature day by day. I watched as they carried him towards the small rise which lay beyond the old Roman fort. Magnus must have told them that there was bare ground there.

Rolf and Windar came over to me with frowns on their faces. "It seems we are not destined for peace. The Saxons have slaughtered all at Audun'ston. These are the only survivors. Thrand died on '*Wolf*'. We drove them off but they will return. We will need to keep watch on the river. I would not have Pasgen suffer for us."

They nodded, "It is good hunting and fishing down there. We saw the river and the forests teeming with game. We will send our hunters down there. They will make the best eyes and ears."

Windar was asserting himself already and that was good. "I will go with the people and bury Thrand. I would not like his body to be attacked by the foxes and creatures of the night."

Even though they did not know Thrand they came with me. We found a raised knoll which had rocks upon it. I had the youths lay his body down and I folded his arms across his body. We placed his shield across his chest and his spear by his side. His son kissed his father and then laid the first stone at his head. Each of us in turn laid a stone and soon there was a circle around his body. We continued to build the tomb until there was just a space close to his head. Sigtrygg laid the last stone. Using our shovels we piled earth upon the top of the stones until there was a mound.

I looked at Sigtrygg. "Tomorrow you must catch an animal and we will sacrifice it here at dusk to send your father on his way." I pointed to the women and the children who had stood and watched. "Until they have men to look after them then the three of you are responsible for their care."

The looks on their faces told me that they would be well looked after.

It would be inappropriate for them to sleep in the warrior hall and I said, "It might be better if you sleep aboard '*Wolf*' tonight and tomorrow we can begin your new life."

Chapter 13

The camp still looked like that, a camp but Rolf and Windar were busy making it habitable for the women. The refugees did not want to be parted from me. Perhaps I was seen as a good luck charm I do not know but they came with me as we headed over to my water by the Old Man.

I knew that they had had a hard time and so we used the ten horses we still had. It made the journey somewhat easier. The three youths were much taken by the land through which we travelled. I described it as we marched. "It is an empty country at the moment. That is Lang's Dale over there. He is our only neighbour." I pointed to the valley where Lang and his family farmed. I would have to visit him and tell him he had neighbours although I suspected he knew. This was his land and he knew every branch and stone.

"Will you three be warriors or farmers?"

Sigtrygg spoke, "For me I would be a warrior as my father was and I would use Saxon Killer to avenge him." He clasped the hilt of the sword.

"You have named him?"

"Last night after you had gone to bed I returned to his grave and swore to avenge him. The name came to me as I stood in silence."

"Then that is your father. It is good. And you two."

"We would be both, Jarl. We will fight for our land."

"And it is good land. First we have to build but soon we will grow and we will fight."

"You will seek the Saxons?"

I laughed, "I do not need to do that, Gunnstein, they will seek us. But we will be ready. I have the finest warriors in the world, I have the Ulfheonar."

They had only heard stories about my wolf warriors and I spent the rest of the journey telling them of their deeds and their training. Sigtrygg said, "I would be Ulfheonar."

"Then you must prove yourself to my warriors. You needs must kill a wolf and then prove that you have the skills to join. I do not choose; my Ulfheonar are the judges."

He said, resolutely, "I will show them."

They had made far more progress by the water than at Windar's Mere. I suspected that Erika had been forceful! There were three buildings now each with a roof of turf and the skeletons for others. Smoke billowed from Bjorn's forge and I saw boats made of animal skins and willow fishing in the water.

I had always suspected that Erika had second sight and was a volva. She had the knack of reading a situation instantly. She greeted the women and the children like a mother hen and they were long lost chicks. She had Maewe and Seara gathering the children up while she led the women into one of the new buildings. As she passed me she leaned up and pecked me on the cheek. "You have much to tell me later, husband!"

Haaken and the Ulfheonar were nowhere to be seen. Aiden and Arturus ran to me. "What has happened, Jarl?"

"The Saxons raided Audun'ston. These are the survivors. Where are the Ulfheonar?"

"Haaken took them to Lang's Dale. He thought it right that the Saxon should know he had neighbours and they were going to find stray animals. They did not wish to take any that belonged to him."

Haaken could have been jarl. He was a thinker and a planner. He was doing the right thing. When we had first arrived on Man we had done the same thing. We had been forced to leave most of the animals we had on the island and we had brought breeding pairs of the best animals. Soon we would have large flocks and herds but until then we would have to tighten our belts and live off the land.

"Would you like to see the sword, Jarl Dragon Heart?"

"You have worked on it already?"

"Bjorn had completed much of the work over the winter and I could not wait to get started." He suddenly stopped half way to the smithy, "Unless, of course you only wish to see the completed weapon?"

I laughed, "No, Aiden, I am as keen as you are to see this work in progress."

Bjorn beamed as we entered his smithy, "I am happy that you persuaded me to come here, Jarl. My family feel at home and," he pointed across the water, "it is good to have Old Olaf watching over us."

"It is a remarkable likeness is it not? And you are happy here by the water?" He nodded as he struck a piece of metal. I noticed that his smithy was roofless. But what about a roof?"

"This is much cooler. I am thinking about working in the open the whole time."

Aiden shook his head, "I like a roof for I do not like being wet."

"Go and fetch the sword." All the time we had been speaking Arturus had been craning his neck to see this ancient sword.

Aiden brought it over. It was wrapped in a sheepskin. He opened it and I took the blade by the hilt. Bjorn had done a good job. He had married the old metal with new. The blade was inlaid with some of the copper which made it look like gold. Aiden pointed to the cross piece. It was bigger than our swords and had rounded ends. "I have worked some gold, silver and copper into the crosspiece, see." He pointed to the design which looked like the dragon on the banner. "I have set some of the blue stones here in the pommel but from the picture there should be a red and a green one. We need to find those."

"You have done a fine job, Aiden and Bjorn."

They nodded and smiled. A good workman likes to be praised. Arturus asked, "May I touch the sword please, father?"

"Of course." I handed it to him. It was heavier than he had imagined and, even though he held it in two hands the blade dipped dangerously close to the floor. Aiden caught it before it did.

"Sorry. It is so heavy."

"When you can hold a weapon like this in one hand then you will be ready to be a warrior. Until then you practise!"

The Ulfheonar did not arrive back until late afternoon. They came driving sheep. I heard barking and saw a golden sheepdog at the back. It was beautiful and appeared to have two golden stars; one between the shoulders and one close the tail. It was a striking animal. "Where did you get the dog from?"

"Lang the Saxon. His dog had pups, and this one was spare. She is a little bossy and, I think, he was happy to be rid of her but she is a good sheep dog. He had trained her already. We lost nary a one on our way here."

"Good." I noticed that there were pens already made to collect the animals. "Then when we have enough we will share them out amongst our people." Haaken suddenly noticed the new people we had brought. "Come, let us go to the hall and I will tell you my news."

"Can I play with the dog, father?"

"He is not a toy Arturus, he is a working dog. I will watch them Jarl Dragon Heart." With Aiden as a mentor, my son could not go far wrong.

Our ale wives had not had time to brew any beer and we were forced to drink the brown tinged fell water which bubbled into the mere. It was good water but it had the taste of metal about it. We would have to wait for our ale and our cheese. When I had told them of Audun'ston the Ulfheonar were even more bullish than the others had been.

"We do not wait Jarl Dragon Heart. We visit pain and destruction upon the Saxons. Let us show this Eanred that he does not attack us without suffering."

"It may well be Eorl Osbald. It was his settlement and monastery we destroyed."

Cnut shrugged, "It matters not. We will visit him and show him that we still have teeth."

Perhaps I was caught up in the moment but I agreed with my Ulfheonar and it would mean that Pasgen would be safer. Haaken said, "We could just take one drekar with a double crew.

We are not going for plunder, we are going for blood. Most of the men could stay and build our homes."

I liked that proposal and I nodded. "I am decided. I will speak with my wife and we will leave the day after tomorrow."

When I told her all she was not surprised but she could not resist a dig at me. "The way you keep leaving me makes me think that you have another woman somewhere."

"As if I would. I will only take the Ulfheonar and the youths we rescued. The rest can stay and build up the village."

"Arturus stays this time."

"He stays." I nodded to the pens where he was happily playing with the dog. "It seems he has a new friend."

"Well the dog does not sleep in the hall!"

I laughed for I knew that she would relent especially as I noticed Kara playing with the young dog outside. Over the years I came to thank Lang for his gift. The dog proved a more loyal guard for my children and my wife than any warrior. At that time it was still *'dog'* but when I returned from my raid it would be named.

We asked for volunteers and we had too many. As soon as we said what we intended every warrior wanted to be part of it. I had the Ulfheonar and I had my three new warriors. For the others we took the youngest warriors that we had. I wanted the older, experienced ones to be there to look after our people. It would do the younger ones good to learn how to defeat the Saxons.

We headed down the river. The shallow place we had named Backbarrow for it was like a plunge down into a tomb. Upstream was a hard pull but riding it down stream meant risking ripping the bottom out of the drekar. It was lucky that we always travelled downstream without any weight. Upstream we pulled and used our arms to fight the river.

When we reached the estuary I pulled in close to the bank and headed to the settlement to tell Pasgen what we were about. He met me half way having seen our mast. "You do not need to do this for us, Jarl Dragon Heart. We will hold off the Saxons for a day."

I shook my head, "We do this for us. The Saxons need a lesson and we will teach it to them."

We sailed as far south as the Lune. It was a good place to moor. I left Magnus and the other ship's boys to guard the ship. I hoped they would be safe but I would need every warrior I had brought if we were to achieve what I intended.

"Magnus, if enemies come then cut the anchor and let the river take her out. You can drop the sea anchor and be safe."

"I will keep your drekar safe for you, Jarl Dagon Heart!"

We travelled light. We knew how far we had to travel. Snorri and Beorn led the way and they took with them Erik Short-Toe who had proved to be a good tracker and adept at hiding. He was to be trained so that, one day, he might try to become Ulfheonar.

We had forty warriors. It was not a huge number but half of them had mail of some sort and all had a shield, spear, helmet and sword. They would do. We half ran and half walked down the trail south. With our scouts out we knew that we were safe from ambush. Snorri and Beorn would not let anyone get close to us. Haaken had counselled me to attack the site of the monastery. He was convinced that they would have rebuilt.

"How do you know?"

"This Eorl Osbald feels an attachment to the place. Why else would he return to wreak such vengeance on it? Remember the Abbot told us that he had stored his treasure in that casket you took. He has also promised the king that he will protect the land. He failed to do so. By slaughtering the people he will show his king what kind of leader he is. He will make the town stronger than before. Then he will head north to finish us off. This will be the best time to attack him for he will not be expecting us."

He was right, of course, but it was a risk. How many men did we face? I knew it was the correct decision. We had to make the Saxons fear us as the Hibernians did. The men of Cymru had not feared us and we had lost our golden isle. People would go hungry because we did not have the grain the island produced. When the harvest came then the dragon boats would follow and the people of Anglesey would suffer. I felt sorry for Raibeart and his people but I had my own people to worry about first. We ran hard and we ran until we were ready to drop but we reached the estuary before dark.

I left the warriors to recover whilst I went ahead with Haaken and Cnut to meet with our scouts. They had found a tumble of rocks with weeds and sprouting straggly bushes. It served to hide our profile and we crouched to watch the Saxons. They had not killed all of the villagers. We saw some, women children and youths, who were toiling to dig a ditch and build a palisade. I saw the heads of the Norse defenders impaled upon the walls of Audun'ston. A savage reminder of how precarious life was. The Saxons had not destroyed the village. They were now working to improve the defences we had begun. In another few weeks it would have been too difficult to take without serious losses. As it was we had a chance. We watched as they worked until sunset and then they led the twenty thralls to a compound outside the village watched by four armed guards. That would be one target. The other fifty or so Saxons went into the walled settlement. I noticed that they had no ship moored nearby and that was a good sign. The warriors we faced would not be reinforced.

I returned with the scouts to the rest of my men. "Beorn, choose ten men and rescue the slaves. No matter what happens to us I want you to get them to '*Wolf*' and then safely home."

"I so swear."

I had no doubt that the slaves would be reunited with their families at Windar's Mere. The rest I led forward to the ridge overlooking the walls. I could hear them inside the walls. They were singing their songs of battle. I heard them sing of the slaughter of the Norse. I shook my head. It was a foolish man who sang of success when he had barely a toe hold on the land. I divided the men so that an Ulfheonar was with two warriors. I took Sigtrygg with me and his two companions. I felt responsible for them. My wolf warriors spread out and disappeared like the shadows of the night.

I had three warriors with me and I headed for the gate. It would be the most dangerous place to attack. I hoped to draw the garrison towards me. This would be a good test for the three young men who were bent on revenge. They also knew the layout better than I did.

The Saxons had just finished work for the day and they were all ready for food and ale. The last thing on their minds was defence. As far as they knew we were many miles away and they would have time to prepare for us. I was pleased that I had listened to Haaken; he had been right.

The three youths all had a leather helmet, a sword and a small shield. When we had time we would show them how to make better and bigger ones. I waved them to the side of me and crept forward. I could see, on top of the gate, two Saxons who were talking and looking at the thralls being taken to their pen. I took the opportunity of quickly moving to the shadow of the wall and gate. I could see that Audun had just left the one ditch and we managed to jump that. Had he dug a double ditch he might have survived the attack.

I motioned for Gunnstein and Thorir to stand and hold their shields. They did so and I climbed up with Ragnar's Spirit ready. I waited until both guards had their back to me and I said, "Now!" They were two strong lads and they lifted me up. When I reached the top of the wooden palisade I leapt towards the two guards. All that they saw was a huge wolf with red eyes leaping at them and they froze. I swept Ragnar's Spirit and it bit into the neck of one warrior as his body fell over the wall; in falling he took his companion with him. Sigtrygg had joined me. He pulled up Thorir.

"Get down and open the gate!" They jumped down and Thorir opened the gate while Sigtrygg finished off the stunned guard who had fallen.

I climbed down the ladder and stood facing the Saxons who stared at me. I glanced up and saw that, all along the walls my men were clambering over. As the gate behind me opened to admit the rest, the Saxons ran at me. One warrior, armed with a spear, was ahead of the rest. He was screaming as he ran towards me. He stabbed forward with the spear. I deftly deflected it to one side and angled my sword over the edge of his shield. The momentum of his charge ran him on to the sword which sliced through his neck and throat.

He fell against me and his body pinned my shield close to my armour. Seeing my dilemma a warrior with a war axe sliced down at me. I ripped my blade from the dead man's throat and it hacked into the handle of the axe man's weapon. I pushed the body towards him and he fell to the ground. I had no time to finish him for a mailed warrior with a sword ran at me. It was good mail; I could see that immediately and his shield was a well made one. He held a fine Frankish blade as though he knew how to handle it.

He feinted at my shield. I was not fooled. I heard a groan to my right and made the mistake of glancing down. Sigtrygg had finished off the axe man. My opponent took his chance and thrust his blade towards my throat. I turned my head and dropped to one knee so that the sword went over my head. I slashed, in desperation at his leg. All my weight was behind it and my sword bit into the mail, severing some of the links. I saw a flicker of pain on his face. I had not cut him but I had hurt him. He stepped back and I stood.

Around us the fight had degenerated into individual combats. They had not had time to form a shield wall and that suited my warriors. I had no time to survey the scene I had to fight and defeat this warrior who, I suspected, was the leader of the Saxons.

I went on to the offensive and I brought my sword over my shoulder to hack at his head. At the same time I stepped forward to punch at him with my shield. The boss of my shield caught his knuckles and I saw him wince in pain. He managed to deflect my sword away. We were toe to toe and I head butted him hard. His helmet had a nasal which afforded some protection, but not enough. There was a crack and his eyes closed briefly. He tried to step back but it turned into a stumble. I brought Ragnar's Spirit down hard. He managed to take the blow on his shield but his stumble meant he was lying on his back. I brought the edge of my shield down on to his unprotected neck. There was a loud crack and a gurgle. When his sword fell from his hand then I knew he was dead. I had broken his neck.

I quickly stood and surveyed the scene. The fight had moved on and I was alone amongst the dead and the dying. I ran through the village. My men were winning. The last few Saxons were trying to form shield walls but there were too few and the Ulfheonar and the young warriors ruthlessly despatched them. It had not all gone the way of my men. I saw some of the young warriors who had been eager to join us lying dead amongst the Saxons. Haaken and Cnut led my Ulfheonar and they overcame the resistance of the last few Saxons. They were cut down to a man. We had won. Audun and Thrand had been avenged.

I turned to the warriors closest to me. "Go and free the thralls and bring them here. Thorkell secure the gates. Snorri and Beorn see if any escaped."

I took my helmet off. The cool air felt good on my face. I had been lucky and my lack of concentration had nearly cost me my life. I was thankful for my shield and my sword. They had saved me again. My three new warriors approached me. I could see that they were covered in blood and had not escaped injury. All three had wounds; none were serious but they demonstrated the problem of fighting without mail. They were young warriors and it would take some time to be able to afford mail.

"You did well. Find yourself weapons and helmets from the dead."

When the slaves were freed and brought into the centre of the village they fell at my feet. "Thank you, Jarl Dragon Heart. You have saved us."

"I am sorry that you had to suffer so much death. We now have a new home in the north which is safer than here. Will you come with us?" I hoped they would say yes for to remain at Audun'ston would merely be delaying their enslavement.

A woman stood, she looked to be older than the rest and I vaguely recognised her from our home in Norway. "We will come with you, Jarl, for all we have here are the bones of our dead."

"Find food and we will eat. On the morrow we will leave."

When morning came I realised the size of the problem. We had taken huge amounts of weapons and armour from the Saxons and the village still had much which the people wished to save. Their animals had all been penned and they were loath to leave them. I made a decision.

"Einar take the villagers back to Úlfarrston and ask Pasgen if we can use his Irish ship. The Ulfheonar and I will stay here until you return." The nods from Haaken and Cnut told me that I had made the right decision. It would not, however, be a swift voyage north. They would be overloaded and would not have my men rowing. I suspected we would have another night alone.

Chapter 14

It took a long time to load '*Wolf*'. Einar had to make sure that the drekar was well balanced. With only half a crew he could ill afford mistakes. We watched as he gingerly edged her towards the sea and, when he had safely negotiated the headland, we returned to the village. We spent the day burning the bodies of the Saxons in one pyre and burying our dead in a barrow. As the afternoon drew on we scouted the land round about the monastery gathering sheep.

We managed to collect a larger number than I had anticipated. We use the thrall pens to hold them. I found myself drawn, once again, to the monastery. I revisited the secret chamber we had searched earlier in case we had missed anything but we had not. I found Haaken and Cnut searching the church. The candlesticks and plates had been taken. The light from the dipping sun spread light and shadows across the stone floor of the church. I was about to leave when I noticed that, close to where they had had what the priests called the altar there looked to be a shadow.

I went to the stone and I could see that it was slightly lower than its brothers. Haaken joined me, "What is it, Jarl Dragon Heart?"

"It may be nothing but…" I drew my seax and ran it around the edge of the stone. "I think this may lift up."

"I can see nothing to get hold of."

"I know and that is why I think this is a chamber for secrets. Had the light not shone the way it did then I would have seen nothing."

Haaken nodded and left the church. He returned with the broken axe from the warrior I had killed the previous day. The axe head was long. He laid it in the crack we had widened and he put his foot on it. Surprisingly it began to move quite easily. He kept the pressure on while Cnut and I put our seaxes in the crack to give added leverage. The stone suddenly popped open. A damp musty smell rose. This had not been opened for some time.

Cnut looked down. "It is empty."

I looked and saw that there appeared to be nothing in the hole. "Get a torch."

We had a fire going to cook our evening meal and Cnut went to get a burning brand. When he returned the Ulfheonar were with him, intrigued by our absence. Haaken held the torch so that its light shone into the dark space beneath the church. I looked down and saw another chest. This time it was a plain one but it was large. As soon as I stretched out and put my head and arms inside it became black again. I felt the edge of the casket. I ignored the things which crawled over my hands. I put the spider's web which covered my face from my mind and I concentrated upon tugging the reluctant chest towards the opening. Gradually it moved. The crawling creatures disappeared back into the dark recesses of their underground home. After a few moments I had the box beneath the hole.

I stood for I had lost the feeling in my fingers. Haaken looked at the casket. "It is the same size as the hole. How do we get it out?"

While rubbing the feeling back into my fingers I studied the top of the wooden chest. I knelt down and took out my seax. I ran it along a tiny crack in the top; it was so slight that it looked like a fault in the wood. Dirt and the detritus of its entombment came away and I slowly prised up a metal handle. It was reluctant to rise and I did not want to force it in case I broke the frail looking metal. Eventually after patient prising it popped up. Haaken reached down and lifted the box. He had to do it carefully for it was an exact fit for the hole where the stone had been.

We had been toiling so long that the sun had set and there was the welcome smell of food drifting in to the church and yet no-one moved. Everyone was fascinated by the box. There was a wooden table in the corner; I think it had been used in the rituals of the White Christ. I put the box down. It was not heavy nor was it empty.

"Locked!"

Haaken went for his sword. I restrained him, "Patience! Remember Aiden. Find my some metal from one of the damaged mail shirts." I took out my small dagger; the one I kept in the top of my boots. When Sven returned with three long pieces of mail I was ready. I had watched what Aiden did and I tried to replicate it. I put the dagger in the lock. I could feel a mechanism. I tried to turn the dagger but there was resistance. I wound three of the mail links together and poked that inside. When I felt resistance I twisted the mail links and the dagger. After a few unsuccessful attempts I suddenly felt a movement. Then the dagger and the mail link turned in my hands and the box was unlocked.

I laid the dagger down and slowly opened the box. Inside there were the bones of a hand, a ring and a leather bag. I lifted the bag out first and handed it to Cnut. He opened it and poured the contents on to the table. They were coins! Some were copper, some were silver but half of them were gold.

"A good find." He began to examine one. "It looks like those words that Aiden can read."

I took one and examined it, "It is Latin. These are Roman."

I carefully took out the hand and the ring. I had spied something beneath.

"Who would bury a hand?"

"I don't know, Snorri but as this is a church or was a church, it may be the bones of some saint or other. Deidra and Macha may well know. This is where they lived. We will keep them safe until we get back. The followers of the White Christ will pay good gold for holy relics." I put them down to avoid damaging them. Saint's bones and religious relics were as valuable as gold and the books of the White Christ. This was a valuable find already.

I took out the calfskin which lined the bottom of the casket. When I opened it I saw Latin written all over it and a map. I could not read much but I did see a signature at the bottom, 'Osric'. Aiden and the two nuns would have much work when we returned. I replaced the hand and ring into the box and tucked the calfskin into my leather satchel.

"Replace the stone and then let us eat. Treasure hunting has given me an appetite."

The two ships arrived at noon the next day. We loaded all of the animals and the weapons we had captured on board Pasgen's ship and we boarded '*Wolf*'.

We offloaded a quarter of the animals at Úlfarrston as a payment to Pasgen for the use of his ship. It did no harm to keep our neighbours friendly. We reached Windar's Mere with more difficulty than on previous voyages. The water level of the river was dropping. Soon we would have to carry the boat over a fifty pace section of the river. I decided to speak with Windar and Rolf about sending the ships downriver while we still could.

I had only been away for three days and yet they had made much progress. There more houses and I could see, dotted along the waterside, small huts and farms. It showed confidence that we were secure. I hoped that we were.

The warriors who had rowed '*Wolf*' drove our animals to my settlement. The Ulfheonar escorted the last of the villagers. We stored the weapons until we could transport them to Bjorn. We would be sharing the animals out between both settlements as well as the weapons but that would be easier if completed at my water.

"They are destroyed then?"

"All of them. And we brought back the last of the villagers." I did not mention the treasure for I did not see the need. When I knew what it meant then they would be informed. "We need to decide it we keep the boats here or moor then at Úlfarrston."

"You had difficulty?"

"Aye we scraped the bottom of both ships." I waved as Pasgen's ship turned and headed down the mere. Now that she had been unloaded she would be able to cross the rocks. "I think unloaded we could get downstream but coming upstream will be harder."

Rolf stroked his beard. "It will mean having warriors watch the ships."

"Aye but we could rotate them."

I shook my head, "You are both forgetting that we are still raiders. We will need our ships close to the sea. We can be at the coast in less than half a day on foot. It is no hardship."

"It is your decision, Jarl."

"Yes but I value your opinions. Is there any advantage to be gained from keeping them here?"

They both shook their heads.

"Then we send them back tomorrow. I will have a skeleton crew over by morning."

I took one of the horses we kept by the jetty and put the casket on a second. The two warriors looked at me curiously but said nothing. I had learned that even those I thought were close did not question me. The exceptions were Erika, Haaken and Cnut. Had I become Jarl Harald One-Eye?

Before I left I pointed to the col to the north of the mere. "It might be useful to encourage someone to farm up there. I believe it is good land and it will give early warning of any danger from the north and the east."

"We will see which of our farmers relishes that prospect."

As I passed the end of Lang's Dale I decided that, as soon as my hall was completed, I would ask Lang and his family to visit us. I wanted him as a friend and not an enemy. He guarded, if he did but know it, the north western side of my land. He could give us early warning of any danger.

As I crested the rise close to the water the first thing I noticed was the huddle of huts on the western side of the water. It was flatter land there but less defensible. I frowned slightly. Who had made that decision in my absence? It did not upset me. But I would have liked to have made that decision.

I caught up with the Ulfheonar who were making the journey at the speed of the women and children. Thorkell pointed to the western edge of the water. "Someone has made a good decision."

"How so?"

"The land is flat; it is treeless and does not need clearing. See how there are four farms there already and yet they are not crowded."

He was right. I was irritated that someone had made a decision without consulting me and that was all.

Erika had pushed the men hard and I could now see that there were two halls and many huts nestling from the hillside down to the river. It was then I realised why they had begun to build on the western side. There was no room left on the east. It had been Erika who had made the decision. I was pleased that I had not said anything. I was learning to listen more and speak less as I grew older.

Kara ran to meet me. She was growing rapidly. I dismounted and swept her through the air. She squealed with delight. I heard Erika shout, "She has just eaten, if she is ill then it is you who can clean it up." I knew there was no seriousness in her words for she beamed radiantly at me as she stepped from the newly finished hall.

I put Kara down. "The buildings are coming on."

"Yes. It is why I asked some of the people to settle on the western side of the water." She looked at me from under hooded eyes, "I wondered if you would mind?"

She was a volva! "No, I think it is a good idea although it is harder to defend over there."

"I am not sure that we will be in danger." Just then the Ulfheonar arrived with the last of the refugees. Erika glanced up at me and gently touched my cheek with the back of her hand, "You found more of the villagers then? This is good. Olaf will watch over them."

I untied the casket from the spare horse. "We found some fine treasures too. Come and I will show you."

Kara grabbed Erika's hand and we entered the hall. Someone had made a crude table. It was close to the doorway and in the light. I opened the casket and showed her the coins. When I showed her the bones of the hand and the ring she shook her head,

"I must ask Macha and Deidra why they make such a fuss about some old bones." She picked up the ring. "This is a pretty ring though. See how the green in the middle makes it sparkle and the blue ones make it look like an island in the sea."

I had not noticed that before. As Erika tried it on I saw that it fitted her. I had thought it the ring of a man. Now I realised it could be a woman's. Without the flesh on them it was hard to tell from the bones alone. "Have Seara fetch them for I have need of their knowledge."

Deidra and Macha had been some of the first slaves we had taken. They were what the Saxons called nuns. Nuns were the volva of the White Christ. At first they had been resentful of their enslavement and feared rapine behaviour. When they were treated well and accorded some privacy and dignity they began to change. Once they were put in charge of the cheese making and the education of those who wished to read then they almost became like freewomen. They were both invaluable members of the clan but both of them retained their belief in and worship of the White Christ. They both knew better than to try to convert any of our people. Most of the other priests and nuns, had been sold in the slave markets. Many, especially the Hibernians, liked the priests and bought them so that they could free them and gain favour with the White Christ. We did not mind. We knew that there was an inexhaustible supply of priests and that they brought good money. What their new owners did with them was their business.

I took out the calfskin map and opened it. Erika could not read but she was interested in maps. "What are these?"

"I cannot say, for there is nothing which shows a coast. They could be anywhere. This blue line could be a river or, possibly, a coast. This is why we need the women." I pointed to a strange drawing on the calfskin. "This could be the drawing of a room, but why put it on this document."

"Aiden, could he do it; read the map?"

"He could, but he is not here. Where is he?"

"Bjorn took him and Arturus with some other men to fetch the copper from the mountain."

"When he returns he can confirm what Deidra and Macha have to say."

She gave me a sharp look, "You do not trust them?"

I shrugged, "In most matters, yes I do, but when it comes to the White Christ then I like confirmation."

"You have become less trusting as you grow older."

"We have been betrayed by too many whom we trusted before now."

Deidra and Macha came to the doorway and coughed, I looked up, "You sent for us, Jarl?"

I closed the lid on the box and then turned over the calfskin. I would question them first and see their reactions.

"We returned yesterday to the monastery from which you were taken." I could have predicted what they would do, they both made the sign of the cross. "We killed the Saxons who were there and rescued the slaves."

They smiled and Macha said, "You have a good heart, Jarl Dragon Heart...."

"You mean for a Viking?" She coloured and I held up my hand. "It matters not. Tell me was there a saint connected with your monastery?"

"Saint Brigid. It is why we were there. It was rumoured that there were some of her bones in the church but we never saw them."

They looked at me with curiosity burning in their eyes and on their lips. "Did she have a ring? One with a green stone surrounded by smaller blue ones?"

They looked at each other. Macha said, "The ring of Hibernia. I thought that was a legend."

"Tell me the legend then."

"It sounds too farfetched to believe."

I smiled, "I am open minded, tell me."

She shrugged. "It seems a Roman soldier came from the mainland to ask her a question." She paused, "There were rumours that Saint Brigid had been the slave of a druid, you understand."

"The question?"

"The question was about the safety of Britannia. Saint Brigid said that a warrior would come from the darkness and bring light to the land."

Deidra shook her head as though to rid her mind of the image of an Abbess telling fortunes. "We were convinced that the story had been made up by the pagans to make us believe that Saint Brigid was the Earth mother." They crossed themselves again.

"And the ring?"

"The ring was a gift from the Roman. It was said to represent the island of Hibernia, green, in a blue sea."

"But is all a legend and not to be believed."

I opened the casket and took out the hand and the ring. They both screamed and made the sign of the cross before clutching their own crosses as though their lives depended upon them.

"It is true then?"

"It looks like it. Now," I turned the map over, "what can you tell me about this?"

I think the shock of the ring made them forget that I was pagan and they translated word for word. When Aiden returned he confirmed it.

I write this record knowing that my death is close at hand. I have served my masters well: I devoted my life to God, I helped King Coel and King Urien to protect the frontier and I kept alive the Roman ways. I have done my duty.
The barbarians are coming and I fear that the Warlord will not be able to hold them back forever. I believe with all my heart that there will come a hero as Lann of Stanwyck came from obscurity to hold back the Angles and the Saxons. It will not be in my lifetime.
To that end I have hidden the treasure of Rheged in the old Roman fortress of Luguvalium. The map will help someone to find it. I believe that God will direct some unborn hand to this

end. I have buried it with St. Brigid's hand and ring as a way of telling the finder of the treasure. If the hand is not with this map then the barbarians have won and the treasure of Rheged is lost forever. The priests in this church know not what I do and when I return north they will still be none the wiser.

The true hero will be from the same stock as Lann of Stanwyck and, in him, is the hope for Britannia.

I go to God with a clear conscience,

Osric of Rheged

The letter touched the former nuns. They had heard of this holy man, apparently. He had been another legend of Rheged. It was now obvious to me that he had buried the chest himself knowing that his time on earth was growing short. It explained much. I now had a name for the Warlord; Lann of Stanwyck.

I must have mused for some time for Erika said, "What is it husband?"

I smiled at the two former nuns who looked astounded, "I just find it staggering that I was meant to find this; a religious object and a map hidden by a priest of the White Christ. *Wyrd.*"

I almost burst out laughing when the two women crossed themselves again and then fled back to their cheese making. Erika put her arm around my waist. "And you have been chosen."

"I found the box and there is a connection but this was a follower of the White Christ and I am, what they call, a pagan."

"We cannot know the ways of the Allfather nor the Norns. Perhaps the Allfather and the White Christ are one and the same."

I shook my head vehemently. "No, that cannot be for the White Christ turns the other cheek Odin would never turn the other cheek. But you may be right. I might be the instrument chosen for this task."

When Aiden and Arturus returned the content of the map was confirmed and I had Aiden make a copy of the map. Arturus was excited beyond words. "When do we go for this treasure?"

"There is no hurry and we have far too much to do here. We have a summer to prepare our homes for the winter and my warriors and I will need to gather grain for the winter."

Erika looked at me as I said that. It meant we would be sailing off to raid the Cymri and the Saxons. We would be going to war again.

Chapter 15

There were never enough hours in the day. The Ulfheonar worked from dawn to dusk to finish off the settlement on the east of the water and that on the west. We had to build a palisade for the one on the western shore and that took time. My warriors did not spend all of their time working. Many of the newly arrived refugees were handsome women and girls. All of them loved this new land and wished to lay down roots. There would be many marriages at midsummer.

There were also more mundane things to attend to like the naming of the dog that Lang had given us. Arturus and Kara both badgered about the name. "You said that when you returned from the raid you would name her!"

I had, in truth, forgotten. She had come into the hall which meant Erika had softened her views. She lay next to my weapons which were by the fire. I looked at my shield and said, "Wolf! Call her wolf."

Surprisingly, for they rarely agreed, both of my children loved the name and the golden dog became Wolf.

When the halls and huts were finished we had to begin the work of ensuring supplies for the winter. We sent '*Serpent*' to trade for seeds while Bjorn stopped turning out weapons and began to make ploughs and farming implements. With midsummer approaching I took Aiden, Arturus and the Ulfheonar on a journey west. We knew that the sea was not far from Lang's Dale and we had seen villages there. If we could make those people our friends then it might save us a portage with our boats. It seemed a good idea. We used the horses we had brought and the wild ponies which we had found on the fells. It made the journey a little quicker.

Lang looked pleased to see us. We had not bothered him and Erik had made sure that he and his family were sent gifts of ale and cheese when they were made.

"We would have you and your family come for a feast on Midsummer Day. There will be many warriors marrying and it will be a happy time."

I could see, before he even answered, that his wife was keen to visit. It must have been lonely for her in this lovely valley to be without other women. I had learned that men can be happy with themselves but women grew happier with the company of other women.

"We will be honoured."

"What can you tell me of the land west of here?"

"We have not journeyed that far. The mountains are high and there is little to be gained. I went as far as the high pass and the old Roman fort which is perched there."

"We will ride to the coast and I will speak with you again when I return."

The land did, indeed, climb steeply. I was grateful to those long dead Roman engineers and road builders who had created this cobbled road to the sea. This Osric had obviously been one of them. We halted at the Roman fort to rest the horses and so that I could explore it. I was impressed. It was made of stone and had ditches all around. No one could have crossed the pass without the permission of the garrison. It set me thinking. We had a pass such as this close to the dale where we were planting rye. Two families had settled there. If they could build a tower or a wall then we would have a defence to the north of my little kingdom.

We reached the end of the pass and looked out towards the sea. "Look, Jarl Dragon Heart, it is Man!"

Snorri was right. There, glistening like a green jewel in a blue sea was man. It looked close enough to touch.

Haaken reined in his horse. "Aye but now Erik is no longer Prince he is now King of Man."

There was bitterness in Haaken's voice. "It is a title, nothing more. I think of this land as a kingdom but we need no king do we? What would a king bring except someone before whom we would bow the knee?"

I did not notice the glances shared by my Ulfheonar. They resented the fact that Erik had benefitted from what we had done. I did not mind for he was Erika's brother. He was not blood but he was family.

It was early afternoon when we reached the walled village. We had seen it for the last three miles or so. Aiden was fascinated by the mile markers the Romans had put by the road. He and Arturus discussed the people who had built these roads. It made me think about the mark we left on the land. Our houses were made of wood. If Hrams-a was abandoned then what would remain in the time of Arturus' son? Nothing. We needed to leave our mark on this land.

When the gates slammed shut as we approached I should have known we would not be given a good welcome but I still believed that we could make all believe our true intentions. We were not in war gear although we had swords and bows. The walls were just sixty paces from us and bristled with spears and ancient helmets.

I held out my hands, "I come in peace." I spoke in Saxon for I thought they might understand that. My answer was an arrow which pinged off the cobbles ten paces from me. My horse skittered back a little in fear. My warriors' hands went to their weapons. I held up my hand, "Let us not start a war over this." I tried again, this time in the language of the Welsh. I only had a few words but I hoped they would be enough. "We come in peace."

A greybeard appeared and spoke in halting Saxon to me. "We do not need your peace. We know you for what you are. You are Vikings and you are not to be trusted. Go from this place or we will kill you."

"I am Jarl Dragon Heart and a man of my word. I say that I come in peace."

There was a pause and then I heard laughter from the walls. "That is what your fellow killer, Sihtric Silkbeard, said before he killed the warriors from the next village and enslaved them. We do not trust Vikings."

"I am not Sihtric."

The answer we received was a shower of arrows. They were not intended to kill us but some came perilously close. I led my men away. Einar growled, "Let us go back and get our weapons. We will destroy these insects and raze their little village."

I heard the grumble of agreement. "No. They are doing what we would do. They have every right not to trust us. They are wrong but they do not know that. We will have to win them over."

Haaken looked at the sky which was clouding over. "We will not make the water by night fall."

"I know. We will stay in the old Roman fort."

We reached it before dark and while Snorri and Beorn sought some game I had the others light a fire while I explored the ruins.

I had noticed that all these forts followed the same pattern. They all had four gates, one in each wall. There looked to be long narrow halls which may have been barracks and there were, as usual, a cluster of buildings for eating and cooking. Aiden and I were looking for one with the remnants of a roof.

Aiden spotted the small building which looked to be most intact. It looked to be big enough to accommodate the few men I had brought with us. Leaving Arturus and Aiden to clean it out I went to see to the animals. There was a water trough and enough water in it for the animals. We tethered them on the grass outside the walls and they happily grazed.

I spent some time with Haaken and Cnut admiring the way the fort had been built. We had much to learn from these ancient Romans who were such clever engineers. I heard Arturus shout for me and we ran over, our weapons out. When I saw the grin on his face I sheathed my weapon. "Do not shout like that, you had me worried."

"I am sorry but see what Aiden has found." They had a burning brand and Aiden had discovered another room behind the one in which we would sleep. He pointed to the floor. There was a wooden door with a metal handle. I could see that some of the roof had collapsed and covered it. The two of them had revealed it by their excavations.

Haaken rubbed his hands together. "More treasure!"

"This was a fort and not a church."

Haaken pointed to the hole. "That looks to be the same size as the one we saw in the monastery. We will find out when we open it."

I leaned down and pulled on the handle. It was stiff and the old wood creaked alarmingly. Suddenly the handle and a huge chunk of wood ripped out and I fell backwards, much to the delight of my son. Haaken quickly finished ripping out the rotting wood and thrust the torch inside.

"There is something down here but this looks to be a deeper hole."

The entrance was too small for any of us. Arturus looked up expectantly. "Very well, son, but be careful down there."

He climbed down and we saw that there were small steps. Whoever had gone down had had to be tiny. We passed him a torch and he said, "There are boxes and bags down here."

"Many?" Haaken sounded excited.

"A few," Arturus sounded equally disappointed.

"Can you pass them up?"

His voice became excited as he said, "Yes and they are heavy!"

He lifted one box up which was about the length of his forearm and as thick as Bjorn's mighty leg. Haaken greedily grabbed as Arturus disappeared inside his hole for more. The top was wrenched off to reveal a box of Roman nails. I almost laughed at Haaken's disgust.

"Nails? Why would they hide nails?"

"Macha told me that Roman soldiers used to sole their sandals with nails and when they left their forts the nails remained behind." Aiden had much information stored in his young head.

"They may not be treasure to you Haaken but Bjorn will appreciate them."

Arturus brought up four boxes of nails. "There is a cloth or something here. I will move it." A red cloak was thrust up. It had had a metal attachment but it had broken. I heard a squeal of delight, "I have found a helmet. Can I keep it?"

"We will see." He handed up a helmet which looked nothing like ours. It appeared to be made of a yellow metal like bronze and had a curved piece to protect the back of the neck and two cheek guards. I handed it to Aiden, "This has to be Roman."

I heard an, "Ow!"

"What is it?"

"I picked something up from the floor and it stuck in my finger."

"Leave them then. Is there anything else?"

"There is something in the corner." There was the sound of something being dragged and then his head appeared with two sacks. "These are heavy."

"Probably more nails."

"I told you Haaken, Bjorn will like them."

"I will check the far end. There looks to have been jars of something but the jars have broken."

He disappeared and we opened the sacks. They contained silver Roman coins. "Now this is treasure."

It had been silent for a while and I began to worry about Arturus. What was it about my family and dark holes in the ground? Suddenly a sword appeared from the hole and Arturus held it. "If I cannot have the helmet, can I have this?"

It was a Roman sword. It was about the same length as my seax but much broader. In all conscience I could not deny him. "Yes if you can clean it up."

"I will."

"Is that it?"

"Pass me the helmet and I will collect these things which stuck in my finger."

Haaken asked, "Why?"

"If the Romans put them here then it must be for a purpose. It will not take me long."

Aiden's influence on my son was beginning to pay off. He was thinking well. The helmet came up and then Arturus squirmed out. "Well done son. That was bravely done."

Aiden held the helmet and I took out one of the objects. "What in the name of the Allfather are they?"

I took one out. They looked like four nails welded together. I could not fathom their purpose. Aiden took one and dropped it on the floor. He picked it up and repeated it four or five times. "Do you see, Jarl Dragon Heart? They always land with one spike sticking up. They are intended to stick into men's feet."

"Or horses."

"Indeed, horses. If you put these before a shield wall then they would find it hard to rush at you."

I nodded. "This is '*wyrd*' we found little gold but much treasure. I am pleased we were turned away from the village else we would not have stayed here."

When we reached Waterston I could see the change another day had made. Bjorn was delighted with the nails and intrigued by the four sided object. We had no name for them as yet and Arturus just called them hedgehogs. It seemed as good a name as any. We decided to take some with us the next time we fought. I could not see when we might need them but, so far, I could find no fault with the Roman war machine.

I had time, after we returned to ride to meet with Rolf and Windar. I took Dargh with me. Since we had arrived at the water he had felt a little lost. He and his men had worked hard but they had no place of their own. I had an idea which I wished to put to Rolf. My journey across the Roman Road had set my mind working.

Both of them were intrigued by the hedgehogs and the nails. "It will be interesting to see them used."

"Aye Windar but I think I can see a use for them already. These would hurt horses." Rolf looked at me, "Remember the horsemen on Anglesey? These would have stopped even them."

I led the three of them north from the head of the mere. "How is the crop in Rye Dale coming along?"

"It is good. The water at Rye Dale ensures the crop is well watered. We should have enough grain for the winter."

"Good but what of the danger from the north? I would have a tower or small fort at the col between the waters."

"Where the land is steep and the river flows fast?"

"I would. It would give early warning as well as shelter for the farmers in Rye Dale."

Dargh brightened, "And that is why you brought me?"

"It is indeed. Your men could build it and garrison it. You could patrol as far as the Grassy Mere and hunt. Eventually, when we get enough men I would do the same at Lang's Dale too."

He rubbed his hands together. "When do we start?"

"I would say now but my wife is busy preparing for the weddings and midsummer feast. We will be raiding south after the feast. Begin then."

"Good."

"When you go raiding how many boats will you take. Jarl Dragon Heart?"

"'*Wolf*' and one other. I would have one of you stay here to guard this valley and watch over mine."

Rolf and Windar had grown close and they looked at each other and nodded, "Then I will come with '*Bear*' and Windar can finish the defences."

As I had expected all of my wife's efforts were on the midsummer feast. She explained that it would make our people joined with the land and pointed out that our marriage on Man had done that for us. As Jarl I also had certain responsibilities. I would watch the sun rise over the water as I had watched it rise over the sea when living on Man. Arturus begged to come with me and I acceded. One day he would become Jarl and he ought to know what was expected of him. As we trudged up the trail to the top of Old Man Olaf, as we called the mountain, I explained that he would need to be silent as we watched for the rising of the sun.

"Why?"

"For we are close to the Gods and Valhalla. If we are quiet then they can speak with us."

"They speak with you?"

"Every time I have done this as Jarl I have heard Ragnar's voice in my head or Prince Butar's."

"What do they say?"

I laughed, "That is for a jarl to know but you may hear voices too if you are silent enough."

My words must have had an effect for, when we sat on the peak with our backs to the rocks, he was silent. I pointed out where the eastern skyline began and we sat and waited. I had not been lying to my son. I did hear voices but I could never predict either what they would say or who would speak them.

I saw the thin white line as it appeared over the far mountains. It would be some time before its rays reached us but it was exciting to know that this day would last longer than any other. It was as close to eternity as we would come whilst on this earth. It was my mother's voice which began to whisper in my mind. Her tones were as I remembered them. They took away the chill of the early morning. They told me of her pride in what we had done. She called me her wolf. Suddenly her voice became fearful and her words rang in my head, "Beware the Vikings."

And then, as suddenly as she had come into my head she went and in that instant the sun flashed from behind the distant mountains and bathed us in golden sunlight. I stood and Arturus gripped my hand tightly. I looked down and saw that he had a strange expression on his face.

"What is it my son?"

"I heard a woman in my head and she was gentle. She told me to seek the scabbard." He looked puzzled. "What did she mean?"

I genuinely did not know. "I suspect it means keep your eyes open. Sometimes these things are not meant literally. A scabbard protects a sword from harm perhaps it means look for something to protect that which is valuable."

"I wondered if it meant my new sword; the Roman one."

"It might do but we will have to make you one in any case and so we would not be seeking that one. Do not let it prey on your mind. The spirits have spoken and that means you are a chosen one. When the Gods touched my sword then I knew that I was chosen and had a different path to take from other men."

The sun was fully up over the mountains and as we turned to walk down the path the rays suddenly flashed across the sea to the west and struck Man. "You see how we are linked to our past and to our present. The Allfather is watching us and the Norns are spinning their threads. Now let us descend for today will be a long day. We have much to do."

When the sun was at its height then those who had chosen to marry were joined. There was a large crowd gathered on the western side of the water. Lang and his family had arrived early and I could see that Lang's wife was taken with the ceremony. I suspected she would have liked such a symbolic union. In all, twenty couples were joined. I could see from the full figures of some of the women and girls that their union was already well established. As jarl that pleased me for it meant more children to be born and that could only make my people stronger.

As usual many of the younger men drank too much and there were the usual fights. The Ulfheonar, many of who had married, did not drink as much and a clout from one of those warriors normally ended any fisticuffs and prevented it escalating to weapons. I knew that the men would be the best of friends before the night was over. It was the way of warriors.

For the women it was a chance to meet with other women and exchange ideas and thoughts. Warriors had the advantage of long sea voyages. We did not feel the need to fill the silences as women did. Yet I could understand their need to talk to others of a similar mind. My wife was the perfect hostess and I was pleased to see Kara following her around and learning how to be the wife of a jarl.

Towards sunset we all gathered on the eastern shore close to my hall to watch the sunset over the water. We had done that at Hrams-a but this seemed to be an even better choice. My men had placed a huge stump for me and it was close by the water. I sat facing west. I enjoyed these last moments of the midsummer feast.

We had eaten well and we had drunk well and the gods had shown their favour by keeping all clouds from the skies. I watched as the sun dipped slowly below the craggy face of Old Olaf. It is strange but it seemed to make a crown around his head. It was almost magical.

Suddenly behind me I heard a collective gasp and Windar shouted, "The king has a crown!"

I had thought that they were speaking of Olaf but, as I turned I saw that all were on their knees and even Erika, who stood still, had an amazed look on her face. I could feel the rays on the back of my head but I could not see what they did.

Erika walked up to me and, holding my cheeks in her hands, raised me up and kissed me. "The sun has crowned you, my love. The people saw a crown upon your head." She turned and, linking me, we faced my people. They all stood.

Haaken strode forwards. "We have all struggled with a name for this place but the Allfather and Olaf have given us one, this is Cyninges-tūn, the place of the king."

From that day forth it became the name of our home. No-one dared to call me king but they all knew that the gods had crowned me in gold. It was no mighty leap of faith; they had touched my sword why should they not crown me? In truth I did not mind for I felt that the king was Old Olaf or even Butar for it was the mountain which I had seen crowned.

Chapter 16

It took us almost fifteen days to prepare for our raid. We had to send men down to the sea to prepare our drekar and we had to carry all that we would need down ourselves. Windar promised that, when we returned, he would have small boats to ferry us along the length of the mere. We could have saved time by coming over the ridge which separated the water but we were loath to risk Midgeton, as we called the fly infested forest which divided us, and so we went the way which avoided the biting insects. I was able to see, before we left, the fort built by Dargh. It was not huge but it would shelter the farming families from the Rye Dale and would warn Windar of any attack from the north. I felt happier.

We set sail with '*Serpent*' and headed for Man. I intended to raid the Welsh on Anglesey for they had great quantities of grain and that was what we sought. The gold and holy books had bought fine weapons and some grain but we knew that we could take what we needed. It broke the journey to Anglesey and, besides, I was curious as to what Erik had done with the island now that he was King Erik. I had warned the Ulfheonar to be on their best behaviour. I did not want a blood feud with his oathsworn. I did not fear them but I did not want my men to shed their blood.

The first thing I noticed as we headed down the eastern coast was how derelict Hrams-a looked. There were still people living there but there did not appear to be many. Many of the buildings looked to have been demolished or parts of them taken. I knew that most of the people had left with me but I had assumed that others would have moved in.

In contrast Duboglassio had expanded and now spread north, south and west. I noticed banners hanging from the walls. They appeared to show three legs all joined together. I remembered that had been the design used on the shields of Erik and Erika's father's men. Erik had never bothered with that he had always tried to copy my wolf design. I liked the symbol because it stood out but I wondered why he had reverted to that design.

There were a number of ships tied up and we struggled to find a berth. We tied the other two ships to the seaward side and clambered ashore over the three ships.

We were greeted by mailed warriors whom we recognised. Their smiles and welcome allayed my fears. They were still the same warriors. Haaken could not resist a dig, "You now serve a king eh Knut? Should I bow?" Knut was an old friend and the best warrior Erik had.

Although Knut laughed I could see he was uncomfortable. He made a joke to ease the moment "Only if you wish to kiss my arse."

The joke eased the tension but I hissed in Haaken's ear, "Behave!" Turning to Rolf I said, "I will just enter with the Ulfheonar. Keep your eyes and ears open. See what you can learn."

King Erik had improved his hall. Prince Butar had never gone in for ostentation. Now it seemed to gleam with gilding and beautiful pots. We must have been spotted from afar for Erik and his Queen sat on a raised dais both complete with golden crowns. They did not stand to greet us. The first thing I noticed was how portly Erik had become while Hlif had become even gaunter and sharp featured.

A small officious looking man, dressed like a priest of the White Christ stood by the dais. He had a staff which he banged on the floor. "King Erik of Man and Queen Hlif welcome Jarl Dragon Heart to their home."

I suddenly noticed how everyone else bowed. My men just continued to look at the two of them. The clothes of the King and Queen were brightly coloured and made of a fine and shiny material I had never seen before. They looked grand but we had fought alongside Erik. Warriors did not need to show off to other warriors.

The Queen did not look happy and she hissed, "Men bow to King Erik."

"I thought that he was the brother of my wife. I will greet him as I always do." I strode forward and clasped his right forearm with mine. "It is good to see you brother."

She was white with anger. "Men have been gelded for less!"

I could not help myself and I burst out laughing, "The man that tries that will soon find it to be a mistake."

Erik stood and glared at his wife, "Enough. He is Erika's husband." He led me from the dais. "What brings you visiting?"

"We are raiding." Something in the back of my mind told me to keep our destination secret. "This is a brief visit. I thought it would be discourteous to pass so close and not see you."

I hoped he took the import of my words to heart. "Of course. And how is my sister?"

"Enjoying building somewhere new and organising her people."

"You must excuse Hlif she has worked hard to make this place beautiful. She means nothing by her comments."

I lowered my voice. "The only man I will bow to is now dead. He was Prince Butar."

"I know. I know." He looked anxiously over his shoulder. "It is my wife. Now that I am king…"

"You are king because you call yourself so. If I call myself Emperor would you bow your knee to me?"

"That is ridiculous!"

I smiled, "Of course it is." I decided to change the subject. "What of the Norse who live in Hibernia? What do you hear of them?"

"Sihtric? He has not bothered me although I hear he is casting glances at your land." He added slyly.

"We have had dealings with the Irish. I think we have discouraged them." Was there a hint of disappointment in Erika's brother's voice? Perhaps I was allowing his wife to colour my judgement. I had fought shoulder to shoulder with this man and he had defended my family. "I clasped his arm again. "Beware some of the other Norse; they can be treacherous. Do not lose what many men died to win."

"I am no fool, brother. I know how to deal with other kings and princes."

As I left him I realised that he had already been duped. He thought that he was now in an elite group. He was in the ranks of kings. If that included Sihtric Silkbeard then he was associating with pirates and robbers. As I boarded my drekar I felt good about leaving Man and that was the first time I had felt that way.

As we pulled away from the shore I felt that I was starting anew. When I had left for my new home a piece of me had been left on Man. Hlif had torn it out with her words and Erik with his indifference. I would bow the knee to no man.

We took our time as we headed south. We knew the island of Anglesey well and Thorkell was navigating. He would land us on a quiet part of the coast line and we would be able move towards the farms where we knew they had grain. We would avoid those areas where the people had been kind to us but if it came to it we would take what we had to. It was our people or theirs. Only the strong would survive.

I kept one eye on Thorkell who was at the prow but I was listening to Haaken and Cnut as they told me what they had learned. "Sihtric Silkbeard visited with Erik a month ago." I smiled. Haaken would never bring himself to call Erik, king. "It seems they are great friends."

I snorted, "Then Erik can expect a knife in the back any time soon."

"It seems that Magnus Barelegs has landed close to the monastery we destroyed and calls himself King of the Lune while Ragnar Hairy-Breeches is King of Caerlleon." He shook his head, "What would you like to be king of Cnut? This bench perhaps!"

The Ulfheonar laughed. I did not. This was serious. We had all left a land with virtually no king and now they all wanted to be ruled by one. I could understand this with the Danes. They all had allegiance to a king. I could not even remember the name of the King of Norway although I was sure that Prince Butar had told me. The other worrying thing was that kings liked to have more land to be king over. If Magnus Barelegs cast his eyes north then he would threaten my people. Once we had enough food I would return home and prepare for an autumn of war.

I saw Thorkell wave to steer board and I touched the steering board a little. His hand came up. We were on course. There would be no moon that night. We had not planned it but it would work to our advantage. Soon I saw the white line of breakers on the northern coast of the island. Anglesey was rich farmland and I knew that they grew two crops each year. A winter one, harvested in spring and a summer one harvested in autumn. They would still have the early crop in storage and the first of the autumn harvest would have been gathered in. Four weeks later, when all of the grain was harvested, they would be expecting a raid. I hoped to catch them unawares.

We took down the sail when Thorkell waved his arms. '*Serpent*' would just reduce sail and wait offshore for us. I could vaguely make out a darker line beyond the surf; that had to be Anglesey. Thorkell was a competent seaman and as soon as his arms went aloft we took in the oars and slid up on to the shingle and sand beach. He leapt ashore with shield and sword to give us early warning of an ambush. We worked quickly. Donning helmets and grabbing shields we jumped ashore. We had four ship's boys on each drekar and they would secure them for us. Alf had eight spare sailors and warriors aboard his ship and, for the first time, we were not worried about the safety of our drekar.

Thorkell led the way and we trotted in a single line over the sand dunes towards the farm houses which were hidden in the dark. Rolf and his men followed behind. We had more than enough men for the farmhouses but the large numbers lessened the chance of the farmers fighting back. I had saved these people from the Saxons. I did not want to kill them.

Thorkell held up his hand but I could smell the farm. It was the smell of animals and wood smoke. It was unmistakeable. Thorkell loped off with the Ulfheonar behind him. They would protect us and prevent any of the inhabitants escaping. This was a big farm. The hall looked big enough to accommodate twenty or more people and there was a slave hut. I could see the bar on the door. They could stay there until we had finished.

Rolf and I headed for the hall. It had just one entrance and that was half way up the building. The lower part would have their animals within. I reached the door; I knew that my men were right behind me and I stepped through and into the warm fuggy mass of heaving and sweating bodies. There was a fire burning in the corner. The temperature did not necessitate one but it kept the wildlife out of the roof and made it easier to start a fire each day. Rolf strode up to the fire and thrust a brand into it. As soon as it flamed into life people began to wake. They saw twenty armed Vikings with drawn weapons. The women screamed. One of the men grabbed for his sword. It cost him his hand.

"You all know me. I am Jarl Dragon Heart. I am here to take your grain but you have my word if you do not resist us you shall all live and we will not burn you buildings."

One man, obviously the farmer, shouted, "What will we eat if you take our grain?"

"You will eat your second crop, or you will fish." I shrugged, "When you rebelled against my men you lost any sympathy I might have had. Be thankful farmer that I give you your life." I prodded his stomach with the tip of my sword. "Going without a few meals might be good for you."

I turned and left. Four warriors remained to watch the prisoners. There was little chance they would try anything. I went to the slave hall and we opened it. Inside were slaves from every nation but there were many Norse. They had been taken when the island fell. To them I said, "You are free. Help my men to carry the grain to the ship." There were another ten. All were Saxons. "You will remain slaves but we will treat you well."

They nodded their resignation and three of my warriors tethered them and led them off. Rolf's men were already loading the bags on to the carts they had found to head back to the boats some mile and a half away. We had fewer men now and the second farm would not be as easy.

Dawn was rapidly approaching when Beorn signalled us to halt. This farm was as big as the first one and they must have had sheep for the dogs which guarded them began barking. We knew we had little time to lose and I waved the Ulfheonar forward. They would have to run hard to cut off the farm. As I waved my warriors towards the farmhouse I heard the noise of people within. The dogs had woken them and there was no time to lose. Had it been me and my Ulfheonar attacking alone we might have escaped notice for we dressed all in black but the men I led were not so dressed and must have been spotted by someone within. I heard the cry, "Vikings!"

"Charge!"

There would be no time for a silent and cautious approach. We needed to get to the buildings before they were made defensible. Arrows suddenly began to strike us. One hit my shield and another pinged off my helmet. The warrior next to me, Olaf the Troll, suddenly pitched to the ground with an arrow in his shoulder. It served to spur my men on and we covered the last few paces to the ditch and low wooden wall quickly. The ditch was not wide but it was filled with water and mud. Anything could be lurking in its depths and I leapt the ditch and then hurdled the wooden wall. I caught something moving towards me and instinctively held my shield up. The spear thudded into it. I wrenched it free and held it before me. I would return it with interest.

The wooden hall was similar to the first farm but here they had men in the animal byres loosing arrows. I saw a white face and hurled the spear. I heard a scream and knew I had struck something. The lower section of the building had openings for air and to facilitate cleaning. I threw myself at one of them; it gave way beneath my weight and I crashed through. My shield struck a bowman and pitched him to the floor. I drew my sword and stabbed him in the back. When I rolled him over I saw that he was a youth of no more than twelve summers.

I yelled, "I am Jarl Dragon Heart! If you fight then you will all die!"

A voice shouted, "We will all die anyway!"

"If you throw down your weapons I promise that you will live."

An old man suddenly ran at me with an axe used for chopping wood. He swung it at my shield. I stepped to the side and then smashed the flat of my sword against the back of his head. He pitched to the ground unconscious.

"I could have killed him. Now throw down your weapons before I end the life of this brave but foolish old man!"

I heard the weapons as they clattered to the ground.

"Rolf, tie up the men. Get the slaves freed and the grain loaded. I will find the Ulfheonar."

I was anxious to discover if they had been successful. I ran out and saw the first light of the new day peering over Wyddfa's peak. When I reached the road which ran by the end of the farm I saw them heading towards me. Haaken hung his head. "I am sorry Jarl Dragon Heart but one escaped. We killed one but a second evaded us."

I nodded. "We will need to be swift then. You will be the rearguard."

The dawn had spurred Rolf and the others on. There were only two small ponies but we had attached them to a cart and loaded that with grain. The men had found some handcarts and they too were loaded. Each slave carried a bag of grain.

"Any losses?"

"Olaf the Troll had a wound in his arm but that was the most serious. He can walk."

"Good. A messenger escaped. Get the grain back to the boats."

With luck we would reach the boats before the Welsh could reach us. It was but a few miles. I joined the Ulfheonar at the rear. Snorri and Beorn were a hundred paces behind us. They waited, watched and then ran forward as they guarded the rear of the line.

"Did we do well?"

"Aye Cnut. We have much grain and many slaves. We have also freed some of our people enslaved when they took the island. It has been a good raid."

When we reached the first farm I waved and the four warriors guarding the farm joined us. I smiled, "For today you can be Ulfheonar."

They grinned as though I had given them golden armour rather than putting them in extreme danger. There were now sixteen of us to slow down any pursuit, I was confident that we would do so when I smelled the sea and saw in the distance the masts of my ships touched by the sun's rays.

Snorri raced up. "Horsemen! And some of them have mail!"

That was not what I had expected. Their mailed horsemen were a relic of the days of Rheged and we had met them before. They did not have many of them but they were hard to defeat. I said to one of the four warriors we had picked up, "Thorgir, run and tell Rolf that there are horsemen. He must hurry!"

"Aye my lord." He looked disappointed as he left us. He knew that we would be fighting and any glory that day would be ours.

I could hear the hooves now in the distance. With luck they would visit the farm we had last left and that would delay them a little. We had almost reached the sand dunes when Snorri shouted, "Shield wall!"

All of us obeyed instantly. We turned around and locked shields with the men closest to us. Beorn and Snorri ran behind us and notched arrows. The first horsemen were a hundred paces from us. A pair of arrows soared above us and the horsemen held their shields to catch them. I saw that there were only two mailed warriors and they held lances but there were ten horsemen that I could see and I saw movement beyond them indicating more were arriving.

Four of my men had spears which would give some protection but when the horses struck us they would simply knock us over.

"Wedge on me!" The warriors on either side suddenly slipped behind me so that Haaken and Cnut were to my rear. It gave us the most protection we could hope for. I saw the lance heading for me. As it closed I prepared my shield. As the lance tip touched I angled my shield so that it ran down the side of my shield and then Cnut's. It struck nothing. I brought Ragnar's Spirit over my head and hacked into the neck of the mailed warrior's mount. The beast crumpled to the ground in a torrent of frothy blood. The rider tried to save himself and he pitched from the horse. Cnut leapt forward and skewered him through one of the eye holes in his helmet.

Their loss made the rest wheel and reform. "Back!"

I saw that there were still fifteen of us and we ran. Suddenly one of the men we had brought from the farm fell forward with an arrow in his shoulder. "Pick him up!"

We were on the dunes and I suddenly had an idea. I had brought a handful of the hedgehogs with me and I threw them on the hard ground before me. As the wounded warrior was helped over the dunes the Ulfheonar gathered protectively around me. I watched as the first three horsemen eagerly gathered towards us at the crest of the dune. Two of them suddenly reared and threw their riders from their backs. The rest reined in and began to examine the ground.

"Back to the ships."

I could see that '*Serpent*' had been loaded and was standing off the shore. Rolf had a dozen men with bows ready to support us. We had a hundred paces to run. We would make it. And then Ragnar Siggison tripped. I was closest to him and I stopped and turned. Two horsemen were galloping down the dunes towards us. The soft sand had held them up but now they were on the harder beach and they leaned forwards with their spears. The others were too far away to help and Ragnar locked his shield with mine. "Sorry Dragon Heart!"

"When I say 'now', drop to one knee and be ready to strike at the horse on your left." I had a desperate idea and it relied on the fact that horses do not like to step on men. I turned my shield so that the left and right of our bodies were protected. They were just five paces away when I shouted, "Now!"

We dropped and the spears clattered on our helmets. The horses tried to jump us. As the hooves from the one on the right clipped my shield and knocked me backwards I thrust up into the animal's gut. I was showered in hot red blood. The horse pitched over us and I leapt to my feet ready to finish off the rider. I saw him lying in the sand with a broken neck. Ragnar had killed his horse too but he was lying unconscious. I sheathed my sword and slipped my shield around my back. Grabbing his arms I hauled his inert body over my shoulder. With his mail he was almost too heavy and I felt my feet sinking into the sand. I struggled towards the ships and the sea now just a tantalising fifty paces away.

I heard the whoosh of arrows and then Haaken and Cnut were by my side helping to carry my wounded Ulfheonar. I felt real relief when the salty sea lapped around my feet. Ragnar was hauled on board and I turned. The horsemen were gathered some two hundred paces away. They had only lost two men but we outnumbered them now. As the oars were run out I took off my helmet and saw the dent in one side. Bjorn made good helmets and it had saved my life.

Haaken and Cnut grinned at me as they began to row. "Lucky Dragon Heart once again. What were you thinking, Jarl? That your head is harder than a horse's hoof?"

I laughed. "At least I know that a horse will not step on a hedgehog and tries to avoid a man so it was worth the lesson."

Chapter 17

We did not risk the shallow waters of the river and our new slaves as well as our warriors marched to Cyninges-tūn. It was not as long a journey as that up Windar's Mere. Rolf and his men were also anxious to see the improvements which would have been made in the few days we had been away. Had the winds not been against us we would have been back a whole day earlier but we did not mind. That was a small price to pay for such a rewarding raid.

As we marched up the small river I discussed with Rolf and Haaken the hedgehogs. "They worked. I only had ten or so with me. Had we had many then they would not have been able to advance at all."

They both agreed. "It would be easy to have a bag with each group of warriors."

"These Romans impress me more each day."

Haaken gave me a shrewd look. "Could that be because you think that you were descended from them? That you have Roman blood coursing through your veins?"

He understood me well. "It would explain many things. Why I felt different as a child on the Dunum and what makes me different from warriors such as yourself."

Rolf laughed, "Everyone knows that you are not Norse, Jarl Dragon Heart and that is what makes others, such as Ragnar Hairy-Breeches, fear you. We all know that you do not fight the way the rest of them fight."

"Perhaps that is why we are so successful."

"When we were in Duboglassio we listened as you asked, Jarl, and we heard that Erik, King Erik as he styles himself, wishes to create a kingdom in the west to rival that of the Danes. His men see Northumbria and Mercia as minor kingdoms ripe to be plucked."

I laughed, "Then he will get a shock when he tries. He would need an army; more than that he would need a well organised army. I have heard, from Alf and other captains, that the

Saxons are beginning to build what they called Burghs. They are forts to defend their towns. The days of being able to raid wherever we wish will soon be gone. If they ever learn from the Romans then we will have to find other places to raid like Dál Riata or Hibernia."

Haaken wrinkled his nose. "That does not appeal; you can only tell the difference between their men and women by the length of their beards... the women's are longer!"

We laughed at his joke but I knew that they would both be thinking of my words. Perhaps the other Viking Jarls, now Princes and Kings had been deluded by our small victories, into thinking that they could do the same on a larger scale. It would not happen. Not, at least, until we had a leader who knew how to rule clans who liked to fight as a group and to be able to organise large numbers.

We reached the southern end of The Water as we called it and you could almost feel the relief amongst the men. This was home. The march from the sea seemed to free the mind of the battles and prepare you for the life of peace which we had at home. Many of the men had only recently married and would be looking forward to being with their new wives, even for a short time.

As we walked along the shore I began to think of our next raid and where that would be. We had enough grain but what we would need would be iron. There was Mercia but that was too far away or there was the Dunum, close to my first home. That was a risky sea voyage, around the northern coast of the island of Britannia or a hazardous march across the top of the world into the heartland of Northumbria. I would need to give it some thought.

Those who lived on the western shore reached their homes first. The thralls who had been captured would be taken with us to the eastern halls where they could be held until a thrall hall was built.

As we reached the trail which led to my home Rolf and his twenty remaining warriors said their farewells. They carried half of the grain we had collected and ten of the slaves. I wanted both of the settlements to prosper. This was not Man. We could support each other here. Farms and small settlements might dot the land but we would only need two large settlements. Man had taught us that. You needed somewhere you could protect and a refuge. I was under no illusions we were still vulnerable to attack and my visit to Erik had only fuelled my fears.

We had been seen from the other side of The Water and all were there to greet us. I knew that Erika would be looking to see that Arturus was safe and that we had not lost too many men. Her smiled betrayed her relief.

"A good raid?"

"We have grain for the winter."

"And how is my brother?"

"Not like the brother I first met. Perhaps Hlif has taken his soul for he appears afraid of her. He has also become false. He lied to me."

She nodded as though she was not surprised. She poured me some ale as I described his court, his flag and his ambitions.

"He always felt our father should have fought harder to hold on to what we had. Perhaps he will do that."

I put my horn into the ringed holder on the wooden table. "He is a good warrior but he is not a great warrior and he is not a leader that men will die for. I am sorry to be so blunt about your brother but I have to speak the truth."

She touched my hand, "I know and you are right. He has sown his own seed and he will have to see what grows. As for me I am happy with what we have."

"You do not wish to be Queen?"

She laughed, "As much as you wish to be king I think. Besides what would we gain from a title? Would the people love us any more, or less?"

"You are right."

"Besides, the people think that you are a king for you wore the golden crown on Midsummer's day."

"But that is nonsense. It was the Old Man who wore the crown."

"They believe what they believe. Surely the warrior whose sword is touched by the gods can be crowned by them too."

The next seven days were spent distributing the slaves and the grain. We all shared in the victory although I still retained the greater share. If things became hard I would have a reserve to distribute. Aiden worked busily on my sword which now neared completion. Each day I would walk down to the water and watch the work in progress. Bjorn had a roof over his head and the rains of late summer made him grateful.

Aiden looked up proudly as I entered. "It is almost complete." He pointed to a space close to the pommel. "As soon as we can acquire a red stone then it will be done."

"Good then you have fulfilled your task well. It is now my task to find such a stone. Perhaps I will find one when we travel north for the treasure of the map."

Bjorn came over. "He has done good work there, Jarl Dragon Heart and the blade looks magnificent. I will incorporate some of the ideas into my new swords but I have to tell you that we need Frankish blades and we are short of iron. The new tools we needed have used up my supply. The copper helps but it is too soft for weapons and armour."

"I know. I will take warriors to the Dunum. We will see what we can find there and I will send 'Serpent' and 'Butar' to Frankia. We have more coins than we can use. Let us use our bounty to make us stronger."

Aiden walked with me as we left the smithy. "It is a dangerous journey is it not Jarl Dragon Heart?"

"Not as difficult as the one we took to Hexham. We will have to be careful but the Saxons are not like the Welsh, they do not use horses. We would need to use our skills as trackers and scouts to evade capture. I would not take a large number of warriors, there would be no need."

"You could always trade for it."

"No Aiden, for metal is more precious than gold. It makes weapons which enable men to steal gold. It is good that you worry but we will plan this all very carefully."

Aiden's words preyed on my mind over the next few days as I dealt with all the problems the new village brought. Although Scanlan was a freeman and a farmer he still acted as a kind of steward. He and Maewe were close to both my wife and my family. He took many of the problems away from me.

"We need to work out a fair way to tax the people my lord. We offer them protection and they should pay."

"Are they happy about paying for protection?"

"Most are and if they are not then they can always leave."

"That seems a little harsh, Scanlan."

"You bring grain for them and you bring iron. They could not survive without either. The slaves you bring help them with the work. You are entitled to a greater share than you take. They are happy to pay."

"What do you suggest?"

"A tenth of what they produce seems fair."

What if they do not produce much of anything?"

He shrugged and smiled, "Then it is a tenth of not much of anything."

I could not find fault with his argument. "Then tell the people. If any disagree then ask them to speak with me and if there are difficulties and they do not wish to speak of it then you must tell me."

"I will my lord." He hesitated. "They would pay much more for the peace that you bring. You are being generous."

I took Arturus with me as I rode around our land. I called it our land for, unlike Man, all of the people who lived in it had sworn allegiance to me. I headed for Windar's Mere. There were now two sets of huts. One, the original one, close to the old Roman fort at the northern end of the Mere and the second on the eastern side occupying a flat piece of land. It almost mirrored that at Cyninges-tūn. In addition I could see the smoke from the fires of huts further away. It looked as though they felt confident in our security.

Rolf was away hunting in the forests. I spoke with Windar and explained to him of Scanlan's tax. He chuckled when I told him. "There are many jarls who take it all anyway. You do not take much and you are generous to your men. I do not think there will be complaints." He sighed as looked down the flat waters of the mere. "This is a beautiful spot. Were it not for the flies on the western side of the mere it would be perfection. But I suppose the flies are there to remind us of the perfection of the rest of the land."

"We have yet to winter here."

"True and that in itself will be an adventure."

He was a phlegmatic warrior. Nothing ever seemed to upset him. He looked for the good in all things. I think that was what made him a better leader than Rolf. Rolf was a war leader but for peace, you needed a Windar. They were a good combination and seemed to marry well with each other.

As we headed north to see Dargh and the frontier Arturus asked me question after question. Not only was his body growing but also his mind. "Aiden says you will hunt for iron. Will I be coming with you?"

"No, for I will be taking a small number of men and they must be the best that we have. One day you will be the best but your body and skills will need to improve."

There was a time when such an answer would have infuriated him but his presence on my raids had shown him what I meant.

"Then when you are away I will work hard. When will you go?"

"When we reach home I shall choose the warriors and we will leave."

He questioned me about the detail of the journey and, to be honest, his questions helped me to refine my plan. It had been many years since I had been taken from the Dunum and I only had a vague recollection of the area. It mattered not. All we had to do was to find where they worked their iron and then take what we needed. I also knew that we would leave none behind alive. We would need to be well away from the river before the chase began.

By the time we reached the bubbling river and the small wooden fort I knew what we had to do. To call the building Dargh had erected a fort was a little like building a funeral ship and calling it a drekar. It was only forty paces square with just one gate, facing south. There were no towers but it was on a small knoll which afforded a view to the water in Rye Dale. Inside was a small warrior hall to hold the fifteen or so men who lived there. He and his men were busy digging a ditch in front of the fort as we approached.

He stopped working and walked over. He was dirty and sweating heavily. He pointed to the ditch. "We have learned from the past, Jarl Dragon Heart. If the enemy cannot get to the walls then we are safer. With a deep ditch all the way around then we will have more protection."

I pointed to the dirt and sweat. "It is hard work then?"

"Aye my lord. We chose this place because of the hill but the problem is that the rock is close to the surface. Still it means that we can use some of the rock we take to make our walls stronger."

I pointed to where some of his warriors were working close to the tree line and the low ridge that ran along the side of the valley. "What are they doing?"

He gestured proudly at a low lying piece of ground to the north east of the fort and the knoll. The land there is lower. They are diverting the stream than runs from the fellside and we will make that a swampy area. It will protect that side of the fort."

Arturus said, "Won't the stream go back to its original course eventually?"

Dargh looked impressed, "He is a clever boy, jarl. Aye young Arturus it will but by then there will be a wet barrier there and the stone which lies close to the surface will stop it running away."

"You have thought things through well. I am pleased. And what of the farmers in Rye Dale?"

"Oh they are both good families and we get on well with them. If trouble comes they know they can reach here quickly. I have told them of our defences and they have a good and safe route to reach us." He pointed to the stream to the west. "We have put stepping stones across the river. They are below the surface. Unless you know where to find them you will not be able to cross safely."

I was intrigued, "We are heading west so show me and we will cross them."

We reached the river bank. It was wide and bubbling. I could not see them. "You will find it easier to lead your horses across. I will lead Arturus' horse and show you." He grinned up at my son. "Hold on tightly or you will end up with a ducking!"

I thought he would step up to his waist in the icy stream but then I saw the large flat stones beneath his feet. There was a path beneath the white sparkling water. I led my horse and we soon found ourselves across on the other bank. I had wet feet but that was all.

I clasped his arm. "You have done well Dargh."

He looked embarrassed. "I may not go on raids with you my lord but my men and I serve you as best we can."

Riding west I reflected that I needed to reward the men such as Dargh. The best reward I could give would be women so that they could have their own families and farms. That would be the task I would set myself after I had gathered the iron.

We crossed back over a fellside without a single hut or home. We had room aplenty to grow but it was not on these bare fell sides. It was perfect for sheep but I imagined that in winter, it would be a little bleak. Perhaps it was my thoughts of winter or the gods toying with me but a sudden storm blew up from the north and drove us home, sodden and miserable. It made up my mind for me. We would leave for the Dunum the day after next.

Chapter 18

We had no maps but we had the sun; it was as good a guide as any. I led my thirty warriors and five horses east on a morning with the chill air of a change in the weather. We marched without armour. The mail was unnecessary. With Snorri, Beorn and Erik Short Toe as scouts we would have ample warning of danger.

We had passed another long mere soon after Windar's Mere. I saw some of the men looking at it with interest. It was very narrow and nestled in the shelter of the huge mountain rising high above the valley. I knew that when we returned some of the warriors with me would wish to settle there. The valley beyond was even more attractive rolling eastwards towards the high hills of the middle of the land.

We had not seen any people living there which puzzled me. It looked to be good land for farming. As it was still early autumn we had no chance to judge the weather properly; perhaps a winter would explain things.

We found a Roman Road which ran like an arrow to the east. It was risky to travel on it but as we had seen few signs of human occupation and we decided to use it to save time. Some twenty miles after leaving Windar's Mere we saw the first occupation in this land. There was a huddle of huts on a small hill. There looked to be the remains of an old Roman fort close by. It did not look to be occupied but the people who lived nearby could take shelter there. We avoided contact with the people. There would be time enough later. I was not worried that they would warn Eanred that Vikings were in his land; we travelled without helmets and bare headed. We did not look like Vikings.

We spied one more village, which we avoided, before we began the ascent over the rising hills before us. The winds whipped around us and we drew our cloaks tighter. It was still autumn and yet it was bleak beyond words. There was a beauty about the bleakness but the fells just rolled away to the north and south and seemed to have no end. It was no wonder that the Saxons had not wanted this land. Three days after leaving Windar's Mere we began to descend and I saw the green and verdant valley that was the Dunum. We spied many villages, none of them large but all of them Saxon. I knew that we had thirty miles or so to go from the mile markers on the Roman Road and so we donned helmets and armour. We were now in enemy territory.

I was heading for the northern bank of the Dunum, a few miles from the mouth. I remembered the smith from my village travelling there to barter for the iron ore he used to make the tools we used. It meant crossing the Dunum and we found a Roman bridge. There was, however, a Saxon village hard by. I did not want to alert them to our presence and so we waited until dark. The village might be a problem when we returned but we would deal with that when we had to. Rather than risk the noise of the horses' hooves on the cobbled bridge five of my younger warriors who had no armour swam the horses across. The river was gently flowing at this point but we made them enter the water well above the bridge and the village. When they mounted the bank and walked downstream then we risked the crossing. We did so in groups of twos and threes. Snorri, Beorn and Erik made the last group. Save for a bark from a village dog we were undetected and our first major obstacle had been surmounted.

We camped in a small wooded dell close to the river but a few miles from the village. Our scouts had a short sleep and then rose mid-morning to scout out the next twenty miles. We used the opportunity to rest. The horses grazed and we put a few guards around the wood in case any unwelcome visitors arrived. We were not worried. Here was the heartland of Northumbria. The Saxons had occupied old Roman forts to the north and the south which they used to protect their land and here, far from the estuary, their people were safe. I knew that we were the first to come from the west. We had seen no-one. They would not be expecting us. I also knew that once we had raided then we would not be able to repeat the feat.

As soon as we had crossed the mountainous divide then the weather had changed. There was a chill wind blowing from the east and we were all grateful for our cloaks. There was little rain but we all felt chilled to the bone. We huddled in the dell while we waited for our scouts.

"If there is copper in our mountains then why not iron ore too?"

"I know not, Haaken. Perhaps the gods do not want to make it easy for us. Aiden tells me that there is a kind of thin rock on the old man which might make good roofing material." We all knew that while turf was good, easy to cut and kept you warm if you had a really bad rainstorm then it would come through. Aiden had told me that the thin rock was light enough to put on a roof and waterproof. We were going to try it on the smithy roof. Bjorn had decided that he wanted one for the winter and the heat of the forge would kill a turf roof. He and Aiden would make one while we were hunting iron.

"The gods do like to play with us do they not, Dragon Heart?"

"It is to test if we are worthy to go to Valhalla."

"Does not dying with a sword do that?"

"I have thought about this, Haaken. I do not think that some of those who died with a sword would be welcome in Valhalla. Harald One-Eye? Would the gods want to drink with a treacherous snake like him? Perhaps he and Loki are somewhere else."

"Interesting. We shall find out one day."

"True and I hope that my good deeds stand me in good stead."

It was late afternoon when the three scouts returned. They were hungry but happy. "We have found a settlement by the river. They have many smithies there and there were ships tied up to a jetty further downstream."

I nodded, "That would seem a likely place. Is there a palisade?"

"Aye."

"And how far from the river is it?"

"The huts and the wooden wall are on a small hill some three hundred paces from the river."

"And how long to reach it?"

"If we leave now then we could be there by the middle of the night."

"Then rest for a few hours and we will get there at dawn."

I remembered when I had been young enough to manage on a few hours of sleep a night. These were young men and they enjoyed the excitement of what they did. When they grew older and married we would see a change.

We had to tread carefully as we headed east. "There were small villages close to the river. They would not have enough warriors to worry us but we had to avoid detection. Our three scouts rode three of the horses to make the journey easier and they made sure that we skirted every place where dogs might alert the village to our presence.

We reached the stockade a few hours before dawn. There was a wood a few hundred paces from the walls and we tied the horses there. We could smell the smoke from the forges, even though they were not working. I hoped that there would be iron enough to have made the trip worthwhile and the number of forges Snorri had counted, four, looked promising.

We spent some time preparing for war. We had learned our appearance was worth another ten warriors. We would appear as red eyed wolves. The Ulfheonar always led the attack. We were the fiercest warriors and the most frightening in appearance. More importantly we were the best protected.

Beorn had told us there were two gates; one on the northern side and one close to the river. Haaken led half my warriors to the river gate while I took Cnut and the rest to the northern gate. We left the cover of the woods and moved silently across the darkened land before the walls. We had not seen any guards but we assumed they must have some. The warriors who were not Ulfheonar waited in the woods until we reached the walls. It is strange but we had learned how to move as shadows along the ground. No matter how many times we approached in this way, we were never seen. It gave rise to the rumour that we were shape shifters. We were happy to let them believe that but we were just well practised in the art of concealment.

Once we were close to the gate we hoisted Snorri and Beorn over the walls. One of these days the Saxons would realise that they needed higher walls to keep us out. They disappeared from view and we made our way to the gate. We heard nothing until the wooden bar holding the gate in place scraped a little as Snorri and Beorn lifted it.

We stepped inside and I saw the bodies of two sentries with their throats cut. I hoped that the others had been as successful at the second gate. We would soon find out. There was no warrior hall. It seemed that these people were the ones who worked the iron. We waited by the gate until the rest of our men had joined us. I waved Thorkell to take three men and find the iron. The rest were waved to the huts. There were only four huts within the walls. The rest was taken up with the smithies and the storage pits for the iron.

I nodded and my warriors entered each hut. The only noise I heard was a stifled groan and then my warriors emerged. Anything of value, mainly metal was brought from within. Haaken came up to me. "We have cleared our huts." All that would remain in the huts come morning would be the corpses of the dead.

We found Thorkell and his men. He pointed to the baskets containing the iron ore. There were four of them. "We found some completed weapons and farm implements."

Haaken looked over to the ships. "I am guessing that they all contain iron goods they have made. It is low tide and they will be waiting for the high tide."

It was tempting to go to the three ships tied up to the jetty and relieve them of their iron but I deemed it too much of a risk. We only had four horses. Two of them could carry the ore while the rest would carry the weapons. "Einar, fetch the horses. Find something to carry the weapons. When we have loaded the horses we will head west. We can rest in the dell we used yesterday."

The mistake would be to try to move too far. Exhausted men and animals could be caught. Dawn was breaking when we had loaded everything. "Get them moving. Snorri and Beorn, when we have gone, bar the gates again and prop the sentries against the wall." They ran off to obey my orders as we marched from the northern gate and headed west. I hoped that the three ships would be too busy to visit the iron smiths. I knew that they would be discovered; there must be a village close by for we had found no women within its walls. I just wanted to delay discovery for as long as possible. It would be a long morning until we reached our dell.

The sun had just dipped past its zenith when we were safely hidden in the dell. Haaken, Cnut and I stood guard, despite the protestations of the others. I knew that, tired as I was I would not sleep. It would need the sight of the land to the west to put my mind at ease. We were forty miles the wrong side of safety for sleep.

The hills looked tantalisingly close but we knew it was an illusion. It would take us a day to reach the other side and that day would leave us exposed. The Saxons would discover their loss before we had even left the security of the dell. I was hoping that by marching through the night we could avoid detection. Once on the other side we could ambush any pursuers.

By late afternoon we decided that our men had had enough rest to push on. The horses had grazed and we had water from a small stream. The trees had given us shelter from the biting wind and I felt more confident. I was now beyond sleep. My body would complain and when I did sleep it would be for a day but I knew that I could reach home without sleep if I had to.

I thanked the Romans every step of the way as we headed west. Their roads and bridges saved us time and prevented us from being ambushed. We clattered over their old bridge. I cared not if we woke the farmers. By the time they had reached the coast with news of our presence we would be almost home. Besides that our trail would be clear to see. You cannot hide five loaded horses and a heavily armed war band of Vikings. We had our start and we would keep it. Leaving the bridge we planted the horses' hooves on the cobbled stones of the ancient roadway. We plodded on through the night. It grew icily cold as we climbed but our efforts kept us warm. It was after moonrise when we began the descent. The wind was not quite as cold on the western side. I had decided to push on until the horses could go no further. If we did that then we might make the last part of the journey in one day.

The Norns were having none of that and we heard the barking of dogs in the distance before the sun had begun to peep over the horizon. There were more trees around us now and we would see them before they saw us. Our scouts stayed on the road as we pushed on. They would watch for the Saxons and then catch us up.

"Sven, look for an ambush place." He trotted up the road. We might be hidden in the dark but the hounds would smell us.

It was at that point that I saw the shortcomings in the Roman Road; it was straight and an ambush would be difficult to pull off. Although trees and bushes had begun to grow they were far too small for us to use for cover.

We moved more urgently now. I noticed my warriors slipping their swords in and out of the scabbards and tightening their shields. If we were surprised we would be ready for action, instantly.

There was a dip and Sven stood pointing to one side. I could see some rocks and scrubby bushes just thirty paces from the road. It was not much but it would have to do. "Tostig, take the horses and their riders up the road. Keep going and do not stop when you hear the sounds of battle. Save the horses and we will join you."

Even in the dark I could see that he was less than happy to be leaving us but I needed someone I could trust and it to be one of the Ulfheonar who led the warriors. He nodded his agreement.

"You five bring those horses along. Take them off the road and walk along the verge." He was using his head. The horses' hooves would be muffled along the grassy sods.

"Haaken, take half of the men and find somewhere on the southern side of the road." The nearest cover was some gorse bushes but they were sixty paces away. He pointed to the men he would choose and he trotted off in the dark.

I could hear the dogs and they were closer. "The rest of you come with me. Those with bows, string them." I led them to the rocks and bushes and placed them where I wanted them to hide. Returning to the road I drew Ragnar's Spirit. "Allfather and Ragnar guide me this night for we will need your help." The followers of the White Christ would have called it a prayer; in my mind I was talking to an old friend and asking him to intercede with Odin. When I held the sword I felt closer to both the old man and the Allfather.

I heard footsteps coming down the road. I pulled my shield into position. Snorri and the other two scouts stopped before me. "There are forty or so warriors. They have dogs; the big Irish wolfhounds again."

I had sent six warriors away and that left me with enough men to do the job. We needed surprise. "Wait here." I ran to Cnut. "I am going to make the four of us bait. Wait until you cannot miss and then attack. Haaken will join in once they are engaged."

He nodded, "Take care."

I rejoined the others. "Erik, lie down as though you are injured." He grinned as he lay down. "When they see us I will shout and we will run. Pretend we are afraid."

The hard part was waiting but the dogs grew closer. Snorri said, quietly, "They are the big Irish Wolfhounds just like the ones you fought at Úlfarrston."

Erik who was yet to become an Ulfheonar said, "If I kill one of those can I wear its skin, Jarl?"

Beorn snorted, "You can but it will not make you Ulfheonar. You need to kill a wolf for that!"

It is hard to wait when you know that you be fighting for your life within moments. I knew that I trusted the three young warriors who would be at my side. The first tiny sliver of light appeared over the hills. I could now hear the dogs at the top of the hill. "Ready to jump, Erik?"

"Ready!"

I heard a single shout from the hill as the sunlight lit us. "Vikings!"

"Now!" We were play acting no longer we jumped and ran quickly down the road. I knew that the wolfhounds would catch us and I had to time our turn perfectly or the ambush would fail. The sound of the dogs' feet thundering on the road told me when they were close. "Turn!"

Just in time I whirled around as a beast the size of a small pony leapt at me. I swept the sword around in a circle and its head flew from its body. The spattering blood enraged the other five beasts. Beorn stabbed one while Snorri sliced through the throat of a third. Erik had slipped and a wolf hound had fastened his teeth around his forearm. I stabbed into its eye and my sword pinned the body to the ground. The last beast was despatched by Snorri and Beorn.

Erik prised the dead jaws apart and stood. The Saxons were now close to the ambush. "Stand close together as though we expect to die."

Whilst it was play acting it enabled us to keep our shields close together. Only Erik did not have mail and we had him to the left where we could protect him. The Saxon hunters hurled themselves down the Roman Road. We must have appeared as stragglers and they were eager for revenge. They had almost reached us when the first of Cnut's arrows began to fall amongst them. It did not stop them and we braced ourselves to receive the charge.

They struck us as Cnut led the men from one side and Haaken from the other. The light from the sun's rays was behind the Saxons and we were all hidden in the darkness. Confusion reigned amongst them as they could not discern our numbers. I stabbed forward at the spearman who raced at me. He aimed his spear at my head and I brought up the shield. He impaled himself upon my sword. The two warriors with him also fell, one to Erik's sword and the other to Snorri's. Those behind turned to both sides to face the new enemies and it allowed us to attack the side of the warband.

We turned our attention to those fighting Haaken. They had no shields on our side and the first four warriors fell without realising that they had enemies on two sides. I hacked at the unprotected back of those fighting Cnut and it proved too much. Their leaders must have been at the fore and they had fallen. Fifteen or so turned tail and ran into the rising sun. I daresay they would tell tales of shape shifters and impossibly large numbers. How else could they explain the loss of so many men?

I left my warriors to despatch the wounded while I went to tend to Erik and his bite. It was not serious but the skin had been badly broken and he would have a scar for the rest of his life. I laughed as I bound it. "You hated the name Short-Toe we could rename you Erik Dog Bite."

I had meant it as a joke but Erik, who was the youngest warrior we had brought with us nodded, "I am happy for that Jarl Dragon Heart for it will be a reminder of the first time I stood shoulder to shoulder with Jarl Dragon Heart and fought an enemy!"

Two of our young warriors had died. We buried them close to the rocks where we had the ambush. There were plenty of stones to make a grave and then we covered them with turf. We buried them with their swords and I spoke the words to send them to Valhalla.

We made a pile of the Saxon bodies. We identified a chief from his torc and his silver cross of the White Christ. We took his head and placed it on a spear. It would be a warning to the Saxons of the treatment they could expect from us. We gathered their weapons and their armour. Much of it was inferior but there were some good spear heads and we could reuse them. Only one warrior had had mail and I gave that to Erik. He had stood bravely by us despite his lack of armour and he was training to be Ulfheonar.

Chapter 19

A week after we had returned from our successful raid the rains came. It was not a shower for one day and then soft autumnal weather; it rained for seven nights and seven days. Only Bjorn was able to be dry. The thin pieces of stone kept his smithy dry while we suffered the constant drip as the water permeated the turf.

Erika had had enough by the second day of the rain. "Tell Aiden I want a rock roof like Bjorn!"

Her tone told me that she would brook no delay and so I set off with Scanlan, Aiden, Arturus and some slaves to cut the rock for the roof. We took a horse and one of the carts we had captured. I was keen to see how Aiden would cut them. He had with him a hammer and a chisel. I would have thought he needed more.

It was a miserable march and we were soaked before we even made the trail to the Old Man. The rain had formed a low cloud so that it was almost like walking in a fog. He stopped where there appeared to be a rock fall. He pointed to the thin rocks lying on the ground. "We can cut these to size back at the hall." He pointed to the slaves. "Pick those that are this size and no smaller." He held up one of the correct size in two hands.

While they did that he strode off and we joined him. He went to a piece of rock which was shiny and dripping with water. He motioned for us to stand clear and then he placed the chisel in a tiny crack and struck it with the hammer. Nothing seemed to happen. He took out the chisel and moved it up. He repeated it and I saw a definite shaking of the rock. He reached up and did the same thing at the highest point he could reach. There was an enormous crack and a piece of rock the size of four men slid down to the ground. It broke into pieces but all of them were bigger than the pieces the slaves were collecting.

He grinned, "Easy isn't it?"

Scanlan stroked his chin. "With these we could roof the whole town and, perhaps sell them." Scanlan had the mind of a trader.

Aiden broke the larger pieces into more manageable ones and we soon filled the cart. There were still many pieces of the rock lying around and Scanlan said, "I will have these brought over to the town. I think Maewe would like to be dry too."

By the end of the day we had enough of this rock, which Aiden called roof rock, to roof the warrior hall too. The actual process meant a great deal of wetness for a short time while the turf was removed and replaced by roof rock. But when each section had been replaced there were dry areas where the rain could not reach. Erika's forceful personality ensured that our hall was finished by dark!

We used the rain filled days to replace as many roofs as we could. It kept men occupied and the women were pleased. We used the turf from the roofs to make a low wall around the settlement. I had noticed, when we had been on the Roman Wall, that that was what the Romans had done. By sticking a few stakes in the top you had an instant wall.

It was when we were sitting in the warm warrior hall that Haaken and Arturus reminded me of the treasure of Rheged. "Why have you not sought the treasure Jarl Dragon Heart?"

It must have been on Arturus' mind too for he added. "Now would be a good time to go."

I ruffled his head. "We have much to do here and the treasure has lain there a long time. As we have the map then no-one else can get it and it will still be there next month."

"What if someone has already found the treasure?"

Haaken rolled his eyes, "Then," I said, "there is no point going to seek it anyway for it will be a wasted journey."

Aiden smiled at his young acolyte's mistake. "Besides which we have not explored that part of Rheged yet and we know not what to expect."

He was right. We had been as far north as the Grassy Mere. The rest of the land was unknown. I would wait until the winter to make the decision. Part of me worried that I would get there and discover that the treasure had gone. The other reason I was delaying was that Erika was with child again and I was loath to leave her. She thought the child would be born in six months. How women knew this I did not know.

We had just finished roofing all of the houses and sent some of the roof rock to Windar's Mere when we had visitors. A party of warriors marched up the long water to Cyninges-tūn. The day was filled with flecks of snow and a wickedly biting wind from the north east. The party of eight were spotted by some of the fishermen who were braving the water and they sailed over to warn us when they saw them at the southern end of the Water.

When I told Erika she began to make arrangements to house and feed them. I gave her a puzzled look. "They were not invited but we should not upset anyone. We can be polite and hospitable. You never know when you will need friends do you?"

She was of course correct and it would not hurt us to be hospitable. The land teemed with game and we had more than enough food for our people. The warrior hall was half empty as many of the warriors had recently married and were holed up in their newly built and roofed huts making sure that they had heirs to follow in their footsteps. The only ones left in there were the likes of Snorri, Beorn and Erik, the younger ones.

We watched them march along the water to the other huts. They were huddled forward trying to take shelter behind their shields from the biting wind which ripped through every chink in a warrior's byrnie. They seemed to spend an inordinate length of time there and then they began the long slog around the head of The Water to our home. Before they reached us I heard the sound of hooves and Rolf rode in with Magnus, the ship's boy from '*Wolf*'. Poor Magnus looked terrified after the ride and he gripped the reins for dear life.

Rolf dismounted, "Jarl Dragon Heart, four drekar are in the estuary. They have boarded the headman's ship there."

I glanced over to the other side of the water. "Have they attacked?"

Rolf looked up at Magnus. "Magnus here was sent by Alf because he did not like the look of them. They have not ventured up the river yet and our other boats are safe."

I gestured with my thumb behind me. "There are Norse warriors walking here now. They may be connected." I did not like this. If the ships were there in peace then why block the estuary? I would speak with their emissary but make my preparations.

"Rolf, get all the warriors and head down the Mere. Take two small boats with you. Do not let these others see you but be ready to defend our ships."

"And Windar's Mere?"

"Get Dargh to move there and protect it. I will speak with these and then send a message to you."

Erika had been listening behind me. She turned to Aiden. "Go and tell Scanlan to find out what stores of food we have." She saw my look and spread her arms, "This may be war. Let us be prepared."

I kissed her, "I chose the best wife a jarl could ever hope for."

As I pulled away she said, "I know."

I put on my armour and my sword. I was not presenting a warlike attitude but showing them who I was. Arturus looked at me expectantly. "Go on then." He ran off to don the Roman helmet and sword we had found. He now had a scabbard for the sword and it was well decorated. Aiden had helped him and worked strands of copper and blue stones into it. They had both taken my mother's words in the dream to heart. I did not think the dream referred to this sword but it did not hurt for them to take extra care with it. When he returned I said go and tell the Ulfheonar to arm themselves.

The turf walls now had a wooden palisade and a gate. The gate was kept open during the day. The eight warriors stood in the gateway, surprised, I think, by the lack of guards. I strode over to meet with them. They removed their helmets and slid their shields out of sight to show their peaceful intentions. Six of my Ulfheonar appeared behind me. Haaken was clever. By keeping our numbers smaller than theirs he was showing that we did not fear them.

I strode over to their leader. He had had part of his nose sliced off at some time. It must have been before he acquired a nasal helmet. He was shorter than I was but quite broad. He had scars on his arms and when he smiled I saw he was one of those who filed his teeth horizontally to give himself a more fearful expression. The marks were now black and uneven.

"I am Jarl Dragon Heart. Welcome to Cyninges-tūn." I held my arm out and the warrior with the filed teeth clasped my arm.

"I am Ketil Flat Nose and I bring greetings from my King, Thorfinn Skull Splitter."

I kept my face expressionless but I was thinking that the last I had heard of Thorfinn he was just a pirate raiding Dál Riata. "Come inside my hall away from this biting cold." It was not just for his benefit that I led him to the hall. The snow had begun to fall and lie on the ground. Winter weather was coming early. The Ulfheonar flanked the others as we walked to my hall.

"You have a good situation here this is well chosen but you have fewer men than we had heard."

He was fishing for information. Was he a spy sent to scout out our defences? "We do not need more men than this. Who are our enemies? The Saxons are many miles from here and they bother us not."

He smiled, "You are lucky then for it is a dangerous world and there are many treacherous enemies out there."

Erika had some beer warmed with a poker from the fire and there were some warm cakes laden with butter and honey on the table. The smell was enticing. She must have had Seara and the thralls bake them as soon as she had left me. She gave a slight bow. "Welcome to our home."

Ketil bowed and leered at me, "It is true what they say Jarl Dragon Heart you not only have a sword touched by the gods but a wife so beautiful she could be Odin's bride."

"You flatter me sir." She nodded to me. "I will be about my business, husband."

She left and it was then I noticed that the rest of the Ulfheonar were within my hall.

"Sit and take refreshment."

They needed no urging and fell upon the food and ale as though they had not eaten for a week. I caught Haaken's eye. He raised an eyebrow and I gave a slight shrug. I could not answer the unspoken question. I knew not why they were there but I did know it did not bode well.

After they had eaten I asked, "So what does your master, Thorfinn Skull Splitter wish of me?"

King Thorfinn Skull Splitter."

"He is not my king."

I saw a brief look of anger flash across Ketil's face before it dissolved into a false smile. "He wishes to visit with you."

"He is nearby then?"

"His ship is in the estuary. He thought it might appear aggressive if he appeared with his men unannounced."

"He is on his way here then? I should prepare…"

"No, Jarl Dragon Heart, he will wait in the estuary until I return."

I tried to affect a relieved look. "Good for it will take us some time to prepare the hall for visitors."

"This hall looks more than big enough." He swept his arm around the Ulfheonar. "You do not appear to have many warriors although the ones you have look to be well armed. This would be big enough."

I nodded, "It would for, what was it you said? One boat crew?"

He relaxed and drank some more warmed ale. "Aye just the crew of one drekar."

I gave a slight nod to Haaken and Cnut. They would be ready. I said, evenly, "You would swear to that?"

"Why should I swear?" For the first time he lost his confident manner.

"It is a small thing but I do not know you Ketil Flat Nose. It could be that you lost your nose because you lied. It could be that you do not owe allegiance to Thorfinn Skull Splitter at all. So I ask again, would you swear that it is Thorfinn Skull Splitter and one drekar which is moored in the estuary?"

He stood and put his hands between his legs. "I swear."

I nodded, "Then perhaps we should remove them eh, because there are four drekar threatening Úlfarrston? Seize them!"

My men had been awaiting such a command and each of Skull Splitter's men was pinned by two men whilst a third removed their swords. Ketil's face became a mask of fury. "King Thorfinn will come here and eat your heart when I do not return."

I smiled, "Then I am safe because you will return to Thorfinn and I will take you."

"And you will be destroyed. These warriors may be well armed but they will be outnumbered ten to one."

Haaken put his face close to the emissary. "And you should know, little man, that the Ulfheonar think nothing of those odds." He turned to me. "Can I take his little love sacks? They will make such a nice ornament for my helmet."

Ketil's face paled. "Not yet, Haaken, but there is always time for that." I stared at Ketil. "This warrior knows the punishment when you are foresworn!"

I said to my men, "Bind their arms and bring them down to The Water."

I could see the fear on their faces. They were weaponless and a watery grave was not going to see them join their comrades in Valhalla. We reached the smithy. "Bjorn, I want their arms shackling behind with iron."

He nodded, "Do you need a key?"

"No. If we have to remove them then we come back here and if they die then we will just hack their arms off."

Bjorn wandered off to gather what he needed. My warriors held the arms of the eight captives tightly. Haaken began to finger the necklaces around the neck of the warrior he was holding.

"This is a pretty piece of silver. Shall I take it now or wait until he is dead?"

Cnut said, "It would be rude to take it now and a few more moments will not hurt."

I went up to Ketil and stood before him. "Now Ketil Flat Nose, what is Thorfinn's plan?"

He stared resolutely at a point above my head. "Bjorn we will only need seven of these. Haaken take the jewellery."

Haaken took out his knife and slit the throat of the warrior with the necklace. He laid him in the water and then chopped off the dead man's head. After hurling the head into the water he took the necklace. "It saved me having to open the clasp."

There were three younger warriors amongst the others and I could see the fear on their faces. "What was that warrior's name?"

"Thorstein Ill-Luck." Ketil almost spat the words out.

"He lived up to his name then. He will never get to Valhalla and his body will wander Niflheim searching for his head."

"What does Thorfinn intend?" Even Ketil looked nervous now. "I could threaten the blood eagle but that is messy and I want to go and visit with this treacherous leader of yours." I pointed to the forge where Bjorn had almost finished forging the first shackle.

Ketil looked at me in amazement. He nodded with his head, "You would go to fight Thorfinn with just these warriors? Then I will tell you for you and all your men will die."

"As I said, there is no reason not to tell us."

"And then you will let us die with a sword in our hand?"

"I will not be foresworn. I told you what I would do with you; shackle you and return you to your leader."

He shook his head, "The tales they tell about you are true, and you are fearless. We were to scout out your numbers and then he would attack you with his warriors. If you go to him then our job is done."

Haaken smiled as he wiped his dagger on the kyrtle Ketil was wearing, "Now if you had told us then Thorstein Ill-Luck would still be alive."

"Ready, jarl."

We took Ketil over and Bjorn beat the metal ring around his wrists. He was not gentle. He did the same with the other side. I knew that the metal they used was hot for I could smell the burning hair and flesh but none of them made a sound. It took some time to shackle all of them but eventually their arms were behind their backs with a short iron bar between their hands.

The rest of my warriors were ready. We would be outnumbered but we had something on our side which would give us victory; we had surprise on our side.

Chapter 20

I left enough men to protect Erika and my family but Bjorn and the fishermen would all be there too. They would be safe. I led the Ulfheonar and twenty other warriors. I saw the confident looks on the faces of our prisoners. They thought that I was a fool. We marched along the river with the snow flurrying behind us. I had left Arturus, much to his chagrin with Aiden and his mother. I would rather have had Aiden and his agile mind with me but I had a plan already there. I had no intention of sacrificing warriors in a futile attack on Thorfinn. I would use the river, the land and my mind to defeat him.

We reached the place where the river from our water met the larger one. I saw that our ships were still hidden. Although I could not see Thorfinn's ships I knew where they were from the masts sticking up above the river bank. The snow storm had turned into a blizzard. Mercifully it still came from the north and would blind Thorfinn and his men as it drove into their faces and obscured our numbers and our intentions.

Rolf marched his warriors along the river bank to me. He pointed to the two small fishing boats. "I brought them but I do not know why."

I smiled, "We will make them into fire ships." He frowned. "If you were anchored in the river, as Thorfinn is then you would feel confident about being able to defeat any who came down the river. Suppose you suddenly saw two fire ships heading for you?"

He smiled as realisation dawned, "Then I would cut my anchor and try to flee as fast as I could."

"And that is what I am hoping. Have the two boats filled with kindling and hoist the sail. Soak them with pig fat to help the fire take hold. Tell the men to wait for my signal. We will take them with us."

While Rolf had warriors preparing the boats I went with Snorri and Beorn to spy out the enemy. I could see that they had landed many of their men. It looked to me as though he had left half of his crews on board. I had never seen Skull Splitter before but I had heard the legend of a man whose blows with his axe were so powerful that he could split a man's skull in two. I saw a figure I took to be Thorfinn. He was large enough and looked to have fine armour. If you had a reputation, as I had, then you ensured that you had the best armour that money could buy.

There were guards and sentries outside the walls but, crucially, they had not occupied the dell where we had camped. "When we return take the archers we have and occupy the dell. Watch for my signal and keep loosing until they fall back."

"What if they do not fall back?"

"They will fall back."

I returned to the warriors, more confident now of my plan. Before I had seen Thorfinn's dispositions the ideas had been a little vague. His numbers on land would slightly outnumber mine. If he landed his men from the ships then he would overwhelm me. I intended to make him attack me and commit his men and hold him until my fire ships got amongst his. The snow and the oncoming night would both be my allies for we knew this land and he did not.

Snorri and Beorn went to select their archers. I turned to Rolf, Windar and the Ulfheonar. "We will march in a wedge as though we wish to attack. I will use the prisoners as both a shield and a goad. I want him to attack us. When they move to defeat us I will order Snorri and the archers to shower them with arrows. The wind is behind and works in our favour. Then we will send in the fire ships. I hope to make him indecisive and when I see him waver then we will attack him."

My warriors were so confident in our ability that they nodded happily. As soon as I saw Snorri and Beorn lead their men by the secret ways to the dell I prodded the prisoners before me. "You will only live if I choose to let you live. Keep that thought in your heads."

"Will you not free our arms?"

"No, Ketil Flat-Nose, you lost all rights when you told me a falsehood. You are lucky that we do not kill you here and now. Your life lies in the hands of your leader."

I knew that the wedge was forming behind me and we moved forward. As soon as we turned the bend in the river we were seen and I heard the furore as warriors were summoned. I tried to picture it as Skull Splitter might see it. He would see seven of the men he had sent in chains. He had to know now that his plans were now in disarray. He would see that he outnumbered us by a considerable force as there were twenty two warriors hiding in the dell. He could flee or fight. For someone who wished to be a king then he would have no choice, he would have to fight.

Once we were level with the dell we stopped. The snow was still whipping south. Once it neared the sea it became sleet but it lost none of its biting qualities. At the front of the wedge I was totally sheltered and felt, if anything, slightly warm. In the time it took to ensure that the wedge was well formed we were seen and I saw movement amongst Thorfinn and his men. He was not a good leader. If he was he would have had sentries further out to give warning of an attack such as ours.

Thorfinn soon organised his men and they came towards us in four smaller wedges. It was a good tactic and would normally be effective. The middle two wedges had the men with the best armour. The two flanking wedges had men without armour. I saw that the weather still favoured us. Although the snow had abated somewhat it still drove icy flakes into the eyes and faces of the men forming the wedges. I watched as warriors raised their shields a little more to protect their faces from the worst of the snow. The ground was slippery with soft snow fallen on hard ground. The wedges which advanced moved a little more slowly than they might have liked.

When they were a hundred paces from us and well within the bow range of Snorri and his men they halted. Thorfinn stepped forward. He had to shout against the wind. "I see you have captured my emissaries?"

"Aye, although it is a poor leader who sends men to tell a falsehood on his behalf. If you just wanted to battle Dragon Heart all you needed to do was ask."

He laughed, "Your words are a hollow boast, little man. You will all die here. I have more than twice your numbers. If I so wished I could bring all of my warriors ashore and crush you like a cockroach."

"Then stop wasting time and do it. I have a meal waiting for me at home and I hate my food to spoil."

"Let my men go first."

It was my turn to laugh, "Why? It amuses me that they will be the first to die when you attack. I do not like treachery. This is not the blood eagle but it will do for now. Perhaps when I have captured you I will try that too."

I knew I had enraged him now. He suddenly lifted his axe and yelled, "Charge! Kill these insects!"

I shouted, "Now!"

As they charged forward, the snow flying in their faces was joined by twenty two arrows. My archers could launch ten flights before they became tired. The arrows fell amongst them and, because they had neither seen nor expected them, they struck home and warriors fell to the ground pierced by arrows. The left hand wedge disintegrated. Their shields were still to their fore and by the time they raised them there were dead warriors where there should have been shields. They had no defence against arrows.

The screams of the wounded men drew the attention of the other three wedges which faltered slightly when they saw the sudden slaughter of their comrades on their left. Snorri and his men could not be seen. I saw spears hurled from the third ranks of Skull Splitter's wedges and Ketil Flat-Nose fell to the ground, killed by his own warriors. The other spears struck our shields.

I shouted, "Now Rolf!" I knew that Rolf would give the order for the fire ships to be launched. They were quite small and, in the snow, almost invisible to the four ships in the river. With the wind behind and the sails hoisted they would fly towards the waiting ships. The flames which would eventually turn them into a floating inferno would be small at first. The current and the outgoing tide would do the rest. They had anchored their ships so that they filled the river and were an inviting target for the two tiny boats.

I concentrated on the task in hand, the approaching wedge. Snorri and his men were now raining arrows on to Skull Splitter's wedge. Instead of their shields facing us they were facing the arrows. The four prisoners who remained were hacked down by their own countrymen as they closed with us. They were a human shield who died to a man. The advancing warriors then had to climb over the bodies and the slippery ground. It meant that they did not run the last few paces to hit us with their weight. They weakly lurched across the ground to get to us.

Skull Splitter's axe smashed against my shield. I knew what to expect and I angled the shield to deflect the blow into fresh air. I stabbed forwards with Ragnar's Spirit. Thorfinn's shield was giving him protection from the arrows and my blade slid between links and scored a deep cut down his left leg. I lifted the reddened blade for all to see.

Suddenly those at the rear of the right wedge began shouting ,"Fire!"

Skull Splitter tried a second weak blow with his axe but he was peering over his shoulder. I could now see the fire ships; they were burning fiercely and the sails although on fire were filled with the northern wind which sped them towards the wooden wall of drekar. Two of the drekar had tried to move and became entangled in each other's rigging. I could see their ships boys struggling up the mast to cut the ropes which bound them. One ship had managed to turn and was heading out to sea. The last had tried to reach the shore but had been struck by one of the fire ships. It was in the shallows and the crew were trying to douse the flames. It was a disaster and Thorfinn Skull Splitter yelled, "Back to the ships!" He had been wounded, out witted and now his only means of escape was in danger of being lost. He was cutting his losses.

This was too good a chance to miss and I shouted, "Charge!" We hurtled after them. Some of them slipped and tripped over bodies and the mud, snow and ice which made the ground treacherous. The ones who lost their footing were slain where they fell. None had time to help their fallen comrades as it became a foot race to the river. One of the ships which had been entangled had caught fire and both crews were desperately trying to put it out.

I was keen to drive this would be king from my land so that he would never dare to try such a thing again. A handful of his oathsworn stood to delay us while Thorfinn Skull Splitter ran to board one of his ships. The Ulfheonar were with me and they each chose a warrior. A large warrior in an open helmet ran towards me. His shield had three yellow hands painted on it around a red eye. In his hand he held an axe. He was taller than me and I think I detected a hint of Thorfinn in his looks. My shield and my helmet marked me for who I was and I could see that this warrior was keen to earn the praise for the killing of Dragon Heart.

He did not make Thorfinn's mistake of bringing his axe overhand, it was too easy to deflect. Instead he swung it sideways. I had no option but to block it with my shield. He was ready for my stab and as I saw his shield come up I twisted my wrist and hacked across his leg. Although he had a long mail shirt and the blow was not full strength I felt it bite into the mail and he stepped back. I punched forward with my shield before he had the chance to swing his axe and I stamped at his injured leg with my right leg. He stumbled backwards and I swung my sword at his head. He was now in full retreat. His own momentum carried him towards the river bank. He was on lower ground as he descended to the icy waters. An axe is a mighty weapon when you can put your weight behind it and swing easily. He could do neither. I alternated punches with my shield and swings with my sword and I put my whole body weight behind the blows. It was tiring for me but more so for him as he had no idea where he was stepping. When he tripped on the body of the warrior slain by Cnut I took my chance and pinned his head to the ground. My blade went through his eye and killed him instantly.

I withdrew it and looked for another enemy but the only ones who remained were the dead and those about to be despatched. The rest were clambering aboard the three remaining drekar. One of those which floated might not do so for long for it had been burned by the ship which had now sunk. A second ship had some fire damage and he only had one undamaged drekar left to him. I watched as a bedraggled Thorfinn Skull Splitter was hauled aboard his ship. He waved his axe in my direction but the sound of his voice was taken away by the wind. The snow had abated but the wind still whipped wildly. I did not care what he shouted to me; he had been soundly beaten and this had been an expensive venture which had failed. Over forty of his men had been killed and more were about to join the dead as the wounded were killed.

My men began banging their shields and chanting, "Dragon Heart! Dragon Heart!"

Pasgen came from his town with his farmers and fishermen around him. They were armed with the weapons we had given them but they did not look confident. "I am sorry we could not get word to you nor help you."

I shook my head, "We had word and this was not your fight."

"When I saw the numbers I wondered how you could defeat them but you made it look so easy."

I waved Ragnar's Spirit at the dead warriors who littered the ground. "It was not easy but the ones we fought were overconfident. They believed that numbers alone win battles. It is not so. It is heart and skill. My men have both in abundance. However we will build a signal tower here so that we can be warned of danger. This was a lesson which we will heed and learn from. Were any of your people hurt?"

He shook his head, "I think he wanted us as slaves. We were threatened and warned that if we aided you we would all die. He seemed to regard us as his property."

Haaken said, "The sooner you can learn to fight the better."

"You are right but we are herders and fishermen. We are not warriors."

"Then learn to fight with slings and arrows. Those skills will help you to hunt game. You will never be swordsmen but you could be bow men."

Pasgen smiled, "Thank you Haaken. We can do that." He and his people helped us to clear the bank of the dead. We did not want foxes, rats and wolves to be attracted to the village by the smell of flesh.

After we had stripped the enemy dead we burned their bodies and headed back up the trails to our homes with the dead we had suffered. We had not lost as many as Skull Splitter but any loss was one too many. As we trudged through the slushy mass of half melted snow and mud I wondered if we would ever have a time of peace. I had thought to make enemies fear us and leave us alone. It seems that they just craved what we had. We had not spilled blood to gain this piece of land we now ruled and we had taken nothing from anyone. I would not allow enemies such as Skull Splitter to walk in and take what we had earned through hard work and planning.

By the time we reached Cyninges-tūn I was tired but I was also resolved to discover a solution to our problem.

Chapter 21

The snow which had fallen so quickly during the fight disappeared and by mid morning there was not a trace of it. Instead, the ground was sodden and slippery. We had to begin to build paths to help us to walk around the settlement. Aiden had the idea of using some of the smaller pieces of roof rock to give us firmer footing. The snow storm had been brief but had been a warning of the winter to come. My plans for the resolution of our problem had to wait until we had adequately prepared for winter. I did not expect another enemy soon. Thorfinn Skull Splitter's treatment would send out a warning to the other Norse.

Over the next ten days we gathered wood and stone to give us fuel and paths for the winter. Hunters were sent out to gather as much meat as they could. Our salt gatherers had returned from the sea and we had enough salt to preserve all of the meat they had hunted. I remembered that there had been a good source of salt not far from Caerlleon. How we could have used it as we prepared for winter.

The weather suddenly turned icy overnight. It was another warning of winter as had been the early snowstorm. While the weather still held I sent the Ulfheonar down to Úlfarrston to build a tower where the rivers met and another at the end of The Water. When the winter was over we would have two signal towers to warn us of an enemy.

I left with Aiden and Arturus to visit with Rolf and Windar. Thorfinn's attack had made me all too aware of the threat to Windar's Mere. Had Thorfinn just marched up the river he might have been able to surprise Rolf and his people. There were forests all along the side of the Mere which could easily hide an advancing enemy.

They had worked hard to build their two villages and the hall into which Rolf took us was warm and comfortable. "How are those wounded from the battle?"

"They are healing. It is the dead who are more of a problem. We lost some good warriors."

"You have young men?"

"Aye but they are untried."

I laughed, "As we once were. Make them warriors, Rolf." He nodded. "After we returned from the Dunum I worried about an attack from the Saxons in revenge."

"But they did not come."

"No, and I do not think that they will come in the winter but I do not know for certain. Lang tells me that there is no way in or out of this land in winter. I do not think that is true for the sea in the south is close enough for us to reach in half a day, even in snow." I pointed to the line of hills to the east. "The mere we passed on our way east looks to have potential for farming and fishing. See if there are any of the warriors who wish to set up their own village."

I knew that there were warriors such as Windar who were loyal but still wished for the freedom of their own people. Warriors such as Haaken and Cnut, the Ulfheonar were rare. Perhaps there might be another Windar.

"I will ask my people. The fort at the head of the valley, close to the Rye Dale, is finished. Perhaps I will have a tower built on the ridge close to the eastern halls."

"Aye that is a good idea for I cannot believe that the Saxons will allow us to get away with our raid. This Eanred will have to do something about us. We are like the flea which keeps biting him; eventually he will scratch."

All the way back to Cyninges-tūn I chewed the problem over. I found that riding in this beautiful land actually helped my thoughts. I needed to know what was going on in the rest of the world. I left the next day with just Aiden to meet with Alf at Úlfarrston. "I want you to take '*Serpent*' and '*Butar*'. Trade some of the surplus we have with the Saxons in Mercia and Wessex. I need as much information as you can gather about what the other Norse, the Danes and the Saxons are up to. Take your time and have your men keep their ears open."

"What do you want us to trade for?"

"Whatever you can get but the most valuable thing you can bring back is knowledge. Call in at Man too and gauge the mood there."

He gave me a shrewd look. "You fear another Skull Splitter?"

"I think, Alf, that we are friendless. The days of our brothers helping us are long gone. Everyone wishes to be a king. Everyone wants their own kingdom. We are too tempting a prize for our enemies to ignore."

"It will take us a couple of days to be ready."

"Good. Then I will have the trade goods brought down."

Riding back Aiden said, "Copper is our surplus. I believe the roof rock is as valuable but I think that others will not feel that way but our metals, they are worth much."

"Have we much to send?"

"There is a good supply at the bottom of the Old Man. We have enough already to fill two ships and we can collect more easily."

Aiden was a bright young man. He and Scanlan were the two minds which made the task of ruling Cyninges-tūn and Windar's Mere an easy one.

As our first Yule in Cyninges-tūn approached the weather deteriorated rapidly. A last bright day was followed by an icy frost which froze the shallower parts of The Water. The next day began grey and drifted to black as snow clouds piled up on the mountains which surrounded us. Soon Old Olaf had white hair and a beard. We could not see the western village for the thick snow which blanketed Cyninges-tūn Water. The children's pleasure at the flakes of white was soon replaced by the red and blue of icy fingers and feet. They appreciated the warm halls. It snowed for five days.

When it finally abated, albeit briefly, I went with some of my warriors to see how far we could get. The pass to Windar's Mere was higher than a pony and would have taken much work to cut a path through to it. We managed to force our way to the western portion of our people on the other side of Cyninges-tūn Water but that was as far as we could get. Two hardy fishermen ventured down the Water while we waited with Finni, the headman of this village. The days were growing shorter as Yule approached and it was almost dark when they returned. They were blue with cold.

"We are trapped in this valley Jarl Dragon Heart. The stream at the end of the Water is frozen over." He pointed to the water level. "Soon the waters will rise as the melt water fills the Water."

I nodded. "You had better prepare to lose some of the huts which are close to the Water."

Some of the villagers, especially the fishermen had built their huts on the flat land close to the water side. If the water rose it would not take much to flood them. The fishermen nodded glumly. "We will have to try to build a hall yonder." They pointed to the small knoll where Finni's hall stood. There was room for another hall but it would be hard to build in the snow.
"Would you like me to send some men over in the morning to help?"

Finni shook his head and glared at the fishermen, "It is our problem jarl. If some of our people had given more thought to where they built their homes we would not have this problem." He was a hard and uncompromising man. The other settlers had chosen him because he was a leader. I would not have led the way he did but all of us had our own ways.

It was an icy, frozen night as we tramped back to our warm hall. The soft snow we had walked through now became sharp icy shards. Aiden pointed to the clear skies. "They will find it impossible to dig the ground. They will have to lay logs on the ground and make something temporary."

"When you were up Old Olaf did you see any caves?"

"There are caves but until the snow goes it would be too difficult to reach them."

I nodded, "I fear that you and Lang are both correct. We are trapped here until spring."

Aiden smiled, his face lit up by the moon, "Look on the bright side, Jarl Dragon Heart, at least no one can reach us to do harm."

I laughed at his words and clapped his back. Perhaps the Weird Sisters heard me and decided to punish me for he was wrong and soon we would be in the direst of dangers.

The next day, although it began brightly, soon degenerated into another blizzard and the snow fell on hard unyielding ground. During the brighter parts we saw the men of Finni's hall struggling to build a shelter. They had managed to make four walls the height of a man before the snow obliterated our view of them. We were safe from the rising waters. It was just Bjorn's smithy which might become inundated with water. As he said, "It will not harm the forge. The thralls can clean it when the waters recede." He was still working for the snow and the cold did not stop his endeavours. He was busily making more weapons in this quiet time. We had plenty of metal captured from Thorfinn and his men. The inferior metal was melted down to make arrow heads and hedgehogs. The better weapons were repaired and improved.

Mails shirts damaged in the fighting needed the most work. Bjorn had some older girls with nimble fingers who were able to help Bjorn's young apprentice smiths and they repaired what they could and used the ones too badly damaged to create new ones. The smithy was the only place with any activity. All of the rest of my people were in the halls.

My warriors created new songs and stories about their exploits and retold the ones from the past. Men worked on their equipment making scabbards and sheaths or fletching arrows. The women worked at weaving and making items from bone and wood. We made those things which took time but added beauty to our appearance. It was why the gods sent the snow; it made us reflect. None were idle as we hunkered down in this first bleak winter.

The storm continued for two days and we had no sight of Finni's Hall. As dark descended and we sat around our fires we heard the sound which sent a chill though us despite the crackling logs; wolves. They howled in the hills and the high places. The storm had brought them from their forests and dens. Game was scarce and that would force them to risk hunting the most dangerous game of all, man.

Erika and Kara cuddled closer and Arturus drew closer to the fire. "Will they attack us?"

I saw the fear in Kara's eyes and the unspoken question on Erika's lips. "I think that our wall will keep them at bay but I fear for Finni and his people. They have no wall."

The silence was only disturbed by the crackling and spitting of the logs in the fire. Arturus looked up at me and his voice was quiet. "Will you hunt them?"

I could read my son like the priests of the White Christ could read books. He wanted to know could he hunt a wolf and gain his own wolf skin. I did not need the flash in Erika's eyes to warn me of my answer.

"I might go hunting a wolf with some of those who would be Ulfheonar but not you."

The disappointment on his face was matched by the relief on Erika's. "But father you were much my age when you killed your first wolf!"

"Aye but I was not hunting a wolf. I was protecting an old man and the beast nearly did for both of us." I pointed outside where the howling continued still. "And this is not one wolf; this is a pack. I will take warriors hunting but they will be the ones who wish to be Ulfheonar and not those who think it might be exciting."

As we lay down in bed the blizzard abated as did the howling. I thought that the wolves had moved on. I was wrong. I was awoken before dawn by the sounds of screams from across Cyninges-tūn Water. Sound carried on still nights. Erika and I were awake instantly. I leapt from the bed and began to dress. "I will take some warriors."

"Be careful!"

"I will."

I dressed not for battle but for warmth and for hunting. I strapped on Ragnar's Spirit but it was not the weapon I would use.

I took my bow and quiver as well as a spear. I wrapped my wolf cloak about me and left my hall. Ten Ulfheonar had emerged from the warrior hall. I was pleased to see Snorri and Beorn. "I will take Snorri and Beorn. The rest stay here and watch over our people."

Thorkell looked disappointed, "Have we offended you Jarl Dragon Heart?"

"No Thorkell but you wear the wolf cloak. What of those who wish to join us? Is this not their opportunity?"

He nodded, "You are wise Jarl Dragon Heart. I will wake those who wish to join you."

There were six such warriors. Erik Dog Bite was one of them. They began to gather and I gave Thorkell his orders. "Tell them to follow our trail to Finni's Hall."

The gate was blocked with snow and we had to climb the wall and drop down into the drift on the other side. After we had fought our way free we set off down the hill. The snow was deep. No-one had stepped out for many days. The going became a little easier the closer we came to the northern shore of Cyninges-tūn Water. I knew that my two younger warriors were not going as fast as they might have done. They were waiting for me. I was not old but I was getting older. I could not run with the puppies any longer.

It took longer to reach Finni's Hall than normal. When we did reach it we saw a sorry sight. There were blood trails everywhere. Finni and his men were tending to those who had been injured in the attack by the wolves. I had no doubt that it been animals and not man who had caused the screams. Deep down I had known that some of my people would have died but I had hoped that they would not.

Finni greeted me. He was one of my bravest warriors and had been with us since the early days at Hrams-a but he looked sad and old as he gave me the grave news. "They attacked those in the half built hall. There are three missing. They are all girls." He pointed to a body. Siggi died defending his daughter but it was in vain. He wounded one of them."

"My hunters are coming and we will follow the wolves." I stared hard at Finni. "And when I return I will bring my men and will finish this hall so that more people do not die uselessly!"

"I am sorry Dragon Heart. I meant for the best."

I softened my voice a little, "You are headman now Finni and that is harder than standing by my side fighting enemies. You have to use your mind and know your people. I hope the loss of three girls has resulted in some good."

Snorri and Beorn had been scouting the blood trails and they returned. "They headed north; towards Lang's Dale."

I hoped that Lang and his family had not suffered. They were even more isolated than we were. The six young warriors, led by Erik, arrived. I pointed north and Snorri and Beorn trotted off. We followed. The blood trail was clear at first. When it became spots of blood I knew that we were following the wounded wolf. The wolves would have selected the victims they could kill quickly and then carry off. That was why they had chosen the girls. Soon they would stop to tear the bodies apart and share their bounty. That was my hope that we could find them sooner rather than later.

Snow began to fall. It would not affect our ability to follow yet but if it continued then it would. It would hide the prints of the wolves. I hoped to be able to follow them to their lair and destroy this danger to our people.

The pack had flattened the snow a little and our going was made easier. The ground was rising towards the pass leading to Lang's Dale. The blood trail was still strong. One of the wolves had to be weakening. Suddenly Snorri held up his hand and he and Beorn strung their bows. We joined them. There crouching with its back to a tree was the wounded wolf. Of the others there was no sign. This would be a dangerous creature. A wounded animal is a terrifying opponent. I looked at the young warriors behind me. Erik Dog Bite said, "Jarl Dragon Heart, let it be me."

I nodded and handed him my spear. I owed Erik that. He had fought by my side and faced the Saxon Wolfhounds. "Be careful. He will be dangerous."

He sprang forward towards the wolf. The wolf's eyes seemed to burn as they watched the approaching warrior. I could see what Erik was doing, he was using his speed as a weapon. He hoped that the wounded wolf would be slower than he was. It was a risky strategy. If he missed with his spear then he would die. I readied my bow. I saw the wolf crouching as it prepared to pounce. Erik ran fast and used a sword fighting technique. He feinted with his spear and leaned to the right. The wolf leapt, its reddened, snarling teeth dripping with the blood of the warrior it had already killed. Erik's move had put him to the left of the wolf and he stabbed forward with both hands. The head ripped into the wolf's throat. Even as it was dying it tried to turn to attack this young warrior. It landed on Erik, its life blood pumping out on to the white snow.

We dragged the wolf from Erik and helped him to his feet. I pulled out the spear. "You remain here, Erik and skin your wolf. We will return when we have found the rest." I nodded to him. "That was well done!"

The other five looked enviously at the young warrior who was one step closer to becoming an Ulfheonar. We left him as he took out his knife to remove the precious wolf skin before it began to harden. He would take out the guts and leave them for the carrion. The meat would be welcome.

The trail of the wolf pack headed, ominously towards Lang's Dale. There was a little more urgency now for the pack would not be slowed down by their wounded. As we turned into the dale we beheld a horrific sight; the wolves had halted to tear apart their victims. I saw the look of horror on the faces of the young warriors. The bones which remained were a grisly reminder of how fragile life was in this beautiful land. Snorri and Beorn scouted the trail ahead. "There are four wolves left with this pack."

"Any cubs?"

"No Jarl Dragon Heart."

That meant that they would still be in their den and there would be that most dangerous of animals, the she-wolf. Catching the wolves we followed would not end this problem. We needed to destroy them completely or they would grow stronger and return. We trudged on as the first chink of light peered over the eastern skyline. We hurried, eager to catch them before they reached their den. It was either a brave or a foolish hunter who went willingly into the den of a she-wolf and her cubs.

We were nearing Lang's huts when we heard the screams and the sound of snarling. We just ran heedless of the danger. Lang and his family were being attacked. We crested the rise and looked down at the huts. Lang was trying to hold off the wolves with a spear. I could see his wife who was kneeling over a still form in the snow whilst his daughter was cowering behind Lang.

Beorn and Snorri each notched an arrow and let them fly. One struck a wolf which turned yelping. The other missed but the wolves were distracted and I saw Lang's wife dragging the body towards the hut. Tostig Olafson suddenly ran forwards so quickly that I thought he had wings. I ran to catch him and I heard my two scouts curse their annoyance.

Tostig drew back his arm as a mighty he wolf leapt at him. He buried the spear into the wolf's chest but it fixed his teeth around his left hand. I heard the screams of pain. I hurled my spear and it thudded into the wolf's side but it continued to shake its jaws around the savaged hand. I drew my sword and, praying that Ragnar guided my hand I sliced down the back of the wolf's neck. I stopped the blade before it completely severed the head but the wolf was dead. I stabbed my sword into the snow and prised apart the jaws.

The hand was badly mangled. I tore a piece of material from Tostig's kyrtle and wrapped it around the wound. "Keep that pressed against the wound." I turned and saw Harald and Karl stabbing another wolf with their spears. The rest of the pack had fled. I watched which direction they took and ran over to Lang and his family.

He was kneeling over his son. "How is he?"

Lang's wife looked up, her face showing relief. "The wolf knocked him out when he leapt at him but the bite is not serious. My husband stopped him."

I looked at Lang who had a bite mark on his leg. It was bleeding still. "Let me look at that."

He shook his head, "No, I can do that. Get after those three before they escape." I nodded. He grabbed my arm, "Thank you Jarl Dragon Heart, I owe you four lives."

I shook my head, "You are a friend. Look after my wounded warrior eh?"

"I will."

I turned as Karl finally finished off the wolf. "Harald come with us. You may yet achieve your own wolf."

We ran after the last three wolves. It might be dawn but the sky was not lightening. The heavy black clouds were snow filled. Beorn shouted, "They are tiring. One has an arrow and one was wounded by Lang."

We could now see them up ahead as they raced for home. One was easily outstripping the other two who laboured up the dale to the rocky peaks. We knew that the den must be close. Harald was running with Beorn and Snorri now. "Do not be as foolish as Tostig!"

He waved his hand in acknowledgement but I knew he would disregard my advice. He was young and had come close to killing his first wolf. One of the wolves darted up to a clump of snow covered rocks. Harald ran after it. I saw that Snorri and Beorn still followed the other two. I waved at Olaf and Kurt. "Keep with Snorri and Beorn."

I watched as Harald stopped short of the wolf. It was the one struck with the arrow and blood was seeping into the snow staining it bright red. Harald stuck his sword into the ground before him and drew back his spear. He was beyond the leaping distance of the wolf but well within spear range. Tostig's wound had served as a warning. He hurled the spear and it struck the beast in the chest. It gamely tried to run forward. Harald gave it no opportunity and he hacked off its head.

"That was well done Harald. We will find you later."

The snow was now falling and it was a blizzard. I could barely see Harald as I descended to catch the others. When I found them then it was all over. Kurt was already skinning the dead wolf while Olaf looked disconsolately at the other dead wolf. Snorri grinned. "Beorn and I finished this one. Olaf was just a little too slow."

I nodded in an absent minded fashion. My mind was elsewhere. "And the trail to the den?" I had to shout because of the noise of the storm.

Beorn shook his head. "You can see nothing."

I nodded, "Let us get back to Lang's and some warmth."

We used the spears to carry the carcasses back to Lang's. We found Harald and trudged through the snow. I had lost the feeling in my hands. When we reached the haven of Lang's hut we were almost blue with the cold. Leaving the dead beasts outside, we entered the warm home.

Lang's wife gave us some broth to warm us through. I took one sip and said, "How is the boy?"

"He is fine but your warrior is not."

I went over to Tostig. His hand was mangled. He would never use his left hand again. Beorn took one look and said. "The hand needs to come off Jarl Dragon Heart."

"I know." Tostig nodded and gritted his teeth. "Get a brand from the fire. Wrap my cloak around his shoulders and bring him outside."

Tostig knew what I would do. "Jarl, would you use Ragnar's Spirit. It will make the loss easier to bear."

I nodded, "And you can still be a warrior. It is just your left hand. Haaken is Ulfheonar with only one eye. You could be one with one hand."

That seemed to make him happy. We took him outside and he held his hand out. The blizzard raged around us, its noise would mask any sounds which might be made. The others held him. He had the resolve but who knew how he would react. Snorri held the torch and he nodded. I lifted the sword high and brought it down as hard as I could just above the wrist. Tostig made not a sound and the mangled hand dropped to the snow. Snorri quickly applied the burning torch to the wound and Tostig mercifully passed out. The smell of burning flesh filled the air. We plunged the seared stump into the snow where it hissed and steamed. When we withdrew it we saw that there was no blood. He would live.

We quickly took him inside again. We waited until the colour began to return to Tostig's cheeks. He still looked anxious. "Tell me true, Jarl Dragon Heart, if I prove myself a warrior can I become Ulfheonar?"

"You can and as that is your shield arm the only weapon you will not be able to use is a bow. That is not important."

Snorri smiled, "Besides, Tostig Wolf Hand, you have proved you are a wolf warrior today when your brother tried to eat you!"

We all laughed, including Tostig and that is how he gained his name. He did, indeed, become one of the Ulfheonar.

While he recovered a little I asked Lang what had happened. "My children went out to collect some kindling. The wolves attacked and my son did all he could to fight them off. We heard the noise and went outside. Then you came."

"You are more than welcome to stay with us in our hall."

"Thank you but we will stay here. I will just be more careful."

"I think that we have destroyed the pack."

"I hope so."

We did not find Erik where we had left him when we trudged back through the raging storm. I was not worried. There was no sign of the wolf just a pile of offal which would soon be devoured by the rats and foxes. Even as we passed the crows and magpies were gathering in the nearby trees ready to feast. We reached Finni's Hall in early afternoon. We were told that Erik had already left for the eastern hall. The mothers of the dead girls looked tearful as we walked through their village. Their eyes asked the questions that my voice could not answer. Their children had been dead when they had been devoured but that did not mean that they did not suffer. I sought the one whose husband had died.

"Your husband was a brave man who died protecting his family. You are a young woman still, let not your grieving stop you from finding another warrior. It is what he would have wished."

Before I had joined the Norse I had not known the power of a suggestion from a jarl. She nodded and said, "I will obey in all things Jarl Dragon Heart." What I had meant as a kind suggestion she had taken as a command to be obeyed.

Erik's arrival had prompted the others in our village to gather and wait for our arrival. The flurries of snow which had accompanied us all the way home had hidden us from view and they knew not what we brought. When Tostig's mother saw his maimed hand her hand went to her mouth but she was the wife of a warrior and the mother of a warrior. She went to him and led him off. Our rough ministering would be replaced by more tender hands.

Snorri shouted, "We will skin your wolf for you Tostig Wolf Hand and we will all eat well tonight."

When a wolf was slain the meat was cooked and served to the warriors so that they might become better warriors. I know that many of them ate the heart of the beast.

Erika and my family watched from the door of the hall. Erik had told them of the children and I could see that Erika had wept. "Thank you for the wooden walls my husband or else that could have been our children."

"I will make sure that all of our children are safe. When the snow abates I will go with my hunters and end this wolf pack once and for all."

Chapter 22

We had another four days to wait until we could go on the hunt. This time there was just Olaf from the ones who aspired to be part of the Ulfheonar. For the remainder of the pack I took all of the Ulfheonar. We would root out this wolf pack and be free from worry for the remainder of the winter. The sight of Tostig with his maimed hand had dampened the enthusiasm of Arturus to go on the hunt.

The ones who had killed their wolves were busy making their cloaks. Tostig Wolf Hand had his mother to help him. All of them begged Aiden to make them a suitable clasp from finely worked copper and iron. He had been tempted to do it for free until I intervened.

"You are a craftsman and should be paid. Besides these warriors will earn more treasure with a well made cloak. It is an investment for them." And so he charged them. He began to acquire coin of his own.

The snow abated and we left one icy morning a day or two before Yule. We were in the times of the shortest days and we would be lucky to reach their lair and return. We now knew that we would be more than welcome at Lang's Dale; if we did not return that day my wife would not worry.

The frost had hardened the snow. We did not sink in but it was slippery and the spears we carried became staffs to help us keep our footing. As we passed Lang's farm we asked if they had been troubled by the wolves again.

"They have been howling but we have seen nothing." Lang pointed to the snow around the hut. "There are no prints of wolves."

We began to ascend the dale. We would begin our search close to the place where we had killed the last two. The depressions in the snow showed where we had discarded the dead wolves' entrails and they had been devoured by birds, foxes and rats. We saw no signs of wolves. We spread out in a long line and began to ascend the valley sides. It was steep and it was slippery. The snow hid the rocks lurking beneath the snow to trip the unwary. Even though we saw the sun reach its zenith we did not hurry. An accident could be fatal. I had young Olaf on one side of me and Haaken on the other. Cnut flanked Olaf on the far side. Olaf was keen to come to grips with the wolves but we knew how dangerous they were. He needed protection.

Suddenly there was a growl and then a she wolf leapt away along the side of the valley with two large cubs behind her. Snorri and Beorn led the Ulfheonar who were on the right after them. I had marked where they had emerged from the rocks and I readied my spear. I was concentrating so hard on the rocks that I failed to notice that Olaf had lowered his spear. I later realised that he thought the wolves had all gone. He wandered up the slope as though he expected to find an empty den.

The large male leapt from the den and fixed his huge jaws around the young warrior's throat. It shook him savagely from side to side. I heard the neck snap and I was then showered by blood. Throwing the dead body to one side it leapt at Cnut. Cnut was ready and he plunged his spear into the wolf. The wolf was not ready to stop protecting his pack and his teeth fastened on Cnut's arm. I stabbed forward and my spear went in behind the ear of the huge male. I knew it would die but before I could celebrate I was hurled to the ground as the she wolf leapt on me. We rolled down the valley side. Her yellow teeth were seeking a soft spot to make the kill. My spear was still in the male wolf and my fingers sought the eyes of this killer. As we rolled down I ignored the bumps from the hidden rocks and I pushed my fingers into the eye sockets. Her teeth found my arm and they began to bite. I would soon be Dragon Heart the Wolf Arm unless I could do something. I saw her neck and I sank my teeth into her neck. The pain from my arm was excruciating but I kept biting through the stinking fur.

The teeth stopped biting and, as the dead wolf was lifted from my body I saw the concerned face of Haaken and Einar. The blood on the end of their spears showed the cause of the wolf's death. Haaken examined my upper arm. "You are lucky. Another few moments and she would have worked through the leather of your byrnie."

He and Einar pulled me to my feet. "Olaf?"

Einar shook his head. "He is dead."

It was a sad procession which trudged down Lang's Dale. We had the dead wolf pack, including the six cubs we had killed but we also hauled Olaf's body. Another mother would mourn in the village. We left four of the dead cubs with Lang. He could use the skins and cub meat was particularly tender. "Call it a gift for Yule."

"Thank you, Jarl Dragon Heart, my family and I will sleep easier now knowing that the threat has gone."

As we neared home and darkness fell I felt the ache from my arm and the pain in my body from the fall down the hillside. I would be battered and bruised for a few days but at least we had eliminated one threat. If I could do the same with the human one then I would, indeed, be happy.

Erika fussed over me and ensured that I rested. It was a good time to rest for the snow kept us trapped within our settlement. The brief window of days free from snow had only lasted long enough for us to kill the wolf pack. Even Cyninges-tūn Water froze. We all hunkered down to sit out the winter festival but we had food enough and now we had even more tales and songs to keep us entertained.

I wondered how they fared at Windar's Mere. Úlfarrston would be subject to less of the snow as they were on the coast and I knew that the crews of our ships would be sheltering. Alf's two ships, I hoped, would be tied up at Pasgen's jetty and he would be enjoying the hospitality of the village. Lang's prophecy had proved to be true. The snow lasted for another month. It did not fall as heavily but we were still trapped within its white walls. Old Man Olaf was keeping us prisoners.

It was Snorri and the Ulfheonar, bored within the confines of the halls, who first made contact with others. Ten days after the last snows had fallen there was the steady drip of melting ice from the trees. They set off to try to reach Windar's Mere. I still thought it was a risk but they were keen to get out.

They returned four days later. Rolf and Windar had suffered the same privations as we had. The difference was that they had not had the trauma of a wolf attack. I knew that we would learn from that. Finni would be a better leader as a result but it was sad that we had lost three children, two fine young warriors and another had lost his hand to learn that lesson.

The snow and ice were now melting rapidly and Haaken suggested a journey to Úlfarrston. "With the melting snow then we may be able to bring the ships up to Windar's Mere. They will all need work."

I was not convinced until Erika pointed out that Alf would have some of the trade goods that we would need. It was not just food which had been consumed in the winter. There were other things which we needed. Pots broke as did beakers and we had little clay to make our own. That decided me. We left one late winter's morning to head down to Úlfarrston. I took the Ulfheonar and those who had hunted the wolves. We would initiate them in the spring but this would be a good test of their skills.

The trail was almost impossible to find. Nothing had moved down Cyninges-tūn Water since the snows had started. Snorri and Beorn had to use their memory and their skills to help us negotiate the tricky track. The further south we went the easier it became. By the time we reached Pasgen's river the snow was not as deep and we could see signs that the melt was well on its way. The high mountains and valleys stopped the sun doing its work but here, in the south, it shone undiminished. We looked in amazement at Úlfarrston for it was free from snow. '*Serpent*' and '*Butar*' bobbed in the river and we could see the masts of our drekar around the bend in the river. It was like entering a different world.

Pasgen and Alf came out to greet us. "We worried about you when we had not heard of you for so long."

I clasped Pasgen's arm. "The snows prevented us from leaving."

Alf stroked his beard. "We have had no snow for a month or so."

As we entered the village I said, "Perhaps that is why there are so few people in the land of the waters but we survived."

Pasgen ushered us into his hall. "Come we will have food. Alf here has much to tell you and I know that you have much to tell us."

We told him our tales of the wolves and the winter.

"I did not know that wolves were so close to us. We never hear them."

"You may not again. I think we may have destroyed the only pack that was close to our lands. And you, Alf, what of trade and what of the world?"

"The goods we traded are in a hut here in the village. We built it before the snows came. We can load it and sail up to the water when the river is navigable."

Haaken wiped the ale from his beard, "The melting snow will have raised the level. We are going to take '*Wolf*' upstream."

"Good then we will join you. As for the rest." He smiled, "It is now a world of kings. It seems every Viking is no longer content to be a jarl they all give themselves the title of king. Thorfinn, Erik, Sihtric, Ragnar Hairy Breeches and Magnus Bare Legs all title themselves king."

I was bemused, "King of what? I know Erik is King of Man but the others?"

"Sihtric is in Hibernia and he controls some of the coast. Ragnar is down at Caerlleon where he battles the Welsh. Magnus and Thorfinn dispute the land around the Lune just south of here. Each controls one side of the estuary."

"And King Eanred of Northumbria?"

"He just watches. The three kings who are south of here are killing more of each other's warriors than the Saxons. The Saxons in Mercia and Wessex believe he is waiting until they are weak through this fighting and then he will fall upon them."

That was interesting. I wondered why he had not followed up on our raid for iron. If I was Eanred then I would strike in the spring when our warriors were still recovering from a harsh winter. I had not remembered it being as hard on the Dunum when I was growing up. Perhaps the Saxons had fared a little better. No doubt they would put that down to their White Christ.

We spent the next day preparing the ships. They just needed to be able to travel the few miles north to Windar's Mere and then we could begin to work on them. The Ulfheonar were as excited as the young warriors to be back aboard the drekar. Young Magnus had grown over the winter. He would spend the summer learning how to steer the drekar. A good ship's boy made a captain's life much easier. I watched as they rowed up the lively river. Haaken had been right, there was a great deal of melt water and the rowers had to work hard as they fought against the torrent of icy water. They enjoyed the task. A winter of indolence meant that they had muscles to harden and this was the best way. The new rowers fitted in well and I knew that I had more Ulfheonar ready to serve me. I smiled for we would have two Eriks aboard, the Tall and Dog Bite. Then there was Tostig Wolf Hand; even though he had a damaged hand he was still a fine warrior. All of them were better brothers to me than King Erik of Man would ever be.

Rolf and Windar sent their men down to the river to fetch the other drekar. If the other leaders of our people were gearing up for war then we had to be prepared. I would prefer not to fight those who worshipped the same gods as we did but I would not let any destroy what we had gained.

As I lay, that night, with Erika we spoke of her brother and our decision to leave Man.

"When you said that you wished to leave Man I could not understand it, husband. It was the place we had met and seemed to me the most perfect of homes but you were right to do so. This, despite the wolves and the winter is a better land and if my brother is determined to be king then I am pleased we do not have to witness that." She pecked me on the cheek and snuggled in to me. "You could be king you. The people call this the land of the king."

I shook my head, "That king is not me. Even if I wished to be king then the actions of your brother and the others would have dissuaded me from such a course. Prince Butar only accepted that title reluctantly. I am happy to be Dragon Heart for I know that I earned that title and my people love me for who I am and not what I am called."

"I am puzzled. Would you have to bow your knee to a king?"

"Only if he conquered me and so long as I breathe this land will be free from a king. The king of this land is the mountain opposite. It is the Old Man, Olaf the Toothless."

Once the snow began to go it went rapidly. We smiled as it hung around the Old Man giving him a white beard and straggly white hair of which Olaf would have been proud. The shepherds went out to collect those sheep which had evaded capture in the autumn. The time of the lambs began. The ending of the threat of the wolf pack had had benefits for the flocks and they prospered. The wool would be valuable and the animals themselves would ensure that we did to starve. Alf had bought much grain seed and the farmers, especially around the Rye Dale began to sow as soon as the ground could be worked.

The ships were hauled out of the water, their bottoms scraped and sprung boards repaired. '*Man*' and '*Ran*' were old boats. This might be the last time they could be repaired. If it was they would be used to make two new halls. Over the winter many boys had come of age and would be joining the ships as ship's boys whilst others would become either seamen or warriors. Spring was a rite of passage for young men. It was also a time of birth as the marriages of midsummer produce fine healthy babies. Our two communities were growing. The world would have been perfect if it was not for events beyond our land.

When the babies and the lambs were born the warriors took their leave of their families and we headed south. Erika had still to deliver. It was hard to leave her.

Dargh and Windar had more than enough warriors to protect our land and the four drekar sailed south to Úlfarrston with

'*Serpent*' and '*Bear*'. They would trade for we had many sheep skins and many iron goods produced by Bjorn. They would return with more grain seed and Frankish blades.

It was not necessary to use oars as we hurtled down the river. The snow melt and the late winter rains had ensured that the river was a torrent and it took all of my skill to keep the drekar in the river. At times I was sure she wished to fly through the air. The calm waters of the estuary were welcome.

We anchored in the estuary. The voyage down had revealed problems in some of the ships. While we waited we debated where we would raid. Most were all for raiding the Welsh again.

I shook my head after the flurry of suggestions. "You choose the Welsh because they are close and they are not Norse but what would we take from them? Their grain is not ready and we have more than enough sheep. Slaves? I am loath to enslave some of those who have helped us."

"The alternative is to raid Ragnar, Magnus or Thorfinn."

"Or Mercia."

They had not thought of that. "Mercia is powerful."

"Aye but the River Maeresea takes us into the heartland of Mercia beyond the dyke. I am sure that Ragnar Hairy-Breeches is too lazy and too fearful to venture there but we could and there would be great riches to be had."

Our debate went on long into the night. I believe that they would have raided Mercia had we not seen the drekar which loomed up out of a dawn mist. There were five of them. It looked like war had come to my land.

Chapter 23

My warriors had seen them and they raced back to our ships. We had plenty of time. Pasgen looked a little concerned. He stood with Rolf, Haaken and myself as I pondered what to do. "What do they want? Are they here to fight?"

"I do not know."

Haaken might only have one eye but it was a good one. "That is Erik's ship. I do not think Erika's brother would come here to fight."

"No, and besides, we have no need to meet with them. We are secure here."

"Shall I get the Ulfheonar to protect you?"

I smiled at Haaken. "I have you, Rolf, Aiden and Arturus what need have I for protection?" I saw Arturus, who had grown considerably over the winter, stiffen with pride and Pasgen smiled at the youth.

The five ships stopped and lowered their sails. Erik's ship rowed slowly towards us. "It seems your wife's brother is coming to call, Dragon Heart."

We walked towards the jetty. The drekar drew up and Erik clambered ashore. He had put on weight over the winter and it was not the move of a fit warrior. He strode up to me with a smile on his face and his hand outstretched. I was not worried but I was still cautious. "Welcome Erik."

The hint of a frown at the lack of a title flashed briefly across his face and then he clasped my arm. "And you Dragon Heart. You wintered well?"

"We wintered well and your sister and niece are fine. " I smiled and then put my hands on my hips. "Now would you like to come to the point?"

The frown returned. "What is the cause for such aggression? I come in peace."

"You come in peace with five drekar and only one is yours. I think we have every right to be suspicious."

"You have a regal assembly, Jarl Dragon Heart. On those ships are King Magnus, King Ragnar, King Sihtric and King Thorfinn." I saw Pasgen's face as it fell and I sympathised.

"Then we have every right to be cautious for the last time King Thorfinn came here he tried to enslave the village and slaughter me."

"He comes in peace now."

"Not on this beach!"

I had taken Erik aback. "We are here to talk of creating a high king of Britannia. This will be a Norse kingdom. Even though you are not a king we would have you as part of it."

I almost spat a reply out; the arrogance of it! They were trying to rule me and wished my agreement. However, Prince Butar had taught me caution and to keep my counsel, I nodded. "I am willing to talk." Haaken flashed me a look of surprise but I gave the slightest of shakes with my head and he nodded his understanding. He thought I was being taken in but I was not. "But we will not allow any of your friends to land here. There is an island further along the coast. It is bare and it is uninhabited. We can talk there where there can be no hint of treachery."

"None of them will take kindly to those words, brother."

"They can take them or leave them. That is the only place I will talk. I do not need to speak with your friends, it is they who wish to speak with me."

"You are a renowned warrior and known as the bane of the Saxons. It is no surprise that they want you on their side."

I stared at Erik, "Thorfinn sent an emissary last time he came and his task was to lure me into a trap. I would hate to think that you were doing the same. His other emissary's bones lie bleaching the beach."

He looked genuinely shocked, "It is only the love of my sister that stops me from taking offence at that slur."

His indignation was hollow, "I care not. Take offence if you will and we will settle the matter here and now. I am my own man now answer me, is it the island or do we fight?"

He smiled, "The island of course, we are here for peace. But just bring '*Wolf*'." He shrugged apologetically, "That way we each only have one ship."

Haaken laughed, "And we need only one drekar for we are Ulfheonar."

"I can speak for myself, Haaken."

"I will tell the other kings." He strode back to his ship.

Rolf said, "I like this not."

"Haaken was right my one crew are more than a match for anything they have. Arturus you stay here with Pasgen. Rolf command the ships."

"But father…"

I turned and snapped, "Hear my words and obey!" He nodded, "Aiden come with me I need you to read the kings."

Aiden was an astute young man. He understood people the way that Beorn understood animals and their ways. I signalled to my ship and she was rowed across to me. By the time we had boarded Erik's drekar had moved to within hailing distance of the others and they had started to turn to the west. As Haaken took his bench the word spread amongst the Ulfheonar what we were about. I saw Haaken and Cnut exchange a glance then Cnut began to sing the beat. I shook my head as they began to row faster. My warriors intended to reach the island before the others despite their start. It was futile for it was we who would have to lead anyway.

I concentrated on reaching the island. There were a number of uninhabited islands and I just had to choose one. It had always struck me that any of them would make a good site for a fort to protect the estuary. We did not have enough warriors to man one but it was the way that my mind worked.

"What do you expect of me, Jarl Dragon Heart?"

"Watch the others, Aiden. You have the knack of reading men's motives. Who is true and who is false? I can hear their words but I cannot watch all of them. You can."

He nodded, satisfied in his task.

We soon began to open a lead on the other ships. Cnut and Haaken had the bit between their teeth. They would show the others who had the best and fastest ship. I eased the steering board a little as the islands hove into view. "Magnus, get the sail down. Aiden help him."

Lowering the sail would warn the others that we had almost reached our destination. I shook my head as I said to Cnut, "I would appreciate not ripping the hull out of my ship when we near the island."

"Do not worry, Jarl Dragon Heart. We can stop her on the head of a Roman coin. Just let us know how far away we are."

I began to call out the distances. "Three hundred paces, two hundred paces." When I reached 'one hundred paces', I could not keep the urgency from my voice.

Cnut shouted, "Back water!" The rowers, as a man quickly lifted their oars from the sea and then reversed them and began to push backwards. '*Wolf*' suddenly slowed and then came to a gentle stop in the shallows.

I nodded, "That was well done. Magnus over the side and tie us up."

Magnus dropped into waist deep water and ran to the largest rock he could find. He wrapped the rope around one and waved. Aiden threw him a second rope and he tied the stern too. I was ashore with Aiden, Cnut and Haaken before the others had even reached the island.

There a couple of logs which had drifted ashore and we manhandled two of them as improvised benches. As the others descended from their boats I said, "Now you two behave yourself. It is for me to take offence and not you. Watch their guards and tell me later what you think."

The five, so-called, kings all came together. Each had two bodyguards. Erik had a wry smile on his face as he strode up to us. "I see the Ulfheonar were keen to get here quickly."

Haaken smiled disarmingly, "We just wanted to arrange the seats for such exalted guests."

I saw that the sarcasm was not appreciated by the others. I hoped that Haaken would let it lie. He saw me watching him and shrugged an apology.

The others stood with their warriors behind them. I had only met Thorfinn and Ragnar before but I recognised Sihtric by his flowing and oiled beard and I assumed the last to be Magnus. I saw Ragnar Hairy-Breeches grinning at me, "I'll say this for you, Dragon Heart, you are a game 'un. I was certain you were going to rip out your hull."

Thorfinn snapped, "More's the pity."

I had noticed him limping when he had come ashore. "How is the leg Thorfinn?"

"It ached all the way through the winter. I owe you a wound now." He looked darkly at me. "And I owe you a dead brother too."

"At least he stayed to fight and died like a warrior. He did not run with his tail between his legs."

"Do not push me Dragon Heart. My weapon is eager for a skull!"

"Any time you would like to try just let me know. I was barely warmed up the last time before you fled. Did you lose many men when your ships went down?"

His hand went to his axe and Ragnar snapped, "We are here for peace and not for war!"

"Why are we here?" I asked innocently. I knew but I wanted to hear how they phrased it.

Ragnar, who appeared to be the spokesman smiled as he spoke. "The Saxons are finished. They are falling back to the east and Northumbria is like a ripe plum ready for the picking. We are here to decide who will be high king and how we should go about it."

They all nodded. "I thought the High King was Irish? And I know that three of you have land close to the Saxons but two of you live safely on an island. How does this affect you?"

Erik coloured and Sihtric's eyes flashed angrily. He clapped his hand on his sword hilt. "You, young pup! I have ignored your lack of respect to five kings but I will not listen to your insults to me."

I laughed, which enraged him even more. "Then listen to the words of your spokesman. He said that you had land adjacent to the Saxons? Unless the Saxons have become the Irish or fish then you have no rights here. Unless, that is, you intend to ride on the backs of other warriors."

Ragnar came between us. I had not risen but I was ready to in an instant. "Dragon Heart, keep a civil tongue in your head."

I stood, "Why should I? It was you who requested this meeting and not me. Why am I here? The five of you could have carried out your plan without my involvement. You could have defeated the Saxons and then come to me and boasted of your deeds. Why ask me?"

Erik spoke, "You have defeated the Saxons more than any other warrior. With you on our side then none could defeat us."

"And what is in it for me? I am happy in my new land," I looked pointedly at each of them in the eye. "And I need no king to obey. I obey no-one and I will not acknowledge the over lordship of any. If I joined you then it would be as an equal and on my terms."

Magnus Bare Legs spoke for the first time. "But we are all kings!"

"Just because you call yourself a king does not make you one." I had now antagonised all of them and yet they remained on the island and their swords stayed sheathed. They were desperate for me to join them.

Ragnar looked at his fellow and waved both his hands as though to calm them. "We accept your terms. Just join us when we begin our attack and share in the bounty."

I could see nothing wrong in that. "And the idea of a High King?"

"We will decide that amongst ourselves and you would have no say in that."

"Excellent. Then I will return to Úlfarrston and you can bring me the news of who has the title and where we attack." My men followed me and we walked to my drekar leaving five very confused kings on the island.

We began to row back and Haaken laughed loudly, "And you told me to behave! I thought we would have a blood bath on the island."

Ignoring Haaken I said to Aiden, "What did you notice?"

"It is Ragnar Hairy Breeches who is controlling them. They all looked to him when you were speaking to one of the others. King Sihtric looked ready to stick a knife in you. He looked to have a very short temper."

"Thank you. And you two," I said to Haaken and Cnut, "what did you make of Magnus Bare Legs?"

"He does not see a very bright leader but his arms were like tree trunks. He would wield a mighty sword."

"Thank you. That was how I saw them."

"What will we do?"

"If it is in our interest then we will join them. We were going to raid anyway. As for the rest?" I shrugged, "We will take what we can and return to Cyninges-tūn. I want as little to do with them as possible."

When we reached Úlfarrston I signalled Rolf to join me. I explained to both him and Pasgen what was intended. "Do you trust them Jarl Dragon Heart?"

"Of course not, Rolf. Send '*Bear*' beyond the bend in the river. Her crew are here in case of treachery whilst we are away. She is the same size as my drekar and her crew is the most inexperienced but they are young and keen."

Rolf nodded and went off to give the orders. "It would not hurt to improve your defences and to lay in some supplies in case they return. When Alf and the other ship returns tell them what we are about."

"I still do not know why you are going with them, Jarl Dragon Heart."

"Ragnar, the old man who trained me told me something wise once. He said, '*Keep your friends close but your enemies closer still*'. I can watch them if I am with them. Any treachery will be aimed at me and not my people. If I did not go then I would be waiting for them to strike. This is the best way."

"But the most dangerous for you."

"This Warlord of which you speak; did he hang up his sword and enjoy peace?"

"No, he died in battle and his son Hogan Lann became Warlord."

I nodded, "And so it will be with me. The difference is that my people will survive when I am gone. That will be my legacy. Take care, my friend." I clasped his arm and whistled for Arturus who had been waiting, out of earshot.

Once on the ship we prepared for war. The shields were hung from the sides and we donned our red eyes. I led our three ships out to sea and we waited for the others to join us. We waited an hour and then the five ships rowed up to us. Erik shouted, "Your terms are agreed. Come with us and join our other ships."

"Where do we raid?"

"In Mercia along the Maeresea."

I waved my agreement and took position astern of Magnus Barelegs' ship. It was bigger than mine and looked to have thirty oars on each side. *'Wolf'* was the smallest drekar going to war but I knew I had the best crew. Each of them could out fight any other ship which sailed before us.

Once we reached the Lune I saw the other six ships which would be completing the invasion fleet. Aiden voiced my thoughts. "We are providing the most men."

"Aye and it would have been even more had I not left a drekar in the river."

Cnut frowned, "But they will have other ships; mayhap they are up to mischief."

I shook my head, "The very best warriors will be with their leaders. They want us to bleed for them."

"And will we?"

"No, Haaken. We are not to be the goat staked out for the wolf. We are Ulfheonar; we are the wolves!"

We sailed down as far as the Maeresea and headed upriver. I was pleased we were the last ship for it meant I could watch how the others sailed. I also realised that we would be the closest to the sea. That might prove advantageous. As darkness fell we pulled the ships up on the banks of the muddy river. I noticed that we used the south bank. That was the one closest to Caerlleon and Ragnar Hairy-Breeches' domain. He had a refuge close by if things went awry and it was his lands which would be expanded if we were successful. Aiden had been correct, he was the driving force behind this raid. That was confirmed when we made our camp and I was summoned to a meeting of the kings.

I took Rolf, Haaken and Cnut with me. Thorkell commanded the camp in our absence. As before, I made sure that Aiden was close at hand.

Ragnar greeted me as though there had been no harsh words and I was his new best friend. He enclosed me in a bear hug. "Jarl Dragon Heart I am the new High King and you are the champion who will show us how to drive these Saxons to their rat holes in the east."

I noticed that the others, including Erik, kept their distance. It was as though I carried the plague. "Have you a place in mind that you wish to attack?"

Ragnar nodded, "Mammceaster. It is a town further east close to two rivers. Both of them flow into the Maeresea. If we take it then we can use it to attack the rich lands to the south in Mercia. Our ships can be protected from the town and we will have a refuge. My men and I scouted it out last autumn. It will give us a base to delve deeper into the riches of Mercia and Northumbria."

Surprisingly it made sense. There were rich farmlands to the south and I had not heard that the Northumbrians were building burghs. So far I could not fault Ragnar Hairy Breeches' planning. "And when do we attack?"

He hesitated and it was then that I knew where the treachery would come. "If you take your ships tonight then you can capture the town at dawn."

I heard the snort of derision from Haaken and I held my hand to silence him. "So it is my crews who will take all of the risks?"

He smiled, "Everyone knows the skill of the Ulfheonar. Who else could have the honour?"

I nodded and I saw the looks of surprise on the faces of the four kings. "Then we will keep all that we take. We take the risks; we take the prize."

Sihtric's mouth opened and closed like a fish. He wanted to object but they had agreed to my terms. Ragnar gave a gracious bow, "Of course. That is how it should be. Those who dare take the gold."

"I will need a guide. One of your men who knows where the confluence of these rivers is. I do not want my ships stranded on a Saxon shore."

Ragnar nodded and waved forward a stocky warrior with a half mail coat. "This is Hermund the Bent. He is one of my oathsworn and knows the place well."

Hermund grunted. Conversation was not one of his skills. "We will sail now."

"We will sail at dawn and follow you."

I could almost see the treachery in his mind. We would fight and capture the town. When he arrived with fresh men he could, if he so wished, take it from us. I would have to ensure that he did not. As we began to row up river I said quietly to Aiden, "You stay aboard '*Wolf*' and guard Arturus." He nodded. I turned to Hermund. "How far along the river?"

He shrugged. "I will tell you when you are close." That was not helpful but it was about all that I could hope for.

As he rowed Haaken said, "How big is this town?"

He shrugged again, "As big as your town on the coast."

Haaken turned to Cnut and said, "They should have called him Hermund the Shrugger and not Hermund the Bent." Hermund frowned and Haaken laughed, "If you do not like it little man we can settle it when we have captured this town." Hermund smiled and nodded. I would put my money on Haaken. He was one of the fastest with a blade in all of the Ulfheonar.

Chapter 24

We had sailed some ten miles or so up river and it was narrowing alarmingly when Hermund said, "It is close."

I signalled to Rolf in '**Man**' to slow down. Cnut slowed down our oars. Suddenly the river widened as another river joined it. Hermund pointed up the other river. "It is up there."

"How far? Can we sail any closer?"

"It is not far. A mile, perhaps two."

That made the decision for me. Here we had room to turn the ships around and space to anchor. We pulled in to the shore. If Mammceaster was as big as Úlfarrston then I would not need three boat crews. I would rely on the skill of the Ulfheonar and Rolf. Asbjorn Word Master could keep his crew to watch all the boats and prevent treachery.

I gathered my men on the shore and told Asbjorn Word Master to spread his men out in all three drekar. Hermund frowned. "You will not take all your men?"

I realised then that my guess had been correct. "If what you said is true then I will not need them. You did not speak a lie did you?"

He shrugged again and Haaken rolled his eye, "No, but if you bring the warriors then why not use them?"

Haaken answered coldly, "For we are Ulfheonar and we do not need extra warriors. Jarl Dragon Heart does not need a second boat to take one Saxon town."

Hermund did not look as confident as we walked alongside the small river. Snorri, Beorn and Erik Dog Bite were scouting and they would easily find the town. I did not need Hermund but I would not let him out of my sight. He pointed up ahead and I put my finger to my lips.

Erik Dog Bite ghosted into view and whispered, "The town is ahead. They have no guards but there are dogs."

"How many huts?"

"Two halls and twenty huts."

That meant that there could be fifty or sixty men in the town. If half of them were warriors then this might not be difficult. I turned to Haaken. "Take the Ulfheonar and get around the other side. We will drive them again." It was a tactic we had often used and it rarely failed.

The Ulfheonar disappeared into the dark. The sky was beginning to lighten in the east and I knew that the town would soon be coming to life. It was a dog which alerted them. Hermund was not as silent as my men and he had a rank smell about him which had grown more pungent as the night wore on. I knew that the dogs would smell him first. As soon as the dog barked then all need for silence was gone. We were almost inside the settlement anyway. With no gate to speak of we had no obstacles before us. Rolf and his men raced into the town. They split up into groups and ran to the huts. This would be easy.

Suddenly the doors of the two halls opened and warriors poured out. There were many more than sixty. It was a trap. I shouted, "Shield wall." As Rolf and his men formed up around me I yelled, at the top of my voice, "Ulfheonar!" There would be no refugees fleeing into Haaken's hands. They would have to save us. I looked around and saw that Hermund had fled. I knew not if he was aware of the trap or he was just a coward but there would be a reckoning.

I drew Ragnar's Spirit as the Saxons raced towards us. I had forty men with me and Haaken led fifteen Ulfheonar. We would be outnumbered. I knew not how many villagers there were but there were at least sixty warriors racing towards us. Perhaps they expected us to flee; I know not why but they seemed to think that they would roll over us.

The ones in mail came directly for me. My wolf shield and helmet marked me out clearly as Jarl Dragon Heart. I had Rolf on one side with Ham the Silent and Erik the Redhead. On the other side was Windar's brother, Lars the Grim. He had a full mail shirt and a mighty sword. The five of us would anchor the middle of the line.

The Saxons liked to use spears. They worked well against weaker foes and poor shields. We were neither and the warrior who stabbed at me was surprised when his spear slid down my shield and stuck in the wood of Lars'. I thrust forward with my sword and pierced his neck above his mail shirt. I twisted as I pulled and was rewarded with a shower of bright blood. The warrior next to him tried to stab me above my shield. Lars lifted his own shield and the shaft of the dead warrior's spear cracked again the man's chin. He looked surprised until Lars split his head in two.

Although the five of us were holding our own the ones around us were being forced back. I used it our advantage. "Wedge!" There was a gap before me and I stepped into it and skewered the next warrior who was not expecting the blow. We now had a proper wedge and I yelled, "Forward!"

They were not expecting us to attack. Vikings liked to fight as individuals. I had learned that we were more powerful if we fought as a band. I stepped over the dead man and swung Ragnar's Spirit overhand. The warrior before me put his shield up to fend off the blow. He had no metal on the edge and it was poorly made. My sword sliced it in two and the arm which held it. The joy of battle was upon me. I swung Ragnar's Spirit before me and none could stand in my way. The euphoria of the enemy had evaporated like a morning mist. They had thought to fall upon a band of warriors and make them flee. We had done nothing of the sort. We had stood and we had fought back.

When Haaken and the Ulfheonar fell upon the rear of their lines it was they who tried to flee but there was nowhere for them to run. My wedge became a circle of iron and we fought our way through them until they were all gone.

As I stood there panting and dripping the blood of my enemies I looked around for Hermund. He was nowhere to be seen. "Snorri and Beorn, find Hermund and bring him to me. Rolf have your men collect any treasure and Haaken, despatch the wounded."

I turned and walked back to the scene of the first fight. I took off my helmet. The cool morning air felt good. The sun was just rising and showed me a sad sight. Fifteen of my warriors lay dead and dying. They were good men. What had killed them? Had it been my arrogance or had we been led into a trap. I would find out.

"Jarl Dragon Heart," I looked down and saw Harald Bagsecgson, Bjorn's second brother. He had been gutted and his entrails lay before him. He still held his sword. "Please send me to Valhalla and tell my brother I kept my oath."

I nodded, "And your sword?"

"Give it to my son. I would have him follow the Dragon Heart."

I stood and unsheathed my sword, "Go to your father and wait for us." Standing behind him I plunged it into his neck killing him instantly. I took the sword from his dead fingers and replaced it in his sheath. I put the sword and belt around my shoulders. Rolf and his men gathered the slaves together. They were terrified. I saw a whitebeard and I beckoned him over.

"You were expecting us?"

He nodded, "We were raided last month by Vikings such as you. We beat you off but the king sent some of his warriors in case you returned again."

"When did the king send the warriors?"

"Just after the new moon."

That was ten days ago. "Did you see any such as us after that?"

"Aye, two days after."

I nodded, "Rolf, let this man and his family go."I turned to the whitebeard. "Which is your family?" Two women and three small children ran to him. "You may go. Jarl Dragon Heart rewards those who help him." The older woman, the greybeard's wife, kissed my hand. "Go mother and find a new life."

The warriors began to head back down the river to the ship. Haaken and the Ulfheonar kept watch. I heard a scuffle and saw Snorri and Beorn dragging a bleeding Hermund. "Why do you bind me? I have done nothing wrong."

"Hold him here. Rolf, load '***Ran***' and put the wounded warriors as well as the older warriors on board as crew. Do not answer any of Ragnar's questions." I waited until all the slaves had been moved and there were just the Ulfheonar surrounding the warrior.

I drew my seax and placed it between his legs. "Why did you run?"

He said nothing and I ripped the knife to tear his breeks. "You know you will tell what I want to know. The question is how much pain will it take and which parts will I remove? Why did you run?" My seax was razor sharp and I applied a little more pressure as I sliced a second time. He winced and the seax came away bloody.

"You knew there were warriors waiting did you not?" I barely moved the seax and he nodded vigorously. "Ragnar knew too did he not?" Again he nodded.

I turned to Haaken, "Now why would Ragnar send me to a defended village without warning me?" I whipped around and put the seax so that the tip was a thumb's width from his right eye. "What were your orders?"

I saw a puddle appear between his legs. I cocked my head to one side and nodded. The words poured from him. "I was to wait until you were attacked and then return to Ragnar and tell him."

"He thought we would all be killed." Another nod told me that I was on the right track. "And any who survived would be killed by his men?" A last nod. I smiled. "You have been true to your master." I turned to Snorri, "Give him his sword."

There was clear relief on the man's face. "Haaken you and Hermund here had something to decide did you not?"

Haaken grinned as he unsheathed his sword. "Aye Dragon Heart."

"But I told you what you wanted to know."

"This is nothing to do with me. Haaken and you need to settle your differences... or would you rather just have your throat slit?" I pointed my seax to the skies. "At least this way you have a chance of going to Valhalla; a slim one but a chance none the less."

Haaken handed his shield to Cnut and approached Hermund. The outcome was never in doubt. Hermund was a blow hard. He was not a true warrior as Haaken was. It took three blows and it was over. We took Hermund's weapons and left him for the crows and magpies which were gathering in the trees.

We marched down the trail. "Will you confront Ragnar?"

"There is little point for he will deny it. No, we will say that Hermund died in the fighting. Ragnar will not believe it but he will not be able to disprove it."

"What if he decides to attack us?"

I laughed, "Then we will kill them all and go home."

"We could just go home anyway. Why fight for someone else?"

"Because we always planned this raid and we might as well become richer for it. I am intrigued as to their next move. Erik is no hero. He will not face me. Magnus seems rather slow. Thorfinn fears us already which leaves just Sihtric and Ragnar. Sihtric might bring things into the open but Ragnar will continue to be devious. He will greet us with open arms and beaming smile."

"We stay then?"

"Not all of us." Einar had suffered a slight wound to his leg and was limping a little. "I will send Einar with the slaves, the booty and the wounded back to Úlfarrston. '*Bear*' can join us here in case we need more men. Ragnar will not know where she is and will worry."

We reached the river and saw the ships of the others rowing up river. They were not rushing. I suspect they were hoping that the Saxons would have finished us off and they would be able to race in and slaughter them. It was a perfect plan, if it had come off. It would have eliminated a large number of the king's men while giving Ragnar a base and, at the same time, ridding them of the thorn in their side, Jarl Dragon Heart.

Rolf had done as I asked. I turned to Einar. "Be careful as you travel north. I do not know if there are other drekar waiting to ambush you. You are a clever sailor." I handed him the sword of Harald Bagsecgson. "Give this to Harald's son and tell Bjorn that his brother died well." As I climbed aboard my boat I saw the relief on the faces of Arturus and Aiden.

Ragnar stopped his drekar next to mine. "Did you not attack the village?"

"We did. The slaves are aboard '*Ran*' and the king's men all lie dead."

He frowned, "Where is Hermund? And how did you manage to avoid losing more men."

He had slipped up there. "Then you knew there were more men in the village than I expected?"

"No, but we both know how sneaky the Saxons can be." He was a quick and devious man.

I let the words hang in the air like insects buzzing above a pond. "You are right Ragnar Hairy-Breeches we both know how treacherous men can be."

He glared at me and snapped out, "Where is Hermund?"

"He died with a sword in his hand fighting for his life. He will be in Valhalla." He could not dispute that statement as much as he might want to. "What will you do now Ragnar?"

I was taunting him. I was speaking of one thing but meaning another. "We will rest in the hall and then tomorrow cross the Maeresea and begin to raid the lands of Mercia and Northumbria."

"Good. We will sleep aboard our ships for we are tired and need not another march. We will watch your ships for you."

I heard Haaken stifle a laugh as he realised I had outwitted Ragnar. He could not argue with my reasons for staying and yet he was risking me being as treacherous as he was. I saw the argument in his head before he smiled and said, "You deserve the rest. I will leave a few men on board our ships. I will speak with the others."

Their ships were soon unloaded and the warriors headed up the trail to the village. They would find Hermund and see that I spoke true. They would just not know that it was Haaken who was responsible.

As soon as they were out of sight I waved to Einar and '*Ran*' began to head downstream and then home. "Get some food for us. I am starving and then, after we have eaten, half the crew sleep. The other half can sleep in a few hours time. I want a good watch kept tonight."

I took off my mail, with the aid of Aiden and washed the red dye from my eyes. I would have bathed in the river but I could see that it was stained from the blood in the village. I would wait until I was near the sea. Magnus Larsson brought us a bowl of some sort of fish stew which had been cooked on the shore. I smiled at him.

"I forgot to reward you when you brought us news of Thorfinn Skull Splitter." I slid my seax out and handed it to him. "Here, Magnus, is you first weapon. It was my first weapon too and I took it from a raider when we lived in Norway."

His eyes widened and he took it as though it was hot enough to burn. He looked at me. "Erik Dog Bite says that you helped Harald Bagsecgson to go to Valhalla." I nodded, "You gave him the warrior's death?"

"If I am too wounded to carry on then I hope that you too, Magnus Larsson, will do the same for me and I will thank you when you join me and Harald in Valhalla."

He said, in all seriousness, "I will, my jarl. That I swear."

As we ate our stew Arturus said, "How do you do that father?"

"Do what?"

"Make men be so loyal to you that they will not betray you?"

"Do not lie to your friends nor your men and never let them down. Even if your life is in danger you must remain true to your oathsworn and they will be true to you. That is why Harald One Eye was doomed. He left his men to die at Hrams-a. If he had stayed with them they might have escaped and they would have been more loyal. It is where Ragnar and the others go wrong. They have given themselves the title of king and think that makes them more important than the rest of their men. It is not the king who is important it is the kingdom."

Aiden nodded, "And we have a kingdom but we do not have a king."

"That is what I believe, Aiden. The Saxons use the term Viking as an insult. I take it as praise for we are not Dane, we are not Norse and we are not Saxon. We are something more. If people ask me where I live I shall tell them, the Viking kingdom."

Aiden said quietly, "Cyninges-tūn."

I nodded at Arturus, "Do you see how Aiden understands? When the midsummer sun touched me and Old Olaf it was crowning not a king, but a kingdom."

We all ate in silence until Arturus said, "Then why do we stay here with these false kings? Why do we not go home?"

I laughed so loudly that some of my men started. "This voyage has been worth it already for you are learning wisdom beyond your years. I would have more treasure and I would see what treachery the others have planned for me. If they are treacherous here then your mother and sister will be safe. Our people will be safe. If I leave I may be inviting even more. No, we shall stay but we will keep our wits about us."

Chapter 25

I think that Ragnar did try something in the night but the vigilance of our men prevented anyone coming close. My guards heard movement in the water but their presence deterred whatever it was. I noticed a few bleary eyed warriors when we gathered at the river the next morning. Sihtric snarled, "Where has your other drekar gone?"

"Home to Cyninges-tūn. I had wounded men and slaves. There was no point in leaving them here. Now we all have two drekar."

Ragnar swept his hand towards the south. "We will cross the river and leave our ships anchored in the middle."

Erik asked, "How long do we raid for?"

Thorfinn laughed, "Until we have so much that we have to bury some."

We rowed the boats across the river. I made sure that my two were on the downstream side. I chose my crews carefully so that I had good men on board. Arturus was staying along with Aiden but I knew that they would be in good hands. I left Snorri with them. He had turned his ankle when pursuing Hermund the Bent. He could rest and take charge. He had been a ship's boy before now and knew how to sail a drekar.

We set off towards the south east. This was all new country to me. It was Ragnar who supplied the scouts for his land was the closest and his men had travelled far to the east. The hills rose sharply to the east and we skirted them as we headed for the place of the pots. The Saxons made fine bowls using the clay from the plains ahead. The men who made them were rich. Rich men liked fine churches and so we knew that the books of the White Christ and gold awaited us. I also resolved to capture some of the pots. They might not be as attractive as gold but we needed to buy them anyway.

We halted at a river. Ragnar told us that there was a town not far ahead where they had great quantities of salt. This was valuable but I questioned how we would transport it.

The others seemed dismissive of my query. I now knew why they had sought me out. They did not think things through.

"Are there any religious houses close by?"

Ragnar summoned his scouts over. "Are there churches of the White Christ close by?"

One of them pointed to the east where the land began to rise toward the distant hills. "There is one but it has a ditch and a wall."

I shook my head in disbelief. A ditch and a wall meant that there was something to protect. "How far away is it?"

"Just two Roman miles away." Ragnar looked at me expectantly.

I shook my head. It was as though they had never raided before. "If they protect the church then there has to be a reason. There will be things of value within."

"But the salt is just ten miles away."

"And it will still be there when we have liberated the books of the White Christ."

That convinced them and we headed east. I heard the bells tolling long before we reached the knoll where the monastery was situated. Ragnar's scouts could not differentiate between the churches and monasteries. The wooden wall was as high as two men and there was a stout gate. That meant it had items of value. I could see a number of buildings within and a church with the cross of the White Christ on the top.

Even the dull and unimaginative Magnus Bare Legs conceded that it might have things worth stealing within. He grudgingly admitted that it might be a better decision than a salt house. Once we had collected enough treasure I would head back to Cyninges-tūn. These kings were poor raiders. It was no surprise that their men had less armour than mine and their weapons were inferior, bending at the wrong time.

We surrounded the monastery. My men were given the task of attacking the front gate while Sihtric and Thorfinn took the rear gate. Beorn and Erik clambered over a quiet part of the wall and we waited. Sihtric and Thorfinn were less patient and we heard the hack of axes on the rear gate which was followed by the pealing of the bell in alarm.

Our gate swung open and we poured in. The monks and priests were fleeing with whatever they could carry. My men merely knocked them down and held them but Ragnar's men were killing the valuable priests who could be sold. The whole monastery was subdued in quick time but there were just ten of the monks left at the end of the unnecessary slaughter and they had been captured by my men.

Ragnar was beside himself with joy for we had not lost a single warrior. I spat with disgust. I had yet to lose a man attacking an unguarded monastery. The reason for the fence and the ditch became apparent when we entered the church. They had small golden crosses and silver candlesticks. They had fine lace and, in one room they had eight of the books so prized by the Saxon kings.

I even saw Sihtric smile. "And only three of their priests escaped. A mighty victory."

I could not believe my ears. "Three escaped! Why did you not capture them?"

"We were too busy ensuring that the rest of you did not rob us!"

"You are a fool! They will bring help!"

His hand went to his sword. "I have taken enough from you, whelp."

Ragnar's Spirit was out in an instant. "Let us try then and see who the gods favour."

Ragnar roared, "Enough. The Dragon Heart is right. They should not have been allowed to escape. But there are no warriors close by. The nearest are on the borders near to the Dyke built by Offa. We still have time to get to the salt houses and return to our ships."

"We do not! My men and I will head back as soon as we have divided the treasure." I was not foolish enough to wait around for the King of Mercia and his men to descend upon us.

Thorfinn shook his head in disgust, "You would flee at the first sign of trouble? I think you do not deserve your reputation as a fearless warrior; fearful more like."

I did not remind him again of our first encounter. His opinion did not matter. "Think what you will, we will leave as soon as we have our two slaves, our gold and our two books."

"What if we choose not to share them?"

"Then I will save the Saxons the pleasure of dealing with you when they come. I will kill you all and take the treasure."

"We outnumber you." Sihtric said darkly.

"So far I have seen you kill priests and let three of them escape. We took a village and fought two warrior halls filled with Saxons." I turned to Ragnar. "As you knew when you sent us into the trap!" My sword was still out and I saw fear upon his face.

He began to back away. "I will not command you to stay. Take your share and go." He pointed to me. "You are alone now. I am High King and I forbid any of our people to give you aid or succour."

I shrugged, "I have never asked for any. Rolf, get the slaves. Haaken, get the books, Cnut, get the gold and silver. Take just what we are due."

We left not long before dark. There were comments hurled at my men by the bodyguards of the kings. Rolf and the Ulfheonar ensured that we did not respond. I did not want a bloodbath. Already some of the warriors who remained were drinking from the holy wine they had found. Soon it would be a roaring, drunken camp and I knew that blood would be spilled. The sooner we were away the better.

As we marched along the old Roman Road Rolf asked, "Will we try to reach the Maeresea tonight?"

"Aye I will feel safer afloat and then hence to home."

"Was Ragnar right? Could we have raided for the salt and other treasures?"

"If that had been men commanded by Prince Butar and the old Jarl Erik then I believe we could. That which we left was a rabble. They were like Harald One Eye's men. King Coenwulf of Mercia is not going to allow his land to be raided. Neither will King Cynan of Gwynedd take kindly to a Norse warband on his door step. Had we been raiding I would have stayed closer to the river." I pointed north east where the sun was beginning to set. "There would have been many places just on the other side of Mammceaster where we could have raided and reached our ships easily. Those five men were all taken in by the titles they gave themselves. As for me? I am grateful that we lost so few men."

"Had we raided ourselves we might have lost those."

I shook my head, "No, Rolf, for we took the word of Ragnar and Hermund. Had we been alone we would have scouted better and known that there were more warriors. This is a lesson learned. From now on we fight alongside no man."

We found the ford some eight miles from the river and we halted. Our two priests were tiring and we needed a little food. Suddenly we heard, in the near distance the sound of voices. The noise was coming from the road we had just travelled. My men immediately grabbed their weapons and went into a defensive stance.

Warriors appeared along the road. It was Erik and he had fifteen or so of his men with him. They had been bloodied. I did not relax my guard as he ran up to me.

"Thank the Allfather that I found you! King Coenwulf surprised us. He and his men fell upon the camp. We were lucky to escape with our lives."

"Where are the Mercians?"

"They are pursuing us!"

"Rolf, get the slaves and the treasure and head to the ships. We will catch you."

"And you?"

"This ford is the only place they can cross; if we can delay them then it gives us more chance to escape."

Erik looked appalled as Rolf marched the men off. "We cannot stay here. We will die!"

I turned and barked at him. "We will die if they catch us on the road and ambush us. Get some backbone, man!" I turned to his men. "You have a choice, fight with me and live or flee with this and die!"

They had all fought with me before. They were warriors of Man and they nodded. The leader of the oathsworn, Knut the Bold said, "We will fight with the Dragon Heart." He looked in disgust at Erik. "I, for one, have had enough of dishonour. This day I will gain honour and fight amongst real warriors." As he stepped back I noticed his wild eyes. You can push men so far and then they break. This was one angry warrior and his voice swayed the others who stood behind him.

Erik had no choice. He had to stay. "Those with bows hide in the bushes above the ford. Thorkell command them. You know what to do. The rest of you come with me." I led the others a little way from the ford so that we were hidden by the slight rise where the road climbed from the river. If we crouched we could delay when the pursuers saw us.

We did not have long to wait. I heard the hooves of horses as the Mercians came resolutely on. I could not see faces for night had fallen but I saw the shadows as they approached the ford. The shadows told me that they had at least six horsemen. They masked the others who were behind. I crept forwards slowly, crawling along the ground. I reached into my leather satchel and took out two handfuls of hedgehogs. I could not risk throwing them in case they made a noise. I spread them along the road in a line and began to creep back.

I had almost made it when I heard a shout, "Up ahead! I can see a movement."

There was little point in hiding any longer and I stood and shouted, "Go home Saxons for I am Jarl Dragon Heart. I am the Saxon's Bane and I will destroy you."

I knew that Haaken would keep the others hidden and Thorkell would choose his moment well. I wanted their attention on me.

I heard a laugh. "I am Aelle the leader of King Coenwulf's warriors and I am not afraid of one Viking even if he does possess a famous sword. Charge!"

The problem the horsemen had was that they had to slow down once they hit the bubbling ford and they had to watch their footing. Thorkell timed his volley of arrows to perfection. Three riders and two horses were struck. The two wounded horses bucked, reared and then fled back up the slope disrupting the warriors who hurtled after their leader. One of the riders struck fell into the stream but the other three came on. The leader was unwounded, well armoured and wielded a mighty axe. He urged his horse up the slope towards me. Swinging his axe he anticipated striking me as I stood, apparently alone and facing him. When his horse stepped on to the hedgehogs it stood on its hind legs as though stung. The leader could not keep his saddle and he rolled backwards over the rump of the horse to be deposited into the stream.

One of the wounded horsemen fell from his saddle and I strode forward to finish him off. The last horseman came at me but, at that moment Haaken and the rest of my warriors launched themselves at oncoming Saxons. The horseman wheeled to face this new danger. In the dark it was hard to estimate numbers but it mattered not. We either held them or we died. Haaken and Cnut finished off the wounded man and I strode down to meet the leader who had recovered enough to stand.

He roared at me and I saw the spearman behind racing to protect their Eorl. I had the advantage of height and I used it. As his axe swung at me I jumped and it missed me completely. The swing took the axe all the way around and when I landed I struck down with Ragnar's Spirit. He barely deflected my sword and he stumbled again. I stepped towards him. Before he could recover I sliced across him and ripped though his mail and his throat. He fell to the stream bloodily bubbling his life away.

Suddenly I heard a roar. Knut had thrown away his shield and his byrnie and he ran, almost naked, across the stream roaring his war cry. He was going berserk. None of my warriors had ever been taken by the blood fury of the berserker and it was terrifying to behold. The Saxons stood terrified as he swung his sword before him. He seemed impervious to their spear thrusts as he took the heads and arms of all those before him.

Thorkell and the archers rained death upon those behind. "Come let us help our brother!" I led the rest of Erik's men and the Ulfheonar. It was hard to keep pace with the wild Knut. I saw that his body was covered in blood; some of it was his own. We despatched all those whom he had wounded and ran to reach him. Eventually he outran the arrows of Thorkell and his men. He was surrounded by a ring of spearmen. Even so he continued to fight until they hacked his head from his body. We reached him but too late to save him. None of his killers returned to Mercia. He was our only loss.

I turned to Erik's men, of their king there was no sign. "Carry this warrior's body to the ford and we will bury him with honour here at Knut's Ford. Let his body watch over this place of glory. Long will we remember him and his brave end. The Allfather and Ragnar will welcome him even now."

As they reverently carried his body my Ulfheonar stripped the Saxons of their weapons. Beorn and Thorkell had captured four of the horses and we would be able to take these weapons back to our ships.

We buried the brave Knut by the ford which bears his name still. We killed his sword and laid it with him and covered him with stones. None of his men could bring themselves to look at Erik who emerged, guiltily, as we buried him. It was almost dawn as we headed north to the river. We had lost a brave man but Erik's men had regained some of their honour.

I smiled when I saw Sven collecting the undamaged hedgehogs. "These are worth their weight in gold, Jarl Dragon Heart. I will fear no horseman so long as I have these."

I almost felt sorry for Erik as we trudged along the Roman road. His men avoided him as though he was diseased. Beorn and Erik Dog Bite, even though they were tired to the point of exhaustion, ranged far ahead. Erik sidled up to Haaken and me. "I have not always made the right decisions."

Haaken merely shook his head in disbelief. I remembered that he was Erika's elder brother. "Perhaps it was my fault for leaving Man."

Haaken could not contain himself. "A man makes his own decisions and does what is right." He pointed at Erik, "Who makes the decisions in your hall?"

"Enough. You do not criticise the way another man runs his home." I softened my voice. "You can still redeem the situation. Show your warriors that you are their leader and they will follow you again."

He pointed to his men who were twenty paces ahead. "Not these men."

"Perhaps not, for they saw the fall of Knut. Just decide what you wish to be. What happened to the others?"

"Ragnar led them west to Caerlleon."

I saw that Ragnar was as careful as ever. His home would be defended by the warriors who survived the Saxons. "The slaves and the treasure?"

"Sihtric slaughtered the slaves as soon as we were attacked and every warrior, who could, grabbed whatever there was."

I looked at him. "And you have nothing?"

"Nothing."

Our conversation was ended as Beorn and Erik raced towards us. "Rolf and his men have been ambushed by Saxons."

"Erik, stay with the horses." The wounded men were leading the horses but I wanted Erik to understand responsibility. He would be guarding the weapons and the wounded.

As I crested the rise which led down to the river I saw a knot of warriors. I recognised Ham the Silent and Erik the Redhead. I caught my breath as I realised that Rolf was lying on the floor. He was not moving. There were just fifteen warriors there and no sign of the slaves or the others. I could see, beyond the trees at the riverside, the masts of the ships.

There were forty Saxons. I saw, in an instant, that King Coenwulf had sent two forces; one to capture the raiders and the other to capture the ships. He was a thinker and not a Ragnar or a Thorfinn.

"Ulfheonar, let us show these Saxons how to fight."

Erik's men joined us as we hurtled down the Roman Road. Knut was still in our minds as we fell upon the unsuspecting Saxons. They were too busy trying to destroy the remnants of Rolf's men. We were outnumbered and we were exhausted but Rolf was one of us and we would avenge his death. Haaken killed the first Saxon and the two next to him whirled around with their swords and shields ready for battle. I hacked down at the shield of one while Cnut skewered the other. The Saxon I fought was a strong man and he bravely held his shield up. I was in no mood to be kind and I punched him with the boss of my shield and then whipped my sword across his unguarded throat.

The Saxons locked shields and I could see, beyond the last one, Ham the Silent fall, mortally wounded, to the ground. Erik the Redhead still fought on. I remembered Knut. He had fought on beyond reason. It inspired me and I recklessly laid about me with Ragnar's Spirit. I would reach Rolf or die trying. I owed him that much. I felt blows striking my shield but I ignored them. I felt swords striking my mail and my helmet but I put them from my mind and I sliced and slashed at all before me. I could see the fear in men's eyes as my deadly blade killed all who stood in my way. Finally I reached a huge warrior completely encased in mail and with a full face helmet. He had an axe and, even as I watched he took Erik the Redhead's helmet and head.

I roared a, "No!" and smashed down with my sword. He was quick for a big man and he spun around to block the blow with his shield. It did him little good. I kicked as hard as I could and, as he reeled back, connected with his groin. He fell as though I had struck him with a hammer. He lay stunned on the ground and I took his head with one might swing. I grabbed his head and helmet and waved it above my head. It was more than enough for the rest. Those who could fled, pursued by Erik's men who were keen to prove their courage to me.

I knelt down next to the body of Rolf. I took his helmet off. I heard a noise coming from the river but I need not have worried. It was Snorri, Aiden and the rest of the crew we had left at the river. Snorri shouted, "We came as soon as we heard the fighting." He saw Ham and Erik, they were both dead and he saw Rolf lying there. "Is he dead?"

Aiden knelt down and put his ear to Rolf's mouth. "No! He lives still!"

I left Haaken and the others to see to the Saxons. I had my oathsworn to tend. Aiden ran his hands over Rolf's body. "I can see no wound."

I looked inside the helmet. There was a patch of blood. I carefully moved some hair. There was a hole in the side of his skull. Aiden lifted a flap of skin and I could see his brain. The young warrior said, "Find the bone from his skull."

I looked down to where his helmet had lain and I found a piece of bone the size of Kara's hand. I gave it to Aiden. He had quick and nimble fingers. He took out a bone needle and some cat gut. "Jarl Dragon Heart, get some honey."

I had no idea where he thought I would get honey from. I stood and shouted, "We need honey now!"

One of Erik's men ran to the horses which were now standing patiently waiting for us. He reached into a saddlebag and drew out a small jar. He looked at me sheepishly, "I found it there earlier and I have a sweet tooth."

"If this works you can have all the honey in the world."

I handed it to Aiden who smeared some around the edge of the skull and then on the edge of the bone. He carefully replaced the piece of bone and then roughly sewed the flap of skin to hold it in place. He stood.

"Will he live?"

"That is in the hands of the Allfather but we must move him carefully so as not to disturb him too much."

Haaken came up to me. "We had better leave while we can. There may be more." He looked at Rolf. "Is he alive?"

"He is. Use the shields and spears to make a litter for him carry him carefully to the ship. Aiden take charge." As they obeyed my orders I turned to Snorri, "Bring our dead with us. We will bury them at sea. They deserve that honour."

When we reached the river I saw that the other drekar were still there. I turned to Erik. "You had better tell the others that their kings are fled."

He nodded and turned to his men. "Come let us go to our ship."

They stood there defiantly and reminded me of Kara when she was asked to do something she didn't want to do. The warrior who had given me the honey, Stig Sweet Tooth said, "I am sorry King Erik but we wish to serve Jarl Dragon Heart."

That was the way it was with warriors. These were not oathsworn and they could choose whom they followed. Erik looked as though his heart had been ripped out. He nodded glumly and went to the bank to signal his ship.

I turned to the warriors, "Are you sure? I am no king and life is hard in Cyninges-tūn."

They knelt and held their swords before them. "We swear to be your men Jarl Dragon Heart and your oathsworn. You are Prince Butar reborn and he was a fair and honest leader. We will take our chances with you."

"I told you, I am no king."

"You need not be a king Jarl Dragon Heart for wherever you are is the Viking Kingdom and we are your men."

And so the men I had lost were made up from other warriors of Man and they proved as loyal and brave as any. Some good had come of Erik's lassitude.

Epilogue

It took three days to return to Cyninges-tūn. We reached
Úlfarrston in two and then rowed as slowly as we dared up the
river to Windar's Mere. All of the time we went north Aiden lay
with Rolf. He dripped water and honey into his mouth and bathed
him. Arturus helped his friend and I was touched by the way they
worked together. Rolf showed little sign of life save a chest rising
and falling slowly. When we reached his hall he was carried by
the Ulfheonar and laid on his bed. Perhaps the Norns had had
enough of playing with us for, as we turned to leave, we heard a
sigh and when we turned he opened his eyes.

Aiden ran to him and gave him a horn of ale laced with
honey. I stood and watched. His eyes were open but what had the
wound done to him? He saw me, "Jarl Dragon Heart. What
happened?"

"What do you remember?"

"We left you at the ford and…." He closed his eyes. "And
that is all."

"You were ambushed and nearly lost your life but Ham
and Erik saved you."

He smiled, "I can always rely on them. Where are they so
that I can thank them?"

"You will have to wait until you reach Valhalla for they
died so that the Saxons could not have your body."

His eyes closed and his voice was almost a whisper. "I had
sailed with them for fifteen years. They were closer to me than my
brothers and now they are gone."

I put my hand on his shoulder. "And what better way
could they have shown their love for their jarl?"

I left him in Aiden's care and went with Arturus back to
Cyninges-tūn. We had come back with treasure and we were
richer but we had lost three warriors who were irreplaceable. We
were now alone. I would not talk with those so called kings again.
I would stay in my land or I would raid alone and if they came

close then we would fight. The land of the waters and meres was now my kingdom. I would rule in the name of Butar, Ragnar and the Old man, Olaf. I had seen what titles would do and I would have none of it.

When Erika stood at my gate with our new child in her arms and Kara rushed up to greet her father I knew that I would never leave this land.

The End

Glossary

Áed Oirdnide –King of Tara 797

Bebbanburgh- Bamburgh Castle, Northumbria

Blót – a blood sacrifice made by a jarl

Byrnie- a mail shirt reaching down to the knees

Caerlleon- Welsh for Chester

Chape- the tip of a scabbard

Cherestanc- Garstang (Lancashire)

Cymri- Welsh

Cymru- Wales

Cyninges-tūn – Coniston. It means the estate of the king (Cumbria)

Drekar- a Dragon ship (a Viking warship)

Duboglassio –Douglas, Isle of Man

Ein-mánuðr- middle of March to the middle of April

Fey- having second sight

Frankia- France and part of Germany

Garth- Dragon heart

Gaill- Irish for foreigners

Galdramenn- wizard

Glaesum –amber

Gói- the end of February to the middle of March

Haughs- small hills in Norse (As in Tarn Hows)

Hel - Queen of Niflheim, the Norse underworld.

Hrams-a – Ramsey, Isle of Man

Jarl- Norse earl or lord

Joro-goddess of the earth

Kyrtle-woven top

Lochlannach – Irish for Northerners (Vikings)

Legacaestir- Anglo Saxon for Chester

Mammceaster- Manchester

Manau – The Isle of Man (Saxon)

Midden- a place where they dumped human waste

Njoror- God of the sea

Nithing- A man without honour (Saxon)

Odin - The "All Father" God of war, also associated with wisdom, poetry, and magic (The Ruler of the gods).

Orkneyjar-Orkney

Ran- Goddess of the sea

Roof rock- slate

Rinaz –The Rhine

St. Cybi- Holyhead

Seax – short sword

Skeggox – an axe with a shorter beard on one side of the blade

Sigismund- Frankish trader living in Cologne

Sif- Goddess of battle and the name of Harald's ship

Tadgh- a former slave and renegade Viking

Tarn- small lake (Norse)

The Norns- Fate

Thing-Norse for a parliament or a debate (Tynwald)

Thor's day- Thursday

Threttanessa- a drekar with 13 oars on each side.

Thrall- slave

Tynwald- the Parliament on the Isle of Man

Úlfarr- Wolf Warrior

Úlfarrston- Ulverston

Ullr-Norse God of Hunting

Ulfheonar-an elite Norse warrior who wore a wolf skin over his armour

Volva- a witch or healing woman in Norse culture

Woden's day- Wednesday

Wulfhere-Old English for Wolf Army

Wyrd- Fate

Maps

Coniston Water

Courtesy of Wikipedia

The Rise of
Northumbria
(Bernicia, Deira)
600 - 700

Northumbria circa 800 AD

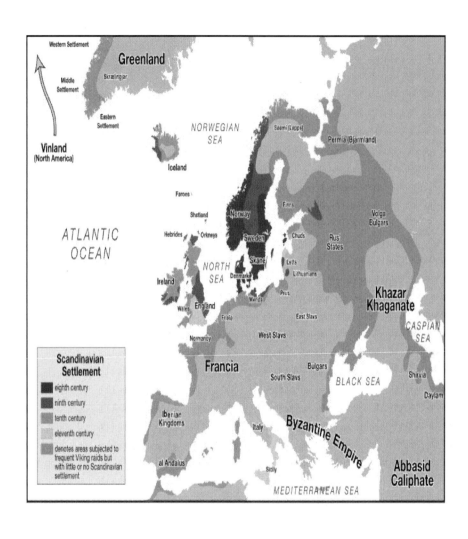

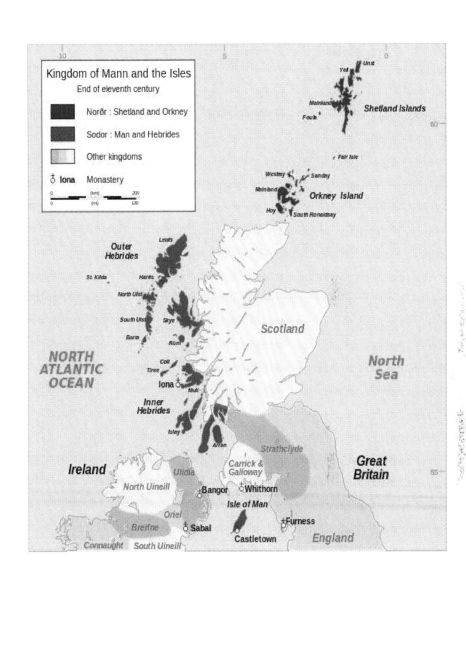

10 5 0

Kingdom of Mann and the Isles

End of eleventh century

Norðr : Shetland and Orkney

Sodor : Man and Hebrides

Other kingdoms

Iona   Monastery

Historical note

The Viking raids began, according to records left by the monks, in the 790s when Lindisfarne was pillaged. However, there were many small settlements along the east coast and most were undefended. I have chosen a fictitious village on the Tees as the home of Garth who is enslaved and then, when he gains his freedom, becomes Dragon Heart. As buildings were all made of wood then any evidence would have long rotted save for a few post holes. My raiders represent the Norse warriors who wanted the plunder of the soft Saxon kingdom. There is a myth that the Vikings raided in large numbers but this is not so. It was only in the tenth and eleventh centuries that the numbers grew. They also did not have allegiances to kings. The Norse settlements were often isolated family groups. The term Viking was not used in what we now term the Viking age. Warriors went a-Viking which meant that they sailed for adventure or pirating. Their lives were hard. Slavery was commonplace. The Norse for slave is thrall and I have used both terms.

It was more dangerous to drink the water in those times and so most people, including children drank beer or ale. The process killed the bacteria which could hurt them. It might sound as though they were on a permanent pub crawl but in reality they were drinking the healthiest drink that was available to them.

I have recently used the British Museum book and research about the Vikings. Apparently, rather like punks and Goths, the men did wear eye makeup. It would make them appear more frightening. There is also evidence that they filed their teeth. The leaders of warriors built up a large retinue by paying them and giving them gifts such as the wolf arm ring. This was seen as a sort of bond between leader and warrior. There was no national identity. They operated in small bands of free booters loyal to their leader. The idea of sword killing was to render a weapon unusable by anyone else. On a simplistic level this could just be a bend but I have seen examples which are tightly curled like a spring.

The length of the swords in this period was not the same as in the later medieval period. By the year 850 they were only 76cm long and in the eighth century they were shorter still. The first sword Dragon Heart used, Ragnar's, was probably only 60-65cm long. This would only have been slightly longer than a Roman gladius. At this time the sword, not the axe was the main weapon. The best swords came from Frankia, and were probably German in origin. A sword was considered a special weapon and a good one would be handed from father to son. A warrior with a famous blade would be sought out on the battlefield. There was little mail around at the time and warriors learned to be agile to avoid being struck. A skeggox was an axe with a shorter edge on one side. The use of an aventail (a chain mail extension of a helmet) began at about this time. The highly decorated scabbard also began at this time.

The blood eagle was performed by cutting the skin of the victim by the spine, breaking the ribs so they resembled blood-stained wings, and pulling the lungs out through the wounds in the victim's back.

Honey was used as an antiseptic in both ancient and modern times.

The Bangor I refer to (there were many) was called Bangor is-y-coed by the Welsh but I assumed that the Vikings would just use the first part of the place name. From the seventeenth century the place was known as Bangor of the Monks (Bangor Monachorum). Dolgellau was mined for gold by people as far back as the Romans and deposits have been discovered as late as the twenty first century. Having found gold in a stream at Mungrisedale in the Lake District I know how exciting it is to see the golden flecks in the black sand. The siege of the fort is not in itself remarkable. When Harlech was besieged in the middle ages two knights and fifteen men at arms held off a large army.

Anglesey was considered the bread basket of Wales even as far back as the Roman Invasion; the combination of the Gulf

Stream and the soil meant that it could provide grain for many people. In the eighth to tenth centuries, grain was more valuable than gold.

When writing about the raids I have tried to recreate those early days of the Viking raider. The Saxons had driven the native inhabitants to the extremes of Wales, Cornwall and Scotland. The Irish were always too busy fighting amongst themselves. It must have come as a real shock to be attacked in their own settlements. By the time of King Alfred almost sixty years later they were better prepared. This was also about the time that Saxon England converted completely to Christianity. The last place to do so was the Isle of Wight. There is no reason to believe that the Vikings would have had any sympathy for their religion and would, in fact, have taken advantage of their ceremonies and rituals not to mention their riches.

There was a warrior called Ragnar Hairy-Breeches. Although he lived a little later than my book is set I could not resist using the name of such an interesting sounding character. Most of the names such as Silkbeard, Hairy-Breeches etc are genuine Viking names. I have merely transported them all into one book. I also amended some of my names- I used Eric in the earlier books and it should have been Erik. I have now changed the later editions of the first two books in the series.

Eardwulf was king of Northumbria twice: first from 796-806 and from 808-810. The king who deposed him was Elfwald II. This period was a turbulent one for the kings of Northumbria and marked a decline in their fortunes until it was taken over by the Danes in 867.

Slavery was far more common in the ancient world. When the Normans finally made England their own they showed that they understood the power of words and propaganda by making the slaves into serfs. This was a brilliant strategy as it forced their former slaves to provide their own food whilst still working for their lords and masters for nothing. Manumission was possible as Garth showed in the first book in this series. Scanlan's training is also a sign that not all of the slaves suffered. It was a hard and cruel time- it was ruled by the strong.

The Vikings did use trickery when besieging their enemies and would use any means possible. They did not have siege weapons and had to rely on guile and courage to prevail. The siege of Paris in 845 A.D. was one such example.

The Isle of Man is reputed to have the earliest surviving Parliament, the Tynwald although there is evidence that there were others amongst the Viking colonies on Orkney and in Iceland. I have used this idea for Prince Butar's meetings of Jarls.

The blue stone they seek is Aquamarine or beryl. It is found in granite. The rocks around the Mawddach are largely granite and although I have no evidence of beryl being found there. I have used the idea of a small deposit being found to tie the story together.

The sailors and warriors we call Vikings were very adaptable and could, indeed, carry their long ships over hills to travel from one river to the next.

The early ninth century saw Britain converted to Christianity and there were many monasteries which flourished. These were often mixed. These were not the huge stone edifices such as Whitby and Fountain's Abbey; these were wooden structures. As such their remains have disappeared, along with the bones of those early Christian priests. Hexham was a major monastery in the early Saxon period. I do not know it they had warriors to protect the priests but having given them a treasure to watch over I thought that some warriors might be useful too.

I use Roman forts in all of my books. Although we now see ruins when they were abandoned the only things which would have been damaged would have been the gates. Anything of value would have been buried in case they wished to return. By 'of value' I do not mean coins but things such as nails and weapons. Such objects have been discovered. Many of the forts were abandoned in a hurry. Hardknott fort, for example, was built in the 120s but abandoned twenty or so years later. When the Antonine Wall was abandoned in the 180s Hardknott was reoccupied until

Roman soldiers finally withdrew from northern Britain. I think that, until the late Saxon period and early Norman period, there would have been many forts which would have looked habitable. The Vikings and the Saxons did not build in stone. It was only when the castle builders, the Normans arrive that stone would be robbed from Roman forts and those defences destroyed by an invader who was in the minority.

The place names are accurate and the mountain above Coniston is called the Old Man. The river is not navigable up to Windermere but I have allowed my warriors to carry their drekar as they did in the land of the Rus.

I used the British Museum Book- '*Vikings- Life and Legends*', the Osprey book '*Saxon, Norman and Viking*' by Terence Wise as well as the Ian Heath book- '*The Vikings*'.

Griff Hosker July 2014

Other books

by

Griff Hosker

If you enjoyed reading this book, then why not read
another one by the author?
Ancient History
The Sword of Cartimandua Series (Germania and
Britannia 50A.D. – 128 A.D.)
    Ulpius Felix- Roman Warrior (prequel)
    Book 1 The Sword of Cartimandua
    Book 2 The Horse Warriors
    Book 3 Invasion Caledonia
    Book 4 Roman Retreat
    Book 5 Revolt of the Red Witch
    Book 6 Druid's Gold
    Book 7 Trajan's Hunters
    Book 8 The Last Frontier
    Book 9 Hero of Rome
    Book 10 Roman Hawk
    Book 11 Roman Treachery
    Book 12 Roman Wall

    The Aelfraed Series (Britain and Byzantium 1050 A.D. -
1085 A.D.
    Book 1 Housecarl
    Book 2 Outlaw
    Book 3 Varangian

    The Wolf Warrior series (Britain in the late 6th Century)
    Book 1 Saxon Dawn

Book 2 Saxon Revenge
Book 3 Saxon England
Book 4 Saxon Blood
Book 5 Saxon Slayer
Book 6 Saxon Slaughter
Book 7 Saxon Bane
Book 8 Saxon Fall: Rise of the Warlord
Book 9 Saxon Throne

The Dragon Heart Series
Book 1 Viking Slave
Book 2 Viking Warrior
Book 3 Viking Jarl
Book 4 Viking Kingdom
Book 5 Viking Wolf
Book 6 Viking War
Book 7 Viking Sword
Book 8 Viking Wrath
Book 9 Viking Raid
Book 10 Viking Legend
Book 11 Viking Vengeance
Book 12 Viking Dragon
Book 13 Viking Treasure
Book 14 Viking Enemy
Book 15 Viking Witch
Bool 16 Viking Blood
Book 17 Viking Weregeld
Book 18 Viking Storm
Book 19 Viking Warband

The Norman Genesis Series
Rolf
Horseman
The Battle for a Home
Revenge of the Franks
The Land of the Northmen

Ragnvald Hrolfsson
Brothers in Blood

The Anarchy Series England 1120-1180
English Knight
Knight of the Empress
Northern Knight
Baron of the North
Earl
King Henry's Champion
The King is Dead
Warlord of the North
Enemy at the Gate
Warlord's War
Kingmaker
Henry II
Crusader
The Welsh Marches
Irish War

Border Knight 1190-1300
Sword for Hire

Modern History
The Napoleonic Horseman Series
Book 1 Chasseur a Cheval
Book 2 Napoleon's Guard
Book 3 British Light Dragoon
Book 4 Soldier Spy
Book 5 1808: The Road to Corunna
Waterloo

The Lucky Jack American Civil War series
Rebel Raiders
Confederate Rangers
The Road to Gettysburg

The British Ace Series
1914
1915 Fokker Scourge
1916 Angels over the Somme
1917 Eagles Fall
1918 We will remember them
From Arctic Snow to Desert Sand
Wings over Persia

Combined Operations series 1940-1945
Commando
Raider
Behind Enemy Lines
Dieppe
Toehold in Europe
Sword Beach
Breakout
The Battle for Antwerp
King Tiger
Beyond the Rhine

Other Books
Carnage at Cannes (a thriller)
Great Granny's Ghost (Aimed at 9-14-year-old young people)
Adventure at 63-Backpacking to Istanbul

For more information on all of the books then please visit the author's web site at http://www.griffhosker.com where there is a link to contact him.

Made in the USA
Columbia, SC
27 July 2021